HER

LAST

GOODBYE

BOOKS BY CARLA KOVACH

HER

LAST

GOODBYE

CARLA KOVACH

bookouture

Published by Bookouture in 2024

An imprint of Storyfire Ltd.
Carmelite House
50 Victoria Embankment
London EC4Y 0DZ

www.bookouture.com

ISBN: 978-1-83525-189-8
eBook ISBN: 978-1-83525-188-1

To the children in our lives. The little ones and the big ones. We never stop caring, despite how old you are.

PROLOGUE

Twenty Years Ago

I take another swig of the revolting whisky and as I swallow it burns my throat and my poor stomach is on fire. Our bonehead of a friend only managed to swipe this from the supermarket. It was okay us putting in an order for vodka, or maybe even a peach schnapps, but whisky is horrendous. I guess beggars can't be choosers as Mum would say. It's not like we actually paid for it.

I swallow and try to quell the nausea that is building deep within me. It doesn't feel right being here tonight, not without the other member of our little gang. As I exhale, coils of my breath dissipate into the air. Mum said I had to look after my little sister while she worked her evening shift at the petrol station, but my sister's fine. Guilt begins to gnaw at me. I glance at my phone. It lights up the edge of the lake as the water laps near my feet. My mum doesn't finish work until midnight so she'll never know, which is good as I'd definitely get a slap for being here. I have a couple of hours so I pop the phone back into my bag.

One of the outcasts snatches the bottle from me. I snigger at that name. We are the outcasts, the ones who teachers love to hate, the ones who turn up late, who sneak out of lessons early and the ones who get caught smoking. When you realise that the world won't stop spinning if you don't do science homework, you become free; that's what we tell ourselves. I open my mouth to say that I should go home to my sister but I think better of it. They won't understand.

Mum says I hang out with the wrong crowd but I love being with them. They're exciting and fun, but right now it doesn't feel right. I shouldn't be here. I should be at home with Shrimp. That's what I call my sis. When she was a baby, I said to Mum that she looked like a little shrimp and it stuck.

'Hey, I found a boat,' Ollie says as he snatches the whisky and gulps.

The two girls fist bump and cheer.

I don't think it's a good idea. It's cold. Going out on a dark lake where there is no one around, in the middle of a frosty February night is foolish. I might buy into the non-conformist stuff and I love a smoke. I've even popped the odd pill but there's something about cold water that stiffens me. I remove one of my trainers and then a sock, and I push my toe into the water. Instantly, I withdraw it and shiver. It's deathly cold. Even wearing my huge quilted coat and a couple of layers my whole body is freezing to the core, fast. 'I'll pass. I feel like I'll chuck if I get on a boat. Shouldn't have had that whisky.'

Ollie bursts into howls of laughter, spraying me with the mouthful of whisky he's just taken, which definitely nauseates me even more. I can smell his breath as he steps closer to me. 'When has that ever stopped you? Scared one of us will push you in?'

I stare at him and I can tell he's not going to take no for an answer. As for being pushed, I wouldn't put it past any of them. The other two furrow their brows. Before I get a chance to put my sock back on, they snatch my bag from across my body, ruffling up my hair and making me step in cold water. Heart pounding, I finish putting my sock and trainer back on my wet foot. 'Give it back.' I go to snatch it off Ollie but he jumps back. A huge grin spreads across his face.

'No. You can have it back when you get in the boat. I'm not letting you bore off on us. Follow me.'

The others get up and head towards him, leaving me alone in the middle of nowhere, sitting by a fishing lake that is literally abandoned. I glance at some of the old rotten wooden pegs. All the fish died a couple of years ago, something to do with toxic algae. My heart sinks. I really don't want to end up in that lake drinking toxic algae. The old clubhouse that was known as The Lodge is now a wreck. No one goes there any more. We used to hang out there until they sealed it up and barbed wired the perimeter. Again, I'm aware of how dangerous this is. A homeless person died in that building, that's why it's sealed up. Something to do with a main artery being pierced by a broken floorboard. My stare fixes on it. I'm sure I saw a shadow. I press my eyes together and look again. There is nothing there. My imagination is in overdrive, probably because I don't want to get in that boat.

Raucous jeers fill the air, then I hear a crash in the water. A chill runs through me as I glance back at the old oak trees behind me. I don't know what it is about being here but I don't feel alone. There are always animals rustling around and it's creepy. The snap of a branch keeps me still and listening for more. What if someone is watching us? 'Hello.' I don't have my phone and my friends are about to get into the boat. Again, my imagination is just out to scare me. Right now, I hate Ollie. If only I'd gone to see my bestie and taken Shrimp with me, everything would be okay, but she hates me now. I have so much making up to do.

I'm taken by surprise as I hear a cough coming from behind a tree trunk.

'This isn't funny.' It has to be one of the other guys from school. Even though I feel as though I'm struggling for breath and might very well have a panic attack, I have to play it cool. If I let any of those shitheads think that I'm scared, they'll love it. I march up to the trees and snatch a hanging branch out of the way and my heart sinks. 'Shrimp.' My little sister looks up at me and nervously balls her hands.

'Your bag is going in the water if you don't get on this boat right now.' I glance back at Ollie, angry that he's threatening to ruin all my things. He's standing on the boat, struggling to stay upright as it rocks.

'What do you think you're doing? I told you to stay at home.'

Shrimp shrugs. 'Didn't want to stay at home. It's boring.'

Ollie waves my bag above the water. If he drops my phone in the water, Mum will kill me, but then again she'll kill me if anything happens to my ten-year-old sister.

I go to shout at her, to tell her to go but I can't let her walk all the way home on her own. If anything happened to her, I'd never forgive myself. I glance at The Lodge again, wondering if I did see a shadow. No, Shrimp is staying with me where she's safe. I grab her hand and take her with me to the others.

'Ollie, give me my bag back. I have to go.' The girls are sitting at the back of the boat. One of them holds a paddle and mutters something under her breath. I think she called me a wuss but I choose to ignore her. 'My sister followed us.'

Shrimp lets go of my hand. 'I don't want to go home. I want to go on the boat. Either I go on the boat with you or I'll tell Mum everything. I'll tell her you're drunk and that you stole from the shop.'

'I didn't steal.'

She shrugs, not caring if she shares this half-truth with our mum. Ollie stole the whisky, not me. My sister is the biggest snitch I know and sometimes I hate her for it.

'See, even little sis is more fun than you.' Ollie is getting on my nerves now. Tomorrow, when he's sober, I'm going to have words with him. I think Mum was right – my friends are trouble. This is too stressful.

Before I get a chance to say anything, Shrimp darts through the shallow water up to her shins and she lets out an excited scream as the cold hits. Before I have the chance to protest, she's climbed into the boat. 'She can't swim.'

'She best not fall in the water then.' Ollie rolls his eyes.

He's right and Shrimp looks so excited. Even though she drives me mad, it feels good to be a cool big sister. 'Five minutes and we get off and I take her home, okay?'

Ollie nods. 'I promise.'

I reluctantly step into the lake and feel the chill of the water as it seeps through my trainers and socks. The hems of my fur-lined leggings soak up the water.

'You need to push us out. I'll help.' He grabs an oar from one of the girls and begins to bury the end in the bank to push out as I put all my strength into it too. The boat's soon floating and I'm now waist high in the water with chattering teeth. The others pull me in and Ollie takes his coat off for me to snuggle under. Sometimes I hate him, other times he can be kind. I swallow, still feeling mean for not spending tonight with my bestie.

Darkness surrounds us and one of the girls plays music on an iPod while drinking and laughing.

'Here, have this. It'll loosen you up.' He offers me a pill. As I go to protest, he throws it in my mouth and clasps it shut. 'Swallow.'

I don't want to swallow. His gaze bores into mine and it's like a switch has gone off in him and he's scaring me slightly. I pretend to do as he says. As he turns to the others, he snatches the bottle and yells with glee. I slip the pill from under my tongue and throw it overboard. Even with the half-hearted paddling that's going on we're nearly at the centre of the lake and panic builds up inside me. I grab Shrimp and pull her close to me, but she bats me off. I'm just grateful she didn't get offered a pill otherwise I'd be trying to fight that from her clutches. She's growing up far too fast. I'm fifteen now but at ten I was still into plastic ponies. Shrimp already asks to try one of my cigarettes and I know she's helped herself to the odd glass of Mum's wine when Mum has been out of it.

A club beat starts playing and the girls stand and start to dance and giggle. Maybe if I join them, I'll warm up a bit and I won't need Ollie's coat. Shrimp's face lights up with joy as she twirls in the middle of the boat. Ollie has started to prance around like he's playing air guitar, which is stupid as there is no guitar in the tune. I need to loosen up, maybe give Shrimp a nice memory to take from all this. In five minutes, we'll head back to shore, hurry through the woods and back home. Then I'll put our clothes in the dryer and Shrimp will be in bed before Mum gets off shift.

Ollie grabs my hand and as we dance, the boat sways. I catch Shrimp picking up the bottle and swigging from it. That's all I need.

'We're going to fall in,' I yell, but no one is listening. They're all high and Shrimp thinks it's the best night ever. 'Stop!'

Ollie stares at me as he dances, a sinister look on his face as he purposely wobbles the boat and points at me. I catch a shimmer of light in The Lodge. Something's not right. All I know is that Shrimp and I have to get off this boat. The others surround me as they sway the boat and I hold Shrimp close to me and close my eyes.

The screams of fun turn into screams of terror as the boat capsizes. As I plunge into the smelly water, it takes my breath away. I can't breathe. I can't move and I can't see the others as I swim for the surface. I see one of the girls and there's a lot of thrashing, then someone grabs my leg from under the water, pulling me down. I kick them away to save myself.

'Shrimp,' I call while spluttering. I can't see her. Maybe it was her grabbing me. I hold my breath and dive under but I can't see her. I can't see anything or anyone. As I reach the surface again, I inhale a huge gulp of air. Maybe it wasn't Shrimp, maybe someone was trying to pull me under. I think of Ollie and the pills. Everyone was high.

Sloshing sounds come from all around but since the phones went in the water, it's pitch black apart from the moon and the stars. 'Shrimp. She can't swim. Shrimp,' I cry, through chattering teeth. I glance across the lake, looking for her and that figure by The Lodge catches my eye again.

'Shrimp,' I keep calling through chattering teeth but I can't see her. My sister, she's gone. I killed my sister. As I go to swim towards the muddy bank, I'm once again pulled under and in panic, I breathe in the water, filling my lungs and I know it's the end for me too.

ONE

BERYL

Friday, 1 March

A man cleared his throat and entered the dining room while Beryl carried a handful of tablecloths. She still had half the tables left to lay. He placed an iPad down on the table next to the window.

'Sorry, breakfast isn't served until eight.' She glanced up at the wall clock just to make sure she wasn't losing the plot when it came to the time. No, it was only seven.

'No worries, I'll wait. Is there any chance of a pot of tea, though? Thought I'd come and sit here while the missus gets ready.'

'Of course. Do you have anything nice planned today?'

He scrunched his nose. 'Shakespeare's house, unfortunately. My wife likes to pretend she likes Shakespeare so we both have to suffer.'

Beryl disagreed as she loved Shakespeare and his house, but

she smiled nonetheless. It wasn't her place to debate anything with the guests. 'I'll grab you a brew.'

She dumped the tablecloths onto a chair and hurried to the poky kitchen. After flicking the kettle on, she turned the oven on. It wasn't too early to get some sausages in. Maybe she could make his breakfast a bit early. After opening the back door, she trudged across the uneven slabs at the back, grateful that guests never ventured this way. The lightest of frost had formed so she buttoned up her cardigan.

The barn at the far end housed her chest freezer. She'd spent years hoping that the bed and breakfast would generate enough income to have an extension out the back. A bigger kitchen would have helped but, as it stood, she barely had room to cook four breakfasts in one go and keep a fridge in there. As for the bar, that was another ambition down the drain. Thirty years ago she had built the barn with the idea it could be turned into a fabulous games room and bar. She'd never even come close to pulling a pint in there.

As she followed the cracked path, battling her arthritic knees, she stopped. She was sure she'd closed the barn door last night. She always closed it as the foxes got in and messed everywhere. Burglary was always the last thing on her mind so she never locked it. A flash of pink caught her gaze. She lifted the glasses dangling down her front on a chain and perched them on the edge of her nose and squinted. Stepping towards it, she reached out and grabbed the bubblegum-pink felt blanket. Holding it up, she saw that there were white stars all over it.

A loud bang came from inside the barn and Beryl almost stumbled backwards, only getting saved by a rusty old patio table which scraped across the stone tiles. She placed the blanket on it and proceeded towards the barn door. 'Hello.' Reaching into her dress pocket, she gripped her phone. Fox or intruder? She had to be sure before calling the police.

The air smelled musty as it always did in the barn. She flicked the light switch. The vast space was big enough to hold a bar, seating, and a couple of snooker tables at least. The tables she'd intended to use had been piled up along the back for years. A second-hand bar she'd bought from a pub that had closed down sat near the back wall. Cobwebs hung from the strip light. They always made her shudder. The thought of coming face to face with a huge arachnid filled her with fear. She shook her head. If there was anyone in the barn, they would have been startled by her turning up. Maybe the bang came from outside, or maybe the fox had escaped out of one of the many weak spots in the structure. The pink blanket could have blown into the bushes after being dropped by a guest's child.

A shuffle came from behind the bar. Beryl's heart began to race. It had to be an intruder. She glanced at the freezer and wondered if someone was trying to steal her food. She knew the country was in a cost-of-living crisis at the moment and maybe it was worth someone's time to steal sausages.

With trembling hands, she held her phone up. 'I'm calling the police.' The last thing she wanted was to get some desperate person into trouble, but right now she was scared. She thought of the man waiting for his cuppa. Maybe she could ask him to check the barn out. No, she would not risk a bad review or looking stupid if it was just a fox. He was the guest. He didn't need to be troubled by this.

'Look, I don't want to call the police. Just come out. You're not in any trouble, I promise,' she said, her voice nervously quivering. If whoever was there had wanted to hurt her, they'd have done it by now. She took a few steps forwards, ducking to dodge the cobwebs.

The sound of dainty steps echoed in the room and adrenaline coursed through Beryl's body. *Be brave, you can handle this,* she told herself, then the intruder revealed themselves. She gasped as the dot of a shivering girl stood against the back wall, gripping a stuffed dog with a heart key ring dangling from its collar. What was a little girl doing in her barn? Her black hair had leaves caught in it and there was a scratch across her pale cheek; her lemon-coloured dress was shredded in places. There were holes in her thick white tights and her coat was hanging off her shoulders. 'What's your name?'

The girl placed her dirty thumb in her mouth and began to suck it.

Beryl knew something terrible had happened. She took a few more steps towards the little girl, but the girl stepped back to escape Beryl. 'It's okay, I won't hurt you. I live just here. Do you want to come inside and we can get you cleaned up? I can make you some warm milk and I've got chocolate biscuits.' She knew she had to call the police now. 'Where's your mummy or daddy? Or was someone else looking after you?'

The girl's jaw began to shake.

'It's okay, darling. I'm going to call the police, okay?' Beryl didn't want to scare the girl but she had to try to get her away from the tables and the bar. Everything had been stacked precariously. 'We should get out of here with all these spiders, and it's very cold. I don't want you to get a chill.'

The girl nodded and took the few steps needed to reach Beryl. She reached out and held the girl's tiny hand, before leading her through the kitchen and into the comfy lounge. 'What do I call you?'

'Cleo.'

'Cleo is a lovely name. Can you tell me what happened? Why you're here?'

Tears drizzled down her reddening cheeks and she gripped her dog. 'Mummy told me to hide. The scary person took her.'

TWO

Gina woke to the sound of her phone going off. Her throat was so dry she could barely swallow. 'Hello,' she croaked. The hangover from hell had hit. She'd only had about four drinks with Jacob but she wasn't used to it any more. Her stomach groaned and she wasn't sure if she felt sick or hungry. Her phone slipped from her fingers, between the bed and her bedside table. As she held it back to her ear, she continued. 'DI Harte.'

'Morning,' Detective Chief Inspector Briggs said in a slightly offish tone.

He was right to be offish. He'd been on his way over the previous night to talk but she had to cancel on him again because Jacob also needed to talk. She'd been grateful that Jacob hadn't just popped by and saw Briggs turning up. Keeping their relationship secret was important for both of them. Neither wanted to be moved from Cleevesford Police Station. Detective Sergeant Jacob Driscoll had needed her again and she had to be there for him.

'You don't sound so good,' he said.

'Sorry. You know me. I'll come alive once I've had my coffee.' He was also still angry that she'd put herself in direct danger during the last case. She had to make things right again as it was getting awkward between them. He'd been constantly checking up on how she was doing her job and it was starting to get irritating.

He continued. 'I know you're due into the station soon but we've had a report come in and I think you should head straight to Brambles Bed and Breakfast on Meadow Way. Is everything okay?' Briggs waited for her to reply.

'Yes, I'm fine. Jacob and I had a really long chat last night and he's definitely ready to come back today. I know you think it might be too soon as you haven't confirmed that with him, but he needs the team and I need him back.' She paused, knowing that Jacob had expressed that he was ready for active duty again but Briggs hadn't been sure. Being suspected of murder in the last case had really taken it out of him. Gina had spent hours with him, helping him through it. He was a detective through and through and he was more than ready to go back on duty. 'What's happened at the B&B?'

'Suspected kidnap. The owner of the B&B, Beryl Sayer, called in to say that she found a child in her barn. The child told her that someone took her mother in the night and that her mother told her to hide.'

'What's happening right now?'

Briggs continued. 'A couple of uniformed officers are with her. We have also managed to contact the child's uncle, Kyle Fletcher, who is on his way. I'd like you to meet him there. We need to know which route the girl took so we can work out where her mother was taken. There are three roads close by. One narrow country path called Sable Way, the A road that runs along the back and another road that leads to Hutton Village. I don't know how well you know the village but it's a new estate of about thirty cottage-style homes. They're nowhere near anything except a pub so it's quite a remote area, set on the edge of Cleevesford.'

Gina recalled reading about the development when it was being built but she'd never had any reason to venture there. 'Okay, I'm on my way.'

'Call Jacob, tell him he's been cleared for duty. I should have called him. He's had all the meetings. HR are happy with him being back on duty.' Gina exhaled, happy to be giving her colleague good news. She knew that he was ready to be back at work. 'Actually, I'll make the call as I have a few things to go through with him. You need to head there and see the girl. She said she heard her mother's screams as she was bundled into a car. Time is of the essence.'

Gina felt a chill creeping across her shoulders as she pictured the woman being forced into a car as her terrified child ran away. She only hoped that the girl's mother was still alive.

THREE

Several low-lying branches slapped Gina's windscreen as she drove up the gravelly road to Brambles Bed and Breakfast. On reaching the huge ivy-covered house, she pulled up behind the police car. She shivered and did up the top button of her long black overcoat. The birds might be chirping like it was spring but the weather had a lot of catching up to do. She thought of the terrified little girl who had been hiding in the cold barn.

A woman with long grey hair and a portly frame opened the creaky main door. 'Come in, come in,' she said as she waved Gina closer and moved aside to let her in.

'Thank you.' Gina stepped onto the orange and brown geometric tiled floor from where she could hear PC Smith's voice coming from the back of the building. She wondered if Briggs had managed to contact Jacob yet. Glancing back, she hoped to see his car pull up but there was nothing yet. She also wondered if Jacob's head was as bad as hers. Being out drinking hadn't been part of her plan but, up until last night, Jacob had been quite melancholy after the last case and she had been meeting up with him regularly so he could talk.

Gina turned to the woman and nodded as she fully entered the echoey hallway.

'I'm Beryl, by the way. I'd say it was nice to meet you but the circumstances aren't good. I've never seen such a scared little girl.' The woman furrowed her brows. 'I've just told the PCs everything and little Cleo is sitting in the dining room waiting with an officer for her uncle to turn up. Luckily, she managed to describe where he worked. Thank goodness there is only one ice-cream factory in the area. Come through to the lounge at the back. It's a bit warmer in there.'

Gina followed Beryl through the hall and glanced into the dining room on the right. The little girl was seated at a table opposite PC Shafiq Ahmed who was smiling and speaking to her. Another couple sat opposite each other at the table in the bay window at the front, the woman eating toast and the man pouring a cup of tea. The girl broke into the tiniest of smiles as PC Ahmed pulled a dramatic face and told her a story about a magical cat. He did have the ability to bring joy to people in horrible situations.

'Here we are. Take a seat,' Beryl said.

Gina sank into a comfy armchair around the table that PC Smith was already sitting at. A standard lamp lit up the various fingermarks on the mahogany coffee table. The shadows cast from the tassels that hung from it reached across PC Smith's notepad. She knew he would have already taken a statement but she wanted to speak to Beryl Sayer herself, just to get an overview of what happened before Cleo's uncle turned up. 'Thank you. Do you mind running through the events of this morning again?'

'Of course not. Not if it will help find the poor mite's mother. I tell you, hearing what she said has knocked me sick. Would you like a coffee?'

'Yes, please. That would be most welcome.' Hopefully it would lift the fogginess and wake her up.

Beryl picked up a cup from the tray, placed it in front of Gina and poured the black liquid, its aroma teasing Gina. She reached for the coffee and sipped her first drink of the day.

'I'll tell you what I've already told the officer here. I keep some of my food in a freezer in the barn. It's out the back. When I got there, I saw that the barn door was open and I also found the pink blanket with the stars on it just outside. Cleo wanted it back. She said it was hers so she has it now. The child just emerged from the back of the barn and she said that her mum told her to hide and that the scary person took her mum. She seemed terrified but it's not surprising, considering what's happened. I managed to get her into the lounge and I called you. She wanted some warm milk and a couple of biscuits.'

PC Smith pressed his thin lips together as he remained poised to write down any potential new information.

Gina cleared her throat. 'Did you see or hear anything suspicious during the night?'

The woman shook her head. 'I only make breakfast here and the guests have a key. I live on the other side of the house. When you enter, there is a door to the left of the stairs, that's where I live and my bedroom is at the front. I like to keep an eye out for comings and goings but I didn't hear anything out of the ordinary.'

'How many guests are booked in at the moment?'

'Just the couple in the dining room. It's been quiet. I guess there are more modern places to stay.'

PC Smith put his pen down. 'We have their details. They're Mr and Mrs Swadling and we've yet to speak to them.'

'Do you think we can speak to Cleo now?' Gina asked PC Smith.

'She really wanted her uncle when we tried to speak to her earlier.'

Until Cleo's uncle turned up, Gina knew that all she could

do was ask the Swadlings a few questions. 'Did Cleo say how she came to be in your barn?'

Beryl nodded. 'She said she ran away from the scary person. Looking at the state of her tights and dress, I'd say she ran through the back which is dense with bushes. It looks like she got caught in them. Had she come along the front and made her way around the house, she could have used the road, or maybe she got scared off the road. Who knows?'

'Did she tell you which way she came?'

'No, I'm afraid she didn't say much. She seems a bit dumbstruck.'

Gina realised that Beryl had probably told them all she knew. PC Smith handed her Beryl's statement and Gina quickly scanned it. 'I'm glad you were here to look after her.'

'I am too. Who knows what could have happened to her had she been stuck in the fields or woods for the night?'

Gina pictured the terrified little girl running away, thinking that the scary person might be coming after her and she felt her body begin to tense. 'Could we please use this room to speak to Mr and Mrs Swadling?'

'Of course. I'll send them in and put another pot of coffee on. Do whatever you need to do and take all the time you need.'

A few minutes later, the couple were sitting opposite Gina.

Mrs Swadling frowned and began fiddling with the edge of her jumper, while her husband ran his hands through the bit of grey hair he had left on the sides of his head.

Gina leaned back, trying to put them at ease. 'Thank you for speaking to us. As you may have heard, a little girl was found in the barn this morning and we are trying to establish what happened.'

The woman shook her head and moved her twiddling fingers from her jumper to the end of her plait that fell over her shoulder. 'Poor kid. I don't know how we can help but please, ask away,' she said in a Welsh accent.

'When did you check in here?'

'It was about five last night. We have tickets for Shakespeare's house today and we're booked to visit Warwick Castle tomorrow. It's our anniversary so we thought we'd treat ourselves to a few days away.'

Gina watched as PC Smith scrawled in his notebook. 'Did you see anything suspicious on arrival?'

'No, not at all,' she replied. 'We dropped our bag in our room and headed out to The Hare, which is a gastropub just past Hutton Village. We went there to eat and I'm not sure what time we got back.'

The husband chipped in. 'It was around ten thirty. We hung around as there was a quiz on. I remember saying it was about ten when it finished, then I ordered a tea, drank it, and we left so it had to be about half ten. We drove past the newish-looking estate that has a sign up saying two houses left. I remember thinking how nice they looked. We came down the one and only road that leads to the B&B from the village. It had to be around ten thirty.'

'Did you see anyone or anything that you can remember?'

The husband shook his head. Mrs Swadling creased her brows and spoke. 'I don't know if this is relevant but it's really quiet around here so you don't expect to see much. Most of the people in the pub seemed to be locals and were drinking so I'm guessing they didn't drive home. When we left, no one else came out of the pub at the same time...'

'What do you remember, Mrs Swadling?' Gina knew that the woman had something on her mind.

'A car. As we passed the new houses, you were wittering on about how nice it would be to live in Hutton Village' – she gestured to her husband – 'and I saw that a car was parked up. It wasn't outside a house. It was past the village. Anyway, the car alone wasn't odd. The glow of a lit cigarette through the windscreen was the odd thing. It happened so fast I didn't overthink it and, unlike my husband, I hadn't been drinking tea all night. I'd had about four gin and tonics and I was feeling a bit woozy, but I know what I saw. Do you think the person in that car had something to do with whatever has happened?'

Gina felt her heart racing. That was their only lead so far so they needed to pinpoint that location and try to pinpoint Cleo's route from there. 'Maybe. Would you mind going with PC Smith to show us where you saw the car?'

'I can tell you exactly where it was. The bumper was almost parked against the WELCOME TO HUTTON, DRIVE CAREFULLY sign, and was facing the village on the right side of the road, so the wrong side of the road to drive on, if you get what I mean.'

Gina nodded. 'Can you recall the make, colour, or registration number of the car?'

She shook her head. 'All I saw was that glowing cigarette. Wait, maybe it was brown or dark blue, I'm not sure.'

Gina tried to picture where the sign was and how far away it was from the B&B. She guessed at about half a mile which would be a long way for little Cleo to walk, but it was doable. Also, the most direct route would have been along the road. Maybe the little girl hid in the bushes until the scary person went. Maybe the perpetrator was waiting for Cleo's mother to leave wherever she had come from and it was possible that the cigarette butt was now on the verge or road.

Someone knocked at the front door. She listened as Beryl opened it and a man's voice boomed out. 'Where is she? Where's Cleo? Is she okay?'

Gina stood and glanced down the hallway as the man, who looked to be in his mid-to-late thirties, ran into the house calling for his niece. 'Cleo.'

She heard Jacob's voice after as he greeted PC Ahmed.

'She's here,' PC Ahmed called out to the girl's uncle.

'Do you need us for anything else at the moment as we have to get to Stratford?' Mr Swadling asked.

'We may need to speak to you again later. Here's my card. If either of you remember anything else, please call me.'

Mrs Swadling took the card and placed it in her bag.

Gina and Mr Swadling headed to the dining room, where Cleo was hugging her uncle. 'I want Mummy.' She began to sob as Mr Swadling began packing his things away from the dining table.

'It's okay, honey pie. We'll find Mummy, but for now you're going to come back to mine, okay?' Cleo's uncle hugged his niece back.

The little girl nodded. Gina walked over, acknowledged Jacob and addressed the uncle. 'I'm DI Harte. We need to ask you a few questions and would it be possible to speak to Cleo and yourself?'

Just as Mr Swadling hoicked his backpack over his shoulder, Cleo began to scream until her face went red. She ran as fast as she could into the lounge and hid behind the armchair that Gina had been sitting in. The lamp tassels shook as the little girl cowered.

Gina followed the little girl, kneeling down and peering behind the chair. 'Cleo, it's okay. You're safe. I'm Gina. I promise no one will hurt you.'

The little girl remained open-mouthed for several seconds, then let out another piercing cry. What had Cleo seen and what had scared her so much?

FOUR

SHANNON

'Morning, lovely. I am so dying for a coffee.' Shannon was sure she couldn't smell coffee and she needed one more than anything. After glancing across the showroom, she could see that the machine wasn't even plugged in. She'd literally been awake all night and her body wanted nothing more than to sleep right now, but that wasn't possible. Why? Because she had to be here selling cars all day. And not only that, she was rostered on for the whole weekend.

'I'll do it.' Joel, the young trainee, ran over to the machine, plugged it in and popped a pod in it.

'Joel, it isn't your job to make coffee, but thank you. I'll take over.'

'I was trying to be helpful.' At nearly twenty-one, Joel was the youngest person to work at Shoreford's Used Car Dealership. His sockless feet stuffed into smart shoes made Shannon shiver. It was cold but Joel obviously chose to prioritise his image over being warm. His grey trousers were slightly short but the braces and tie he wore had a smartness about them. He was fast becoming a hit with the customers and she could see him smashing his sales targets in no time.

Shannon took a sip of her caramel latte thinking what the hell, she'd claw those calories back at lunchtime because for one, she hadn't bothered making any lunch. 'This is hitting the spot. I can feel the life flowing into me with every sip. Right, let's get those doors open and hope we get more than just browsers today. Is Darcie powdering her face again? She seems to spend forever in the bathroom on her phone.'

'No, she hasn't come in yet.'

Shannon put her lipstick-stained cup down and pressed one of her manicured nails into her chin. 'Really, who opened up?'

'Gordon. He let me in and said he had to be somewhere. He seemed a bit stressed but said he'd be in later.'

'Stressed, he doesn't know the meaning of the word. He sits in that office all day playing stupid games on his phone but I guess as he owns the place, that's okay, but stressed he is not.' She grabbed her drink and finished it off. 'Oh well, he scares the customers off anyway, but don't ever tell him I said that, okay?' She knew their boss wouldn't see the funny side of her joke. Gordon Shoreford never saw the funny side of anything, even though she'd worked for him since leaving school at sixteen. 'Did he say when he'd be back?'

Joel shook his head, releasing a burst of musky aftershave. Just then his phone beeped. He opened up a message.

'Who's the lucky girl?'

'Just someone.' He blushed and smiled.

His phone beeped again.

'She's keen.'

'She is but this is just my mum confirming what time she's picking me up tonight after work. I suppose I best get buffing the bumper of that Merc. Gordon noticed a spider's web trailing from the wing mirror. Don't want to scare anyone off and Gordon said it had to be my first job of the day, then he said it was my turn to clean the loos.'

'Yuck, sorry about that.' Shannon paused. 'Did Darcie say

anything about being off today. My calendar says she's meant to be in. She hasn't called or emailed?'

He shook his head as he grabbed a duster. 'She never said anything to me. Maybe she squared it with Gordon and has a day off.'

'Maybe, but she's meant to get any holiday requests signed off by me first. Maybe Cleo's sick.' She glanced out of the floor-to-ceiling glass frontage, into the foggy distance where she couldn't quite make out the convenience store and the row of houses across the road. She took her phone from her bag and activated it. Darcie hadn't left any messages or tried to call. They'd been friends for years, since childhood. They told each other everything. Well, they did until Finn came into their lives. Things hadn't been the same since.

She checked her watch. He was due to come and collect the Kia that awaited him. It needed a lot of work and a valet. He was meant to be here in half an hour to take it to his garage and she wasn't looking forward to seeing him. In a way, she was glad that Darcie hadn't turned up. It made life easier. That didn't mean she could escape doing her job. If Gordon hadn't agreed for her to be off, it was Shannon's job as Darcie's superior to call her and find out what was going on. She pressed her number and waited, but the call was instantly cut off like the number no longer existed. This wasn't on. She and Darcie weren't exactly getting on but this was work. It had to be separated from their personal lives. She tried again to no avail.

Friendship is fragile as Shannon had come to learn, and she and Darcie were walking on a rope as thin as the spider web that Joel was now dusting away. She glanced at her reflection in the window. Most people guessed she was in her twenties, not her thirties. She had zero baggage. She ran semi-regularly and she worked hard on her appearance most days, so why had Finn cheated on her and worst of all why had Darcie lied?

FIVE

Gina left Kyle Fletcher with his niece and the little girl seemed to be calming down. While he was looking after her in the lounge, Gina returned to Mr Swadling. The man looked horrified at Cleo's outburst and was being comforted by his wife. 'I didn't mean to scare her. Is she okay?'

Kyle popped his head into the dining room. 'She said she was scared by your bag.' Kyle cleared his throat and continued speaking in a broken voice. 'She said the scary person grabbed my sister, and threw her over his shoulder, like you did with your bag.' He took a deep breath. 'What's happened to my sister? Someone has taken her and they're going to kill her. You have to find her, please.'

Gina took a step forward and nodded for Mr and Mrs Swadling to leave. They didn't know the kidnapper's reasons for taking Darcie but she had to consider that Darcie could already be dead. She swallowed and forced her emotions down. As soon as the couple went out the front door with the PCs and Beryl, Gina and Jacob joined Cleo and Kyle in the lounge. 'Mr Fletcher, what is your sister's full name?'

'Darcie Fletcher. She's thirty-five years old and the nicest person you could wish to meet. I don't know who would do this to her.' The man scratched his shaped brown stubble.

'We are going to do everything we can to find her. Do you have an up-to-date photo of her?'

He nodded and scrolled through his phone photos until he found a selfie of him and Darcie together.

'Can you please text that to me?' Gina passed him one of her cards with her phone number on and Kyle Fletcher sent it straight away. 'Would it be okay if we spoke to Cleo with you here?'

Kyle undid his coat and kneeled in front of Cleo. 'Cleo, sweetie, these two people are from the police and they want to help find Mummy. Are you okay to speak to them? I know you're scared and I'm scared too, but all we want is to help Mummy.' Gina could see that Kyle was shaking and doing his best to hide his distress from his niece.

The dot of a girl looked out from behind the armchair and gripped her stuffed dog harder. Then she nodded.

'I think that's a yes,' said Kyle.

'Hello, Cleo. Remember I told you my name was Gina?'

Cleo nodded and began sucking her thumb. A few strands of her black hair had stuck to her face. Kyle reached across and moved them from her mouth. He gently led her from the floor into the chair where he perched on the arm.

'This is Jacob. He works with me.' Jacob smiled. 'Is this your dog?' Cleo nodded. 'What is your dog called?'

'Doggy.'

'Doggy is lovely. I'm glad you had Doggy with you last night as it must have been very scary. Can you tell me what happened?'

Cleo nodded. Kyle held a tissue up to her nose and she blew. After he'd finished wiping her face, she started talking. 'We were at Mummy's friend's house. We left when it was dark.'

'Was it late?'

The little girl nodded. 'I was asleep. When I woke up, we were outside and I saw the scary person picking Mummy up. I was on the grass and it was wet. Mummy screamed and told me to hide from the scary person.'

'I know this is hard for you, Cleo, but did you see the scary person?'

Cleo shook her head. 'Not properly. I was looking at Mummy and I was scared.'

'Were they taller than Mummy?'

She nodded.

Kyle pressed his lips together. 'My sister is only five feet three. Everyone is taller than her.'

'Did this person speak?'

'He shouted at Mummy to shut up.'

'He? Was it a man?'

Cleo nodded.

'Thank you,' Gina said. 'Cleo, you are doing a great job and we will need to speak to you in a minute too, Kyle. But, Cleo, is there anything you can remember at all about him?'

Nodding, the little girl loosened her grip on the stuffed dog. 'Big zip.'

'He had a big zip?'

'Yes.'

'Where was the zip?'

'Here.' Cleo pointed from her groin to her neck. 'The trousers and top were stuck together like my playsuit.'

Gina had the image of a boiler suit in her mind. 'Anything else you remember?'

'No.'

'Did you see the person's face or hair?'

The little girl shook her head. 'He had something on his face.'

'What did it look like?'

'It was all white.' She made the shape of two round circles with her fingertips against her eyes. 'There were holes here and then I looked at Mummy and she said run, so I ran.'

Gina quickly typed in white masks into Google. 'Did it look like any of these?'

Cleo nodded and pointed to a plain white mask that was commonly sold at craft shops, usually bought to decorate. She held it up for Jacob to see so that he could make a note of the type.

'Where did you run to?'

'The trees. I got lost when I was hiding.'

'You must have been very scared there on your own. You did very well to find the barn and hide there. Can you remember where you saw the car? Did you see anything around?'

'I saw a white square with writing on it.'

Gina tried to think what the sign to Hutton Village looked like and it was a huge white square sign, just like Mrs Swadling had described. They needed to find out who was in that car and they had a scene that needed sifting through. She nodded to Jacob who knew that his next call would be to forensics.

'Where had you come from?'

'Anna's house.'

'Who is Anna?'

'Mummy's friend. Mummy and Anna weren't happy.'

Kyle placed an arm around his niece.

'Why do you think they weren't happy?'

'Anna cried and they sounded mad.'

Gina waited for Jacob to catch up with his notes.

Kyle raised his eyebrows. 'I know where Anna lives. I've dropped Darcie off there before. My sister does drive but when she goes over for a drink she doesn't take her car.'

Gina turned to Kyle. 'Do you know of any fallings out that Anna and Darcie had had?'

Kyle shook his head. 'I know Darcie was always trying to set her up on dates as she comes over to mine a lot and tells me things. They go out together sometimes and I normally babysit. Anna usually comes to stay with Darcie on those nights but I don't remember Darcie telling me about a fall out.'

'Just as a process of elimination, could I ask where you were last night between nine and midnight?'

Kyle scrunched his nose and stretched his legs out. 'Really? You think I took my own sister and terrified my niece.'

'It's just a routine question, Mr Fletcher.'

He sighed. 'I was at home all night with my husband, Richard. We were watching the news around ten and we went to bed around eleven.'

Gina waited for Jacob to take a note of that. Kyle Fletcher seemed genuine but, as a matter of routine, his whereabouts would be checked out. 'Thank you. Can I take Anna's address and do you have a surname for her?'

Shaking his head, he opened the messages on his phone and scrolled. 'No to the surname as I don't have it and it was weeks ago when I dropped my sister off. I'm just checking Maps to see where it was. Here, it's Plum Cottage. Number one Plum Walk.'

'Gina,' Cleo said in her sweet child's voice. 'The scary person smelled funny.'

She smiled at the little girl. 'In what way?'

'Like apples.'

'Apples?'

The little girl nodded and rubbed her red eyes.

'Did he say anything else?'

Cleo shrugged and leaned against her uncle.

'I think she's been through enough for now. You have to find my sister. Someone has taken her and we need her back.'

'I couldn't hear what else he said to Mummy. Mummy hit him when he picked her up and he dropped something on the grass. This was before I hid in the bushes.' Her bottom lip began to tremble.

'I know you're scared and you're doing so much to help Mummy. Can you tell me what he dropped?'

Tears slid down the little girl's face and she gripped Doggy. Kyle placed a loving arm around her. 'Mummy screamed. It was a finger. Then Mummy said run.'

SIX

Gina drove to the Hutton Village sign where Bernard Small, the crime scene manager, was already togged up in a crime scene suit, his gangly frame towering over his two assistants. She parked by their cars and vans on the opposite side of the road. The two PCs were still placing cordons around the sign to seal off the area. A notice had already been erected at the roadside appealing for witnesses who had driven through the previous evening to come forward. She stepped out and waited for Jacob to pull up behind her and they hurried over to the boundary.

'Bernard, have you spotted anything?' she asked.

'Not yet, we've only just got here. As you can see, we've requested that the cordon extends from the tree at the junction, past the sign and the fence post back there. We've taken it all the way to the treeline and we know there are a few acres of scrub, marsh and woodland behind it.' The large silver birch branches whipped in the breeze as a gust caught them, a twig hurtled into the road.

'What are you thinking, guv?' Jacob asked.

'After having an argument with her friend, Anna, Darcie must have left her cottage. From what Kyle said, Darcie would leave her car at home if she was having a drink but we obviously need to check that with Anna. We need to head there next.' She paused and gazed beyond the trees, trying to get a glimpse of what Cleo would have battled with. She pictured a terrified little girl, hiding, hoping that the perpetrator wouldn't chase her down too. 'From what I recall, there is a brook and some marsh land beyond that treeline which is guarded by an entanglement of shrubs.' Gina pictured Cleo being carried by Darcie in the dark from Anna's cottage, both of them unaware of what was about to happen. 'Maybe her kidnapper was here waiting for her, or maybe he'd been there all evening after following her here. At ten thirty, he was sitting in his car, smoking, waiting for her to come out of Anna's cottage, if Mrs Swadling's statement is accurate. I'm wondering if he'd been following her for a long time? I can't stop thinking about the finger. I'm hoping Cleo is mistaken as someone out there could be missing a finger, which means we have another victim to consider.'

Gina's mouth started to dry up as she considered the fact that they would come across a body or bodies soon. She coughed and tried to swallow. The cup of coffee that Beryl poured for her hadn't touched the sides. She cleared her dry throat. 'The thought of Darcie screaming and being bundled into a car while poor little Cleo hid in the bushes is really playing on my mind. And if we find a finger, I dread to think what he's going to do with Darcie.' She paused and tried to think of something other than the severed finger. 'From what I know, we don't have any reports of a missing person so if there is a finger, who does it belong to?'

'We'll get to the bottom of it, guv.'

Gina forced a smile. 'I hope so. The alternative doesn't bear thinking about. I'm glad you're back.'

Jacob glanced across at the CSIs working the scene. 'I am too, despite the hangover. I know it hasn't been that long but I've missed this. Well not this, the team.'

'Have you heard from Jennifer?' His ex-fiancée had left him but was due to return to work with Bernard as a CSI. Gina couldn't see her amongst the two CSIs who were placing yellow evidence markers on the ground and taking photos.

'She messaged me a while back.'

'And... sorry. If you don't want to tell me, you don't have to. It really is none of my business.'

Jacob shook his head. 'It's okay.' His clean-shaven face and Clark Kent looks were back intact after the last case had taken all he had. She was pleased he seemed on form again and had been looking after himself. 'She's left the department and moved back in with her parents. She's living in Gloucestershire and applying for jobs over that way. It's the end of an era.' His Adam's apple bobbed as he swallowed and he took a moment. 'I guess it wasn't meant to be. We had our fair share of tragedy, with her being run over and losing the baby and I guess that ended us. If we were meant to be we'd have got through it, but we didn't, so it is what it is. That's where I am.' He took a deep breath and white mist filled the air as he exhaled. 'I didn't even get to keep the rabbit, but then again, I'm glad Thumper is with her. She loves him.'

'I really am sorry. You've been through a lot.'

'Don't be. Right now, I feel like I'm right where I need to be. I have no complications. It's just me. I need some space to digest the past few months. It was hard being treated like a murderer and something I'll never fully get over. I just have to keep going.'

Bernard called to Gina and held a hand up. He placed a yellow marker on the grass. One of the assistant's stepped in front of him to take a photo.

'Bernard, have you found something?' Gina began walking towards the outer cordon, cold hands firmly in her coat pocket.

'We have indeed. We've found a human index finger, right hand,' he called to her as he left the CSI to continue.

Gina swallowed. 'Cleo had been right about the finger. I

was hoping she'd been mistaken. Can you tell me anything else?' The two PCs glanced over. PC Ahmed turned away in disgust and PC Smith furrowed his brows and stared at the digit that was now being placed in an evidence bag.

Bernard pulled his face mask under his chin, releasing his long grey beard as he stood on the other side of the cordon. 'Obviously we need to get it to the lab.'

'I need you to fast track it and by fast track, make it an absolute priority.'

'Will do. From what I can see, the finger has been clean sliced then sawed in a raggedy manner, and there were coarse fibres caught in it.'

'That means there is another victim out there. This isn't Darcie's finger.' Gina shuddered as she thought about the person who was missing a finger.

'Another thing, the victim is wearing red nail polish. Given the new growth at the base of the nail, it looks to have been applied about a month ago. Fingernails grow about three millimetres per month. I don't have anything else at the moment so I'll call you as soon as we have any results on the finger, or if I find anything that will help.'

'Thanks, Bernard. We'll need to check the DNA database, see if we have a match on file.' She had to believe the victim was still alive unless they found a body, but then again, if the kidnapper had cut off a finger, what was to stop them killing their victim? Her mind dished up a picture of a woman with red nails being held down while her finger was being sliced off.

Bernard headed back to his team. Gina took Jacob aside. 'I don't know why; I'm thinking our perpetrator left this for us to find, or maybe he used it to scare Darcie with and dropped it while struggling to get her into his car. Either way, I know time is against us and who knows what he has planned for Darcie. Where are the ANPR cameras around here?'

Automatic Number Plate Recognition might just help them

find the owner of the maybe dark-blue or brown car, although Gina knew that a lot of cars used the A road. It would be like finding a needle in a haystack, but it was a start.

Jacob bit his bottom lip as he thought. 'The A road that leads to Cleevesford. I'll chase that up in a minute.'

'Bernard,' Gina called. 'Do you have anything else for us now? Anything at all?'

He shook his head. 'Sorry. That's it. Like I said, I'll call you if we find anything.'

'Any cigarette butts?'

'Yes, some fresh, others old. There is a fair bit of litter on the roadside as you can appreciate. We have stacks of rubbish to process from the scene. Like most roads, people throw it out of their windows and things get blown around and get caught up in the long grass and the bushes. This scene is going to take a lot of processing. I can get the finger sent to the lab fast but the rest, it's going to take a fair while. I know that's not what you want to hear—'

'I understand,' she interjected. She appreciated the work that went into forensics. It was a long process. 'I won't hold you up any longer.'

He pulled his mask back over his mouth and nose, then rejoined his colleagues.

She turned to Jacob. 'Maybe Darcie opened up to Anna, told her that someone was bothering her or stalking her. Let's head to Anna's place and find out why she and Darcie were arguing last night.'

SEVEN

UNKNOWN

'What do I see? I see kind eyes and a warm smile, not right now but that's how you look when you speak to people. What they don't see is that beneath all that you have no soul and you have no heart. You are a cut-out. You are also someone who needs a reminder of the past and here I am to remind you. Do you know you have no heart, or is it down to me to wake you up and make you see what you've done?' She won't look at me. All she can do is blub and cry and I'm done with her self-pity.

I wonder if she knows she was being watched. I doubt it. I swig from my water bottle and while wiping my face with the back of my hand, take what's left of my lipstick off. 'I'm the song carried by the breeze, telling you of my presence. I'm the scent of a rose that is there to remind you that thorns prick. I'm a beautiful summer's day that is telling you that cancer is the risk you take when you lie in me for too long. Who knows, maybe I'm a cancer. Or maybe you are. It's all about perspective.'

I know she can't answer me with the rag in her mouth and the slip of material tied around her head keeping it in place, but I like that she has to keep her mouth shut and I get to do the talking. No one listened to me back then so here I am. I am making them listen. The drip, drip, drip coming from above is an added bonus as I know it has her thinking.

Her eyes are wide with fear but not for long. I have something that will help. 'Don't look at me like that. You have no right to.'

My hand trembles as the red spreads across her face. I'm finding it too hard to control the rage inside so I use the scalpel again. This is not going to end well for her.

I snatch the pretty locket from around her neck and open it. The cute kid smiles back at me. I fling it on the floor and crush it under my boot, knowing that really, I'm crushing her.

EIGHT

Gina waited while Jacob had grabbed his satchel from the back seat of his car. Anna's cottage looked quite old and quaint. It had been built to look like the older houses that bordered a large green. Weathered-looking brick with cobbled paths and traditional streetlamps adorned the frontage.

'Do we have any more information on Anna, guv?' Jacob walked behind her as Gina stepped onto the cobbles and tapped the brass fox knocker.

'No, nothing. We know that Kyle Fletcher didn't seem to know her that well.'

A woman opened the door and creased her forehead. 'I don't need anything and I don't want to join the church.' She continued to towel dry her hair as she stood there in her blue fluffy dressing gown.

'I'm DI Harte and this is DS Driscoll. We're from Cleevesford Police. Are you Anna?'

Anna tapped her nails on the doorframe as if contemplating how to answer. 'Yes, I'm Anna. Anna Heard. What's happened?'

'It would be best if we came in?'

Anna stepped back into the hallway. 'Is it my sister? Is she okay? Or my mum...'

'We need to speak to you about an incident involving your friend, Darcie Fletcher.'

'Darcie? I only saw her last night.'

'I know and that's what we need to speak to you about.'

'Is she okay?'

Gina stepped further into the hall, hoping they could sit in the lounge or at the dining table. She also took a deep breath, knowing she was about to deliver distressing news. 'We have reason to believe that Darcie was taken by a man in a car when she left your house last night. May we sit down?'

Anna's legs buckled and she dropped the towel on the floor, revealing her damp blonde pixie cut. Gina reached out to steady Anna, then she helped her to the kitchen where she seated her at the table.

'Thank you. Are you sure it was Darcie? Maybe it was someone else. What about Cleo. Is Cleo safe?' Her wide blue eyes started to water slightly.

'We are sure it was Darcie and Cleo is safe with her uncle. She managed to run away and hide. We need to ask you a few questions.'

'Of course. Anything.' She let out a long breath with closed eyes, then opened them again.

'What time did she leave yours?'

Anna shrugged. 'It was late and we'd been drinking wine. She said she was calling an Uber and left.' Anna began scrolling on her phone and she brought her Facebook account up. 'I posted a selfie of us about half an hour before she went. That was at ten thirty so she must have left around eleven or eleven fifteen.'

'Can I see?'

Anna held her phone towards Gina and Jacob. Jacob made a note of the time. Darcie looked like she had in the photo that Kyle had on his phone so they had an up-to-date photo of Darcie. Her dark-brown hair fell over her shoulders in a choppy straight cut that framed her face. There was a light crumple in her nose as she smiled and her high cheekbones had been accentuated with a bronze blusher. 'Was she wearing that top and headband when she left?'

'No, she left the headband in the bathroom. It's mine. She was messing around and came out wearing it. She had the black jumper on though, and that necklace, she wears it all the time. The locket has a photo of Cleo in it.'

'How long have you been friends?'

'Since school. I can't remember which year. We also worked at a summer camp in America together for a season, which we both loved.'

'Do you see each other regularly?'

Shrugging, Anna leaned back on her chair. 'Once a week, sometimes twice. I stay at her house a lot and she sometimes sleeps here when we have a drink. We used to go out a lot but Darcie has Cleo and it's hard for her to get a sitter all the time, so we tend to stay in and watch films or have pamper nights. I know her brother babysits sometimes.'

Jacob shifted his chair closer to the table.

Gina continued. 'Is Darcie in a relationship?'

'No, she split up with Cleo's dad about a year ago. He was really jealous. Poor Darcie couldn't even go to the shop without him questioning her when she got back. But it wasn't him. He wasn't violent, just insecure. I mean, he's with someone else now and they're expecting a baby already, if you can you believe that.'

'What is his name and do you have an address for him?' Alarm bells rang for Gina. Would he still be jealous, even though they had split up?

'Corey Lowe. He lives in Thorne Close, Cleevesford. I don't have the house number but he has previous so you should be able to find him.'

'What does he have previous for?'

'Oh, some man helped Darcie to change a tyre. He came back from work early and they were chatting on the drive. She was only thanking him and had left her boot open to put the jack back inside. Corey grabbed the jack and smashed it through the man's windscreen. He got charged for criminal damage, I think, and I know he had to pay a fine or something.'

Gina bit her bottom lip. So, the man who wasn't violent, was violent. Corey was definitely on her suspect list but then again, would he leave his daughter in the woods? Maybe he panicked. Jacob scrawled his pen along the page of his notebook before coming to a halt. 'Did Darcie mention any problems she was having with anyone lately? Could someone have been harassing her?'

'No... wait. She works at Shoreford's Used Car Dealership. She said that a man kept coming in to test drive cars. At first, she was really keen that he kept asking for her as she would bag the commission if he bought a car, but this week she said when they went out on a test drive he asked her out on a date. Then, there was something else.'

'What's that?'

'When they were in the car, he placed his hand on her knee, then he tried to put his hand up her skirt and touch her. At the lights, she got out and said she was a bit shaken but he apologised and said it was an accident. She got back in as she was stranded at this point, but he drove them both back and that was it. As far as I'm aware, she hasn't seen him since and she did say if he came back to the showroom, she was going to tell him where to go. She said he had no intention of buying a car. Do you think he's been stalking her?'

Gina blew out a breath. 'We need to speak to him for definite. Thank you, we'll get in touch with Shoreford's. If he test drove a car, they'd have his details on file. Did you see anything or anyone suspicious last night?'

She nodded. 'My cat was hissing in the garden around eight last night. I didn't think anything of it until you came but what if this stalker, kidnapper, or whoever he is was in my garden, watching me and Darcie?' Anna stood and hurried over to the patio door and shivered. 'That's where my cat was, right at the back gate, just right of the shed.'

'Is the gate locked?'

'It only has a slide lock. It's quiet around here. I've never been worried before but I'm going to get a padlock now.'

'May we take a look?'

'Please do.' She slid the door open and tied her dressing-gown cord tighter. 'I'm really worried for Darcie. Do you think that whoever has her will hurt her?' Anna's hand trembled slightly.

'We hope not but it's important that we find her, so if you remember anything else, however small, we need to know. It could be the tiniest detail that leads us to her.'

Gina and Jacob stepped out onto the small patio and Gina led the way towards the gate. There were no footsteps on the grass or on the slabs. None of the borders had been disturbed. She popped on a pair of latex gloves and slid the lock. The path behind led to more woodland and brambles.

'Guv, look.'

A fresh cigarette butt lay on the pavement. 'We need to call Bernard, see if he can spare a CSI to check this area out.'

Jacob nodded and stepped aside to make the call. 'He said a CSI will be here in five.'

They hurried back into the house and explained to Anna what would happen. 'Should I be worried? Will whoever took Darcie come for me? They won't kill her, will they? Please say she's going to be okay.'

'We're doing everything we can.' She couldn't tell Anna that Darcie would be fine. She didn't know and, again, the thought of finding the finger made her stomach turn. They were dealing with a dangerous person. Gina glanced at Jacob. She couldn't answer Anna but she needed to consider her safety. 'We'll organise drive-bys so that we can keep an eye on your cottage. Take this.' Gina passed a card to Anna. 'If you see anyone lurking around, call the station or call me. Also, we will need you to head to Cleevesford Station today to make a formal statement.'

'I'll do that. Thank you.'

'One more thing. What did you and Darcie argue about last night?'

Anna scrunched her brow and the slight twitch at her temple told Gina that she probably wasn't going to answer that question truthfully. Sometimes the tiniest reactions gave people away. 'We didn't. I don't know why Cleo said that.'

'I didn't say she did.'

'Oh, I just assumed as there would be no other way of you thinking that. We didn't argue. When Darcie left, she was fine, a little drunk maybe, and said she was going to wait outside with Cleo for an Uber. I went to bed and thought no more of it. Right, I have a lot to do.'

Anna couldn't get them out of her cottage fast enough and Gina wondered why. She sent a quick message to O'Connor, asking him to find Corey Lowe's house number. Before Jacob closed his car door, she leaned in. 'She knows more than she's letting on. Why would she lie about arguing with Darcie? Or maybe Cleo was wrong.' Gina shook her head. 'That little girl told us she saw the perp drop a finger on the ground, in the dark. It was late and she was tired and scared. She's a good witness. I believe Cleo.' Her phone flashed with a message. 'That was quick.'

'What's that?'

'O'Connor has just sent Corey Lowe's full address and we pass it on the way back to the station.'

NINE

Gina quickly read the highlights of Corey Lowe's file and Jacob got into the passenger side of her car while she updated him. 'He does have a record and as Anna Heard said, he was convicted of criminal damage. It wasn't the first time either. He got into a fight and broke a man's nose ten years ago. He's definitely a violent person. Apparently, he is registered as living here with a woman. Twenty-eight-year-old Monica Bell. Let's go and see what he has to say.'

'Guv, I guess we're ruling out kidnapping for ransom as we know there has been another victim and we haven't heard anything from the kidnapper yet?'

Gina pondered for a second over that question. 'We can't rule it out completely but given what we have, it's not looking likely but you never know. Time will tell on that front. Right now, I'm not ruling out murder. I just hope a body doesn't turn up.'

Not wasting any more time, they got out of the car and Gina knocked at the mid-terraced flat-roofed house, but there was no answer. Jacob stepped over a pot to get to the front window and peered through.

'Can you see anything?'

'No, oh wait. There's a woman coming from the kitchen. She's holding a baby.'

The woman opened the door, her thin brown hair piled on her head in a bun as she held her tiny baby. The buttons on her nursing top were only partly done up. 'Hello.'

Gina held up her identification and introduced them both to the woman. 'May we come in?'

She nodded and stepped back to let them through. 'Sorry, the place is a mess. Is there something wrong?'

Gina stood in the middle of the dark lounge, trying not to trip over the changing mat and rattle on the carpet. 'We're looking for Corey Lowe. Is he here?'

Monica placed the sleeping baby into a Moses basket. 'No.' There was a slight quiver in her voice.

'Do you know when he'll be back?'

She folded her arms. 'Hopefully never.'

Gina wanted to sigh. She hoped to be able to speak to Darcie's ex. 'Has something happened?'

'It's kind of private.'

'Miss Bell.'

'Monica.'

'Monica. We are investigating a serious crime and we need to know where he is, so if you have any idea at all, I'd really appreciate it if you told me.'

The woman looked down. 'I told him to leave.' She paused, then gestured for them to follow her into the kitchen.

'What happened in here?' The kitchen window had been boarded up.

Monica's jaw began to tremble and a few strands of hair fell from her bun. 'We had this big argument and he threw the pepper mill at the window.'

'When was this?'

'Last Sunday.'

'What was the argument about?' Gina bit her bottom lip.

'It's just... ever since we had Patsy, he seems to be jealous all the time. If I hug her, he sulks like a child and I don't know what to do. Things went from bad to worse. We've needed a fence panel fixing for ages so I thought I'd try and do it myself. I can be quite handy, so I was out in the garden getting on with it when I saw my neighbour. He came out and started playing with his dog. I asked him if he'd help me slip the panel back in. Corey came home and caught me laughing with the neighbour. He just told a joke and I thought it was funny. Corey went mad. He nudged the neighbour out of the way and shouted at him to get out of our garden and he dragged me into the house. He then accused me of sleeping with the neighbour and questioned whether he was Patsy's dad. The worst thing is, I always see messages from other women popping up on his phone and he keeps telling me I'm paranoid.' She bit the skin around the edge of her nails.

'Do you know who these messages were from?'

Monica shook her head.

'What happened after that?' Gina wondered if Corey had decided to take his anger out on Darcie following this incident. If he treated Monica in that way and with their baby present, why would he care about leaving Cleo at the roadside?

Monica choked on her words but continued. 'I thought he was going to lunge for me but he snatched the pepper mill off the table and threw it. I told him to leave. I was about to call my dad to ask him to come over and help me get Corey out, but he went. My dad pays the rent for me here since I had the baby. Corey doesn't give me anything which is why my dad hates him. I wish I could say he cared about our daughter but he doesn't. Corey only cares about Corey.'

'Do you have any idea where he may have gone?'

'He's contracting in Bristol and staying there from Monday to Friday. I think he went back to his digs on Sunday. I can't see that he'd have anywhere else to go unless he's staying with one of the women he'd been messaging.'

Gina knew that they didn't have a number on file for Corey. 'Do you have his phone number or the address of where he's staying?'

'I know it's near Bristol city centre but I don't have an address. I have his number.'

Gina instructed Monica to WhatsApp the number to her phone, which she did.

Jacob raised his brows at Gina as he noted everything down. She could tell that he too was thinking that they had a suspect.

'What's happened? Has Corey done something?'

Gina knew that the news would soon break about Darcie. In fact, Briggs was probably speaking to the press as they spoke. 'Did he mention his ex-partner much, Darcie Fletcher?' She knew she was answering a question with a question but she didn't want Monica to clam up and hold anything back.

'Only when he drank too much. On a normal day, she was just that bad ex who wouldn't give him access to his child, but I always thought, why didn't he get a solicitor or do something? He told me about his criminal record. He thought that any judge would only believe her so he decided not to bother.'

'Did he ever see his daughter?'

Monica shook her head. 'The fact that he never saw her or said that he missed her should have been a red flag. I saw through him as soon as we had Patsy. He didn't even want to hold her. I feel stupid now and my dad goes on about what a fool I've been, but I have my baby and I love her, so how can I be angry?' She paused. 'You didn't answer my question before.'

'Sorry.' Gina tilted her head. 'Darcie Fletcher has gone missing and we're investigating.'

'And you think Corey was involved?'

'We're investigating all leads. We just need to find him and speak to him.'

The room went silent and Jacob shuffled on the kitchen floor.

'Has he mentioned Darcie recently?' Gina asked.

Monica leaned on the worktop and looked at the boarded-up window. Tears began to slip from her eyes.

'What is it, Monica?'

She grabbed a piece of kitchen roll and wiped her tears away. 'Sorry, my hormones are going berserk at the minute. Just as he was leaving, he told me he'd met up with Darcie again and they'd slept together. He laughed at me as he left. I think he was just saying it to hurt me but I'm not sure. He makes out that she'd take him back any time. I don't believe she would, but what do I know? I've never spoken to Darcie so I have no idea what the truth is.'

The baby began to gurgle in the living room.

'Will you make a statement about him smashing your window?' Gina would love nothing more than to see Corey Lowe arrested again for criminal damage. She looked back at the window and for a second her old life flashed before her. Her dead ex-husband Terry used to scare her by breaking things. That used to be the prelude to him hitting her. She wiped the image away of him lying at the bottom of their stairs all those years ago, as she waited for him to die. She had no regrets. 'I can ask an officer to come over to your house and we can speak to your neighbour too.'

'No, I've started looking for somewhere else to rent. I need to move on from this and concentrate on my studies.'

Gina glanced at the kitchen table to see a pile of social science books from the Open University.

'As for Corey having anything to do with Darcie's disappearance, I couldn't say if he's involved. All I know is that Corey is unpredictable, he's entitled and very jealous. I don't understand him. I wish I did and I wish I could help more, but I can't. Sorry. When he left, I was checking my phone. I don't know why. Something just seemed off. Corey always seemed to know where I was. I found a tracking app on it and a tracker tag in my bag. I've removed the app and I dumped the tag in a public bin. That's a bit stalkerish, if you ask me.'

Gina had to agree. If Corey was involved in taking Darcie, he may have known exactly where she was at all times.

TEN

As Gina entered the station with Jacob, she spotted Nick the desk sergeant booking one of their regular petty criminals in. 'Morning,' she said as she held her phone down and pressed in the door code. There was a chill in the corridor. Detective Constable Paula Wyre caught her attention. She smiled at Gina and began tying her poker-straight black hair into a bun under the nape of her neck.

'The briefing is about to start.' Wyre headed towards the incident room and Gina caught up with her. Briggs had already marked up the board with witness names and as much detail about Darcie Fletcher as they had. He'd stuck a map up on the wall and pinned the entrance to Hutton Village and Anna Heard's cottage.

Gina took a seat next to the one that Briggs had thrown his jacket over and Jacob sat opposite. He pulled a banana from his bag and began eating it. DC Harry O'Connor ambled in with a box and placed it in the middle of the table. 'Iced buns. Mrs O made them last night and you know she always makes a million of everything.' He patted his protruding stomach, his shiny head reflected by the strip light above. Trainee DC Jhanvi Kapoor leaned in and took an iced bun.

'Right, good to have you all here.' Briggs placed his meaty hands down. His blue tie rested on the conference table as he leaned forward. His hair flopped onto his forehead slightly. 'We are treating this as a kidnap case. It looks like our victim, thirty-five-year-old mother and car salesperson, Darcie Fletcher, was bundled into a car at around eleven last night. All we have is that the car might be brown or dark blue. I've marked out the timeline with what we have so far.' He pointed to the board.

Gina glanced at the photo she'd messaged to Briggs, the one of Darcie and Kyle. Briggs had stuck a copy to the board. The photo had been enlarged and cropped to just show Darcie's face. The woman with the choppy haircut wearing a locket around her neck smiled back at them. Briggs continued. 'As you can all see from the map, Darcie's little girl, Cleo, had to have taken this route. We believe she hid out in these bushes and then when the car had gone, she followed the road until she reached the bed and breakfast where she hid out in the barn all night. She can't have gone deeper into the woods as behind the main row of trees, it's marshy. She would have been a lot dirtier and probably wet or, heaven forbid, she may have even drowned. DI Harte, you will be Senior Investigating Officer on this case. We need to find Darcie but given that the perp left a finger behind, we need to expect the worst. It shows what our perp is capable of and I think he wanted us to know that. Can you update us on the crime scene?'

Gina nodded and stood next to Briggs. 'Jacob and I have just got back from visiting the B&B, the scene at the road and Darcie's friend, Anna Heard. We also went to Darcie's ex-partner's house. Bernard is still at the roadside in Hutton Village and PCs Ahmed and Smith are there assisting with traffic management and protecting the cordon until Bernard and his team have finished. The one thing that stands out is that

Bernard found a human fingernail that had been painted red. It looked like approximately a month's growth had occurred since its application. Bernard has already emailed me to say it has been rushed to the lab so I'm hoping they can quickly extract DNA and we can run it through our database. This tells us that there's another victim. Cleo claims that the man who took her mother dropped the finger while he was carrying her to the car.'

Trainee DC Kapoor placed her half-eaten iced bun on the table. She grimaced and leaned back.

'Right, onto the victim. She was visiting Anna Heard last night. A witness, Mrs Swadling, said that when she and her husband left The Hare pub, she saw someone in a car, parked by the Hutton Village sign. All she saw was a glowing cigarette, so we're looking for a smoker. She didn't manage to give a description of the car, apart from it was brown or dark blue. I will update the system next so you'll all have access to this information. Cleo claims that Anna and Darcie argued before they left, but when we asked Anna about that she said they didn't. Anna also told us that Darcie's ex-partner was jealous and that he also has a record. She said he took a jack to someone's car window and all they'd done was help Darcie with a tyre. His name is Corey Lowe. Jacob and I visited Corey Lowe's address when we left the scene as it was on our way back. His current partner, Monica Bell, said that she told him to leave last Sunday.'

Briggs added Sunday the twenty-fifth of February onto the timeline on the board.

Gina continued. 'Before that, there was an incident with a neighbour that was similar to the incident that Anna Heard described when she spoke about Darcie. This time, Lowe got jealous that a neighbour was helping Monica fix their fence. He dragged her into the house. On the Sunday, he threw a pepper mill at their kitchen window, smashing it. He also told Monica that he'd been sleeping with Darcie, but she doesn't know if he was just saying that to be nasty. Monica also discovered that he'd hidden a tag in her handbag and installed a tracker app on her phone, which she has since removed. I told her that we'd like to take a statement from her but she didn't want to give one, unfortunately. What we do know is that he's a contractor and he works in Bristol. He stays there in the week. I've checked the system, there is a Volkswagen Caddy Maxi Van in white registered to him. O'Connor, can I task you with getting all units to look out for his van. With any luck, he'll appear on an ANPR camera?'

'Yep.' O'Connor jotted the details down.

'Right, back to Anna. She mentioned that she heard her cat hissing at someone outside her back gate around eight p.m. last night. Jacob and I checked the area out and we found a fresh cigarette butt so one of Bernard's team is there now checking it out. Cleo went home with her uncle, Kyle Fletcher. He's coming here later to make a statement with her, as is Anna. Wyre?'

DC Wyre smiled and straightened her black jacket. 'Yes.'

'I'd like you to follow up with him and Cleo. I need you to delve into Darcie's social media too. Check Facebook, Threads, X, TikTok and any others you can think of. Also, we now know that there was no phone found at the crime scene. We know Darcie had intended to use it to call an Uber when she left Anna's, so where is it? Did you follow up on that?' She glanced in O'Connor's direction.

'Yes, we have a number provided by her brother and I have checked with her phone provider, but it's now turned off. Records show it was used in the Hutton Village area at around eleven last night but after that, we have nothing. We're waiting for her phone records to come through. Then we'll have her messages and a call log.'

'Great. Anna also told us that Darcie had a problem with a man who came to her workplace. She works for Shoreford's

Used Car Dealership. We need to head over there to find out more about this customer. She said that Darcie had been upset by him, that over the past week he's sexually assaulted her during one of their test drives. Jacob and I will investigate this further. In fact, it's now gone midday so we'll head over after the briefing and the updates. Anything else for now?'

Kapoor raised a hand. 'We've just had an email. One of Anna Heard's neighbours said that his mother who has dementia kept screaming about the man in the mask. He checked to see if there was an intruder but he didn't see anyone. His mother regularly has nightmares and had fallen asleep in front of the back window so he chalked it up to a bad dream at the time. This was around eight thirty.'

Gina swallowed. 'It looks like this man was watching Darcie Fletcher last night. He waited for her to leave and took his opportunity to kidnap her. We need uniform out there, knocking on the other doors. We need to know if any other neighbours saw anyone suspicious hanging around. Right now, all we have is a man in a white mask and we can't even identify the make or colour of the car. Kapoor, can you arrange a team of PCs for the door to door, but be on hand should I need you?'

'Yes, guv.'

'We have a dangerous person out there, a kidnapper at the least and a murderer at worst. This was a targeted attack and there is more than one victim. I want all avenues explored but we also need Corey Lowe brought in as soon as possible. He's a violent, jealous person and it's possible that he's been involved with Darcie recently. Let's find him.'

ELEVEN

SHANNON

'You're late.' Shannon gripped the car key in her hand like she was gripping Finn's neck.

He smirked. 'I've been busy sorting out the garage stuff.'

'The Kia's out the back.' She threw the car keys at Finn. He didn't care that he was late. He and Gordon were good friends and Gordon would never stop using Finn to valet and MOT the cars that got traded in. 'What?' She wished he'd just do one and leave her alone.

He rubbed a bit of oil from his olive-skinned cheek. 'Can't we at least still be friends? I mean we have to work together and neither of us needs this every time I have to collect or return a car.' His dark oily hair shone under the light.

'I don't know, Finn. I guess I don't feel like being friendly with you.' Joel headed her way with a drink in each hand. She gave him the look and he instantly knew to turn around and go back the way he came. Joel was doing a good job of reading the room and she was grateful for that.

'Look, I said I'm sorry. I made a stupid mistake and I know you love me.' The lopsided smile that always tugged at her heart was back.

'It was more than that and you know it.' She stared at him, noticing the scratch on his neck. 'What happened?'

He scrunched his thick brows. 'What do you mean?'

'Your neck?'

He glanced at his reflection in the large window and a trickle of rain trailed down the glass as he felt the scratch. 'I don't know. I was a bit itchy earlier. Maybe I scratched it. It's this new shaving balm. I don't think it agrees with me.'

Shannon sniffed. 'You're right, I don't think it does. It smells like something you'd put down a loo.' She couldn't help having a little dig. His all-in-one overall fit him perfectly and however much she hated him, she still wanted to rip it off and devour him. She hated herself and her emotions. Finn was a player and a cheat and he could be cruel, so why was she still drawn to him.

He glanced around as he jangled the keys. 'No Darcie today?'

Shrugging, Shannon walked off into the kitchenette. She didn't want to discuss Darcie with him. She was still too angry to go down that route. He stormed after her, half-closing the door behind them, his breath hot on her neck. He reached under her blouse and began caressing her right breast and then she wanted him more than anything. His lips brushed her neck. 'Stop.'

'I thought—'

'You thought wrong.' She turned around and slapped him across the face. 'How dare you hurt me, then follow me in here and assault me—'

'Assault you? We both know you want me.' He shook his head and narrowed his eyes. He could tell she wanted him but she couldn't get past how much he'd hurt her. It wasn't just his lies; it was the way he made her feel. One minute she felt like a goddess, the next it was like she was dirt on his shoe. He knew how to play her but she also knew his game now.

She placed her hand on his chest and played with his overall zip, then she pushed him into the back wall and stormed out of the kitchenette. 'Joel, thanks for the drink. Where is it?'

He pointed to the main desk in the showroom. 'Everything okay?'

Finn came out of the kitchenette smoothing his hair down.

Shannon nodded. 'Finn has work to do, don't you?'

The bell rang and a customer entered. Joel hurried over, eager to earn some commission from a sale. Finn stepped closer and brushed his finger across Shannon's cheek. 'Oh, I have a lot of work to do, don't I?'

A shiver ran across the nape of her neck. 'Finn, stop it. Just go, please.' He was a liar and a cheat. It was over.

He leaned forward and kissed her on the forehead. 'We were good together in the sack. Come on, let's keep it casual.'

'Stop it, Finn. You know that's not what I want.'

'It's what I want and you know you can't get rid of me that easily and you also know, I always get what I want.' He placed his hand on her hip.

Shannon shrugged him away. 'Not this time. Get off me.' She was never going near him again.

He let out a laugh. 'I'd say you have someone else but look at you. You try far too hard. That lipstick makes you look like a clown.' He smeared her bottom lip.

'Get off me.'

'I'm not on you.'

'Just go, will you?'

He picked up her coffee and took a long swig before placing the cup back on the desk. 'Only if you say I can come to yours tonight and we can finish what we started. You know she means nothing to me, don't you?'

'You made your bed, Finn.'

Joel hurried over. 'Is everything okay?' Shannon's heart boomed. Joel couldn't have come over at a better time. Finn didn't often make her feel that uncomfortable but his intense stare and the way he stood in her way was unsettling.

Shannon nodded. 'Finn is leaving. He has the Kia to MOT and valet, don't you, Finn?'

He made a clicking sound with his tongue and did a mock salute. 'Yep, see you both later.'

Exhaling, Shannon sat on the edge of the desk.

'You don't look so good.' Joel tilted his head. 'Anything I can do?'

'No, I'm okay. Just a bit worried about Darcie.' That was a lie, but she didn't want to discuss Finn with the young trainee.

'Any news from Darcie?' Joel raised his eyebrows.

She shook her head. 'Nothing and I can't get her on the phone, which is weird.' She watched as Finn drove the Kia away and breathed a sigh of relief. She had no idea what she ever saw in him. To begin with, he'd been like a thrill ride at a theme park. He'd been the risky to her sensible. They'd had sex in odd places like the toilets in a restaurant. She'd never done things like that with anyone before. He'd been fun and slightly intense, but she'd liked it. Now it was nothing more than creepy and she wished Darcie would come in so she could tell her what had just happened. Darcie needed to know what Finn was really like. It was time to forgive her best friend.

'I'm sure it's like you said. Maybe Cleo is ill and she's busy looking after her.'

'I hope so. I'll try calling her again in a bit.'

Joel checked a text that came through.

'Is that your new girlfriend again?'

He smiled. 'It might be.'

A man and a woman entered the showroom. The woman's long black overcoat looked like it pinched a touch around the middle and her brown hair was frizzy from the inclement weather. The man seemed quite a bit younger and was definitely handsome with his chiselled jaw and smart appearance.

He was far sexier than Finn. They didn't look like a couple looking for a car.

The woman pulled some identification from her pocket. 'I'm DI Harte and this is DS Driscoll. We need to speak to someone about Darcie Fletcher. She works here, doesn't she?'

Something bad had happened because why else would the police be here? Despite their differences, Darcie would never ignore her calls. Her heart skipped a beat and she sat back down on the edge of her desk, scared of what the police were about to tell her.

TWELVE

Gina accepted the coffee from the young man. As soon as she'd explained what had happened, Shannon sat and twiddled her hands in shock. 'I mean someone took her but have they hurt her? They won't hurt her, will they?'

Not being able to make any promises on that front, Gina pressed her lips together and smiled sympathetically. 'Can we go somewhere more private to talk?' A customer began to loiter behind them and the young male assistant went over to help them.

Shannon stood and led them to an office at the back of the building. Paperwork spilled from the trays and various certificates on the wall told Gina that the recipient, Gordon Shoreford, had been business person of the year in 2003 and 2006. A more recent photo of him in a newspaper article had been framed and showed him to be a portly man who looked about sixty. His thick moustache almost reached both ends of his face and his eyebrows almost joined into a monobrow above his small eyes.

'Take a seat.' Shannon sat behind the desk and pushed a mouldy cup aside.

The metal frame of the seat bounced as Gina sat. She waited for Jacob to get his notebook out. 'Can I take your full name, please?'

'It's Shannon Calder.' She nervously traced her long nails along the edge of the desk.

'When did you last see Darcie Fletcher?'

'Err, about three yesterday. She leaves early to pick her daughter up from school.'

Gina undid her coat buttons. The radiator beside her pumped out a lot of heat. 'How did she seem?'

'Happy enough. I heard her talking to Joel, that's our trainee. He made them both a coffee. She told him that she was going to her friend's house for a drink later that night. When she didn't come in this morning I thought maybe Cleo was ill, or maybe Darcie had a hangover, but Darcie has never had time off when she went out for a drink. Actually, she barely drinks. Maybe one or two glasses of wine at most.'

'So, she said she was going to a friend's house. Do you know her friend?'

Shannon twitched her nose and exhaled. 'Her name is Anna. Anna has come out with us a couple of times and she comes here quite often to meet Darcie, and they go out to lunch together. I think Anna works locally or for herself. I'm not sure what she does but she used to be a holiday rep.'

'Were they on good terms?'

'I think so. If they weren't, Darcie didn't say anything to me.' Shannon stopped trailing her nails across the desk and placed her hands underneath it.

'Do you know if Darcie was having any problems with anyone?' Shannon pushed her chair back and crossed her legs. Gina could sense she was nervous about something. 'Had she had any issues or conflict recently?'

'Hmm, there is someone. There's a man who's been visiting the showroom for a couple of months. He always asks for Darcie and he definitely has a thing for her, but it's not a two-way thing. He's creepy and I know Darcie thinks the same.'

'So, she has had an issue with a customer?'

Shannon nodded and rolled her shoulders as if trying to loosen a tense muscle. 'Yes. He comes in at least once a week and asks to test drive a car. Darcie didn't like going out with him but he always asked for her. I know you probably won't get why she simply didn't refuse to accompany him, but what you have to understand is that we get commission. Darcie has a little girl and she needs the money, as we all do. Our basic salaries are nothing to write home about. We have to sell.' Shannon hesitated. 'We did start to wonder if he was ever going to buy a car but Darcie was convinced he would when he found the right one. Joel and I knew that he was only coming to see Darcie. We even said as much, but she said we were trying to move in on her customer. She wanted to entertain Mr Creepy, and she told us to back off, so we did. That was until he scared her.'

'How did he scare her?'

'The last time he test drove a car, he groped her. She came back shaken and said it came from nowhere. When he stopped the car at the traffic lights, she jumped out and had people tooting their horns behind them. Anyway, he claimed it was a misunderstanding and she got back in and he drove them back here. She then agreed with us that he was a weirdo, so she said she wasn't going to go out in a car with him again. If he came back, Joel said he was going to go instead but Joel doesn't have a licence, so it was going to have to be me and maybe him too. Bless Joel, he even said if the creep did actually buy a car, Darcie could have the commission.'

'What day was this?' Gina leaned back in the chair and Jacob frantically wrote all the details down.

'Tuesday. It was first thing, so around nine in the morning.'

'Do you have a name for this customer?'

'I can do one better. I have a copy of his driving licence with all his details on. We took this before he drove any of our cars. If you can bear with me for five minutes, I'll get it for you.'

Gina nodded. 'It would be really helpful if you could take a copy for us.'

Shannon stood and left the room, closing Gina and Jacob in.

'It's sounding like this guy had some sort of obsession with Darcie,' Jacob said.

'He's definitely our main person of interest right now.'

Shannon burst back in, flapping a piece of paper in one hand. Gina almost gasped when she saw whose licence had been copied. After quickly speaking to the trainee, Joel, Gina hurried back to her car and passed it to Jacob. 'You know who that is, don't you?'

'I can't say that I do.' He scrunched his brows.

'Registered sex offender, Mitchell Varley. PC Smith has mentioned the case in the past as he was first at the scene when he attacked one of his victims. We need to call this in and pay him a visit, now.'

THIRTEEN
SHANICE

Shanice's mum yelled again. She'd been going on at Shanice to take the rubbish down for about half an hour and rather than wait until Shanice went out, her mum had to have it done right now. Her mother barged into her room just as Shanice was tying her pink scarf around her head. She'd got the position perfect until she'd been scared out of her skin. 'Mum, you promised you'd start knocking.'

'I'll start knocking when you've finished your chores, baby girl.' Her mother turned her bottom lip over and folded her arms which always made Shanice laugh a little. Her mother was all bark and no bite.

''Kay, 'kay.' As Shanice threw the scarf on her desk, she knocked over her nail varnish remover and it spilled all over her A level English revision notes. 'Fuck.'

'Shanice, I didn't bring you up to cuss like that. Go take the rubbish down and then you need to wash that foul mouth of yours out.'

She had embarrassingly dropped the f-bomb in front of her mum. By the time she got back up, Nanna would know about it too. Shanice nodded and hurried to the kitchen. As soon as she sorted the rubbish out, she could get back to her hair and then she was going to meet her bestie.

The lift pinged and she stepped out, her footsteps echoing in the tiled entrance to their block of flats. As she left the building, a chilly breeze caught her. Goosebumps prickled on her bare arms. A skimpy T-shirt wasn't cutting it in this weather. It wasn't summer yet. She heard her nanna's voice in her head. *You'll catch your death, child. Put some clothes on.*

The bin area always gave her the creeps. To get there, she had to walk around the back of the building and enter a huge brick, walled-off area that was full of industrial-sized bins that stank. She nudged the gate open. As usual it creaked. First, she had to pass all the huge recycling containers. One of the bins had been wedged open by a mountain of bags, the ones further away were nicely closed. Shanice stretched her T-shirt over her nose as she approached the bin. The smell always got to her and in the summer, sometimes there would be flies and maggots. At least the cold ensured she wasn't going to be startled by that level of horror today. On approaching the bin farthest away, she grabbed the sliding lid and pushed it back as far as she could and flung the bag inside.

A bang and the sound of murmuring stopped her. A gust caught the gate and it slammed shut. Shanice's heart thrummed as she stared at the graffitied wall next to the last bin. An old water-stained burgundy sofa that had been stacked in front of a dirty mattress had been leaned against the wall. Someone had to be hiding behind it. 'Hello?' She had come across a homeless person before and he'd terrified the life out of her. He'd darted out with a sleeping bag flung over the back of his head and crashed her to the pavement before running off.

She sprinted to the gate, scared it might be someone more dangerous. As she went to open it, heavy footsteps came from the other side. She didn't know whether to lock herself in with the person behind the mattress or go out there and face whoever was standing firm on the other side. Stepping back, she could see the wearer's chunky black boots. 'Hello.' They didn't answer. Whoever was lurking behind the gate certainly wasn't just another resident coming to throw some rubbish out. Her mind flashed back to all the horror stories she heard on the news. She only had to check it out to hear about stabbings and drug crimes, and she wondered if her bin store was the perfect place for a dealer to do business. She shuffled behind the recycling bin and clasped a hand over her mouth. Whoever had been behind the mattress remained there. Maybe they were hiding from the booted person. But she'd said hello. Both strangers knew where she was. Her teeth began to chatter. Maybe it was just Old Mr Turkey, nicknamed that because of his neck. He had a pair of boots like that. It could be him and if he saw her cowering behind a bin, he'd think she was silly.

The wearer of the boots began to walk away. Shanice let out a huge breath and placed a hand over her banging heart. Whoever was out there had gone. It probably was Mr Turkey and now she felt foolish. As she stood, she heard a bang coming from behind the mattress again. Was it too soon to open the gate, especially as it was more than likely Mr Turkey? She rested her trembling fingers on the catch and a few drops of rain speckled her cheeks.

Just then a figure hobbled from behind the mattress, Shanice stared open-mouthed. She'd never seen someone look so emaciated. The woman's straggly brown hair fell all over her face in tangled ribbons. That wasn't the most worrying thing; the woman was naked apart from a pair of dirty white underpants. She staggered forward like something from a horror film, wheezing as she struggled for breath. As she reached the middle of the courtyard, her legs buckled and she stumbled onto the path.

Shanice ran over and held her as she pulled her phone from her pocket and dialled 999. Just as she was connected, she heard a car speeding away. 'It's okay, I'm going to get you some help.' The operator asked what service she required. 'Ambulance, police. Come quick. I've just found a woman and she might be dying.' Tears trickled down Shanice's face as she looked the woman up and down, then she almost heaved when she saw that the woman had a missing finger.

FOURTEEN

Gina ended her hands-free call as she pulled up outside Mitchell Varley's registered address and waited for Jacob. They now had a plan to deal with Varley. She glanced in her rear-view mirror, expecting to see PC Smith and Trainee DC Kapoor. They would soon be in place, ready to take the next steps. A few seconds later, Jacob parked and stepped out of his car. He jogged across the road to meet her, his satchel crossing his body and banging against his hip with each step. 'Guv, what's the plan?'

'We need to wait for Smith and Kapoor before going in.'

'I haven't come across Varley before now so I don't know what we're up against here. What do you know?'

She glanced up and down at the tightly packed, fifties-built terraced houses, with their mishmash of window dressings, some covered in nothing more than a sheet in the many houses of multiple occupancy. She stepped over a puddle to see if anyone from Varley's household had noticed her outside but no one had.

'Here's the quick lowdown. He's been out of prison for five years now but he's on the sex offenders' register. He was convicted of exposure and sexual assault. He terrorised dog walkers and joggers for a year before he was finally caught. One of his victims, a young woman in her early twenties, fought back and broke his wrist during a struggle with him, then she managed to get him on the ground and restrain him while she called the police. He'd picked on a self-defence trainer that day. Anyway, four other people who were assaulted had managed to obtain his DNA whether it was from scratched skin under the nails, or hair. I think a victim's dog also bit him while trying to help its owner. A smear of his blood was found on the dog. We think he committed up to fifteen assaults but unfortunately there wasn't enough evidence to convict him for the others.' She glanced up at his house again and she couldn't see anyone at the window.

'He was a habitual offender, then, which definitely puts him high up on our suspects' list. Can a person like that change?' Jacob adjusted his bag.

'It doesn't look like it, not if he sexually assaulted Darcie Fletcher just before she was taken. I wonder if he's committed any offences that haven't been reported. I know Darcie didn't report him for assaulting her. If he has taken Darcie, I'd say he's escalating. If he's our perp, maybe he's no longer thrilled by exposing himself and sexually assaulting his victims. He's a dangerous man.' Gina blew out a breath and ran her hands through her damp hair. A drop of rain speckled her nose.

'What did he actually do to his victims? I just want to understand what he could be escalating from?'

Gina noticed a blanket covering an upstairs window quivering. Smith and Kapoor still hadn't arrived. 'After wrestling them to the ground and pinning them down, he forced his hands down their underwear and up their tops while touching himself. He wore a balaclava so none of the victims saw his face. After committing the assaults, he'd run away leaving his victims in a state of shock. They were all female. One woman was in her seventies, another girl was seventeen. He didn't seem to have a type as such. Ages aside, they were different ethnicities, builds; had different coloured hair and eyes.'

'Who else is coming?'

'Smith, Kapoor and a team of PCs in cars for backup.'

Smith pulled up at the end of the road. Gina's phone vibrated. She answered and listened. 'It's Smith. Kapoor is in place around the back, just in case he should try to scarper.' Gina gave Jacob the nod and headed up the uneven path, pushing the stray bramble branches aside as she reached the chipped blue door. After knocking, she could hear a grunt from behind the wood, then a man opened it.

'Who are you?' He sniffed and pulled his stained dressing gown across his bare belly and boxer shorts.

The man standing in front of Gina was too old to be Mitchell Varley. His bulbous nose and grey sideburns put him at approximately sixty but Varley was in his late thirties. 'I'm DI Harte and this is DS Driscoll. We need to speak to Mr Varley.'

'Oh, him.' The man left the door open and headed through to the kitchen at the back. 'I'm not standing on the doorstep and you're letting the cold in. Come on in and shut the door.'

Gina took that as an invite to enter. She and Jacob stepped into the dark hall. The first room to the right had a number stuck to it. 56A. She gathered that someone lived in it and the house had been sectioned into bedsits with a shared kitchen. The white woodchip walls were stained by a brown mark that came from the top of the wall and reached the old carpet gripper that had been stuck close to the skirting board.

The man swivelled the numbers on a combination lock to open a cupboard door. 'Everyone robs your stuff in this house.' He pulled a can of cola from the bare shelf and it released a hiss as he opened it. He took a swig and belched. 'Want one?'

Gina shook her head. 'What's your name?'

'Colin.'

'Colin, is Mr Varley in?'

'Nah, he hasn't been in for a week at least.' Gina's shoulders slumped. She gestured to Jacob to keep Smith and Kapoor updated.

'Which room is he in?'

'He shares with me. Look, I don't want to get in any trouble. Before moving in here, I was living on the streets but since getting clean and off the streets, I'm slowly turning my life around. I have a part-time job. I can't lose this room so if I'm square with you, I trust you won't tell the landlord. I just helped a desperate man, that's all. I've been where Varley is and it's hard to drag your arse out of the gutter.' Worry lines spread across the man's forehead as he waited for Gina to answer.

'We just want to find Mr Varley. Do you know where he might be?'

Colin shrugged and scrunched his pink pockmarked nose. 'The last I saw of him, he went off in his fancy pants clothes to see some woman he'd been banging on about for the past few weeks.' Colin let out a snigger. 'He got me to trim his hair. I was a barber in another life. Then he went out to a charity shop and bought some nice jeans and a smart shirt. I kept on at him to use his new-found love of looking good to find a job but he didn't take any notice. I just hoped this new woman was going to be good for him.' He hesitated. 'Is there something wrong with him? Is he hurt? I mean a DI and a DS, that's heavy going. Has he done something?'

'I'm sorry, I can't divulge anything about the case we're working on at the moment but if you know where he could be, it would really help us, and we definitely won't say anything to your landlord. It's admirable that you're turning your life around like this.'

Colin paused and placed his can of pop on the worktop. 'Come up to my room.'

As he turned his back, they followed him up the rickety wooden steps until they reached two other rooms.

'This is mine.' He pushed open the unlocked door to reveal a single bed pushed up against the far wall and a camp bed under the window. A small television with a large back had been placed on a chair in the corner of the room. Even though Colin had nothing, he was sharing it with someone else. 'He's taken his stuff so there's nothing here.'

'Colin, is there anything you can tell us about Mr Varley? Where he goes, who his friends are?' Maybe the clue to finding him was in his habits or something he'd mentioned.

'He's quiet, keeps himself to himself and I know he's done time. You might wonder why I'm helping a crim but you know, shoplifting and breaking into a factory isn't the worst crime a person can commit. He just needs a chance and I thought I'd give him one. He managed to get his driver's licence and said he was going to get a job as a courier.'

Gina wondered what Colin would think if he knew he was sharing his room with a violent sex offender. 'Did he mention his girlfriend's name?'

'Darcie. I laughed and said her name sounded posh. He said she has a little girl too and that he'd love to be a dad one day.' Colin walked over to his back window and pulled the net aside. He turned back to Gina and went to say something.

'What is it?' Colin had a concern, she could tell.

'I'm the type of person that wants to believe the best in people. Despite what I've been through, I'm an optimist and I like to help people.'

'Is something about Mr Varley worrying you?' Gina paused, wondering how much she should divulge. 'Colin, I know you're a good person and you want to help. We believe that Mr Varley could be about to do something that there is no coming back from. If you want to help him, you need to tell us what you know.'

Colin walked over to the camp bed and reached under the pillow. He pulled a balaclava from underneath it and threw it on the blankets. 'I'm worried he's planning a robbery and going back to his old ways. Please find him. We can stop this. Look for Darcie. She works at a car showroom. Find him and stop him before he ruins his life again.'

'Thank you, you've been really helpful. I can't divulge any details about the case, but I'd ask that you call us immediately if he turns up, and don't let him stay with you.'

Gina's phone beeped and Briggs's name popped up. She opened the message.

Gina, a woman has been taken to Cleevesford General Hospital and she has a missing finger. O'Connor has headed over to interview the witness who found her. We have the first victim. I need you over there now. It's touch and go. Word from the hospital is she probably won't make it and was left for dead.

FIFTEEN

SHANNON

A gale whipped up Shannon's hair. She pulled up her fur-lined hood and zipped her coat up to her chin as she tottered off the bus towards the dog-sitter's house. Having to part with her beloved Volkswagen Passat had hurt but she couldn't afford to keep it any more because Barney had cost her a fortune over the past year. Joel's mother had picked him up from the showroom. Worried after what had happened to Darcie, they'd offered her a lift home but it didn't seem right to ask them to collect her dog first, besides, she'd still had work to do at the showroom and Barney sometimes got car sick.

She pulled her phone from her pocket, hoping that Darcie had messaged her with some big misunderstanding as to why she'd vanished from a roadside last night. No, that was wishful thinking. Her friend had been taken by some psycho. Her jellied legs prompted her to glance over her shoulder to check she wasn't being followed.

The streetlights flickered on and lit up the path ahead, making her feel slightly safer. It was still early. Nothing happened to people at teatime, did it? She couldn't wait to get home and into her pyjamas. Maybe she'd try to make friends with Anna on Facebook, see if she'd heard anything about Darcie. It's not as if the police would tell her if she called and asked, although she did have the detective's card, so she could call. She searched her pockets for the card. Damn, she'd left it on Gordon's desk with a note for him to call the police too. Come to think of it, Gordon hadn't been back all day which was odd. He never stayed away that long, preferring to be in the showroom so he could scrutinise how hard they all worked.

The trees whooshed in the breeze and a cat jumped from a branch before scarpering behind a dustbin, then under a fence. She placed a hand on her banging heart. It was just a cat.

A message flashed on her phone. What did Finn want? He'd been horrible to her earlier.

Shannon, soz about before. I just miss you and I lashed out like an idiot. I said some horrible things and as soon as I left, I felt bad, but you can't deny that we still have that spark. Come out with me later. We can have a laugh and get smashed.

She wasn't falling for the nice guy act. However much she'd like to meet up with him, get smashed, and take him home with her, he'd acted in an unforgivable way. The things he'd said were awful. It wasn't just the way he played Mr Horrible one moment, followed by Mr Nice the next, it was also him, Darcie and the lies. She wondered if she should have mentioned those to the detective but then again, that had nothing to do with Darcie's disappearance. Finn was many things but he wasn't a kidnapper. He didn't have to kidnap women. For some reason, they fell at his feet. She'd well and truly seen through him at last. Besides, she had Darcie to think about now. She thought about the weirdo, Mitchell Varley. If only they'd called the police on the day he had assaulted Darcie. Maybe they'd have picked him up. It had to be him.

'Shannon.' It was as if the breeze had carried a haunting whisper with it.

Was that her name being called? She stopped walking. The sound of her own blood pumping through her body threatened to deafen her, and she tried to listen for the voice through it. She glanced back and all she could see were trees. Squinting, she tried to focus on the darkest voids between the trees without success. Her mind was playing tricks on her. Darcie had been taken and that had shaken her up. Hell, Darcie might not even be alive now and that scared Shannon more. Poor Cleo had been left alone in the night. The whole thing was tricking her into thinking she'd heard a voice. It was the stress of the situation. She waited for her heart to realise there was no threat but it was taking its time to stop rendering her breathless.

'Shannon.' This time it was even softer, but it was unmistakably her name being called. She ran on her heels, her soles burning every time she pounded hard on the pavement. Then one of her heels got caught in the crack of a paving stone. However hard she pulled, she couldn't free her shoe.

'Who's out there?' she called out, before gulping down the lump in her throat.

The breeze whipped violently just as the weather forecast had promised. Shannon didn't know where to look. She looked to her left, then her right, then over her shoulder before staring ahead again. She couldn't watch all directions at once. Stepping out of her shoe, she bent down to pull it and as it released, she almost stumbled back. She placed it back on her foot and ran away from the trees as fast as her shaking legs would allow.

She turned into the estate and leaned over to get her breath back. Before continuing, she turned and stared at the path she'd just ran from wondering if the person calling her name would appear. Her phone beeped again. It was Finn.

It's a horrible night to be outside. It's not safe for a woman all on her own. You need me. X

It had to be Finn who was calling her name. Mr Nice Guy hadn't lasted long and he did have a tendency to know where she was at any given time which was always odd. At first, she'd thought it was romantic when he 'bumped' into her while she was on a night out with friends. He'd claimed that it was the universe telling them they should get together but now, after all that had happened, it was freaking her out a little, especially as he'd made it clear that he wasn't the committed relationship type. Understanding him was impossible. He just wanted to control her more than anything. She could see that now. She hit reply.

Just leave me alone. Don't call me. Don't text, and don't ever come to my house again!

'Get lost, Finn, or I'll call the police,' she yelled at the path behind her, knowing that he'd hear her from wherever he was lurking. He didn't reply. He was gone, for now. To him, it was a game, but it wasn't funny to her. She pictured him sniggering as he listened to her shout.

She reached the house on the end and opened the gate. Her dog carer was already waiting at the door, passing Barney's lead to her before Shannon could say a word. 'Sorry, I have to go and pick the kids up from my friend's. Barney's had a good day and he's been adorable as usual and he's still doing well. No rashes.'

Shannon glanced down at her furry friend. Just before Christmas he'd come down with some rash and he had to wear a cone on his neck, and he'd needed a never-ending supply of steroids from the vets. Even so, she always got the dog carer to keep an eye on him now so that she'd know if he was having a flare up. The carer pulled her door closed and ran to her car. 'I'll see you in the morning.' In a flash, she'd reversed off her drive and sped off.

Shannon bent down and patted the black Labrador's head. 'Come on, Barney. Let's go home.' There was no way she was taking the same path back to hers. It might only be a ten-minute walk away but she was going to walk the long way around.

Several minutes later, she reached her end of terrace house and flinched as her back gate banged against the frame. She was sure she'd closed it. There was a padlock but she never used it. Nudging it open, Barney dragged her alongside the house. Odd, the security light didn't come on. 'Barney, stop it.' She gave his lead a gentle tug, not wanting to go any further. Something didn't feel right. That's when she saw the man peering through her kitchen window. Before she could run away, he was already behind her.

SIXTEEN

Gina peered through the glass window of the treatment room, the smell of bodily fluids and disinfectant turning her empty stomach. She hated hospitals. Jacob had gone to get them a drink while she waited to see if they'd be able to speak to the victim. The victim had no name, no address and no details whatsoever. The young woman's sunken eyes and deeply cracked lips drew Gina's focus and she wanted so much to turn away but she couldn't.

'Guv.'

She flinched. 'Shaf, tell me what we have so far?'

PC Ahmed put the chocolate bar he was carrying into his trouser pocket. 'I came straight from the Hutton Village scene as instructed by DCI Briggs. I supervised the doctor in charge as he managed to calm the victim down enough to take some nail clippings, blood and swabs. The nursing staff removed the underpants she was wearing when they cleaned her up so I bagged those too. They should be on their way to the lab. I spoke to Keith and he said the samples would be fast-tracked. She wasn't wearing anything else.'

As Jacob approached them he almost threw the coffee at

Gina when the woman let out a piercing scream. Her wide-eyed stare darted all over the room as if she was seeing things. 'I think Briggs was being optimistic when he thought we might be able to interview her this evening.' He held Gina's coffee out.

Gina took the drink. 'Thank you.' She looked towards PC Ahmed so he could continue.

'They said she's been drugged but I know the doctor who treated her wants to speak to you.' PC Ahmed glanced up and down, as if looking for him. 'I can't see him around but his name is Doctor Alessi.'

'What can you tell me about the victim or where she was found?'

The PC cleared his throat. 'She was found in the bin store of Broadwas Mews by a teenage girl. Her mother had asked her to take the rubbish out. She also said she heard someone walking behind the gate that separates the bin store from the road, then they sped off in a car.'

'Is there any CCTV?'

'No, guv. The residents have apparently campaigned for it as a lot of low-level crime goes on by that bin store, but the council refused on the basis of lack of funding.'

'Did she see this person or the car?' Gina knew of Broadwas Mews. It was a several storeys high block of flats. 'With so many people living in such close proximity, someone must have seen who was lurking outside.'

'No, she was in this walled-off courtyard where the bins are kept. All she saw was a pair of heavy black boots when she looked under the gate which has a large gap underneath it. She described them as work boots. She said she thought they might have been slightly stained, oily maybe. Her statement has already been uploaded to the system but she didn't say much else of any help. A team of PCs are interviewing everyone in the flats to see if they saw anything, but that will take a while as most of the residents were at work or out. A crime scene assistant attended a short while later.' Shaf removed his police hat and ruffled his flattened hair. 'It's always hot in hospitals, isn't it?'

Gina nodded and took another sip of coffee. Her stomach rumbled for food. 'Anything else?'

'She just kept shouting words that made no sense. She also smashed the wall clock as they wheeled her into the treatment room. Everything she said sounded like gibberish, if I'm honest. Sorry, guv. Wish I knew more.'

'I'm Doctor Alessi,' said the tall man standing behind Gina. Wispy curls framed his face and he smiled. 'Shall we talk in a side room?'

'Yes, please.' Gina finished her drink and dropped the paper cup into a bin. 'Shaf, can you stay here and keep an eye on the patient? I don't want her left alone tonight. She's not safe until we catch the perp.'

He dragged a chair outside the room and pulled his chocolate bar from his pocket. ''Course.'

Jacob walked with her behind the doctor until he managed to find a room that was free. Doctor Alessi opened the door and waited for the strip light to come on. After they sat, the doctor began. 'We don't have a name or any information but what we do have is one very sick patient. If she had been out there any longer, she'd be dead now. She has acute pancreatitis. We suspect it has been caused by severe malnutrition and she's also very underweight. She came in dehydrated and we detected a slight bit of fluid in her lungs too. On arrival, she was coughing a lot and had been vomiting in the ambulance. We also found track marks on various parts of her body, some old, some new.'

'So, drugs were involved?' Gina wondered if their Jane Doe had been drugged or was on drugs. The two were very different. If someone had been holding their unnamed victim, they could have been injecting her to control her.

Doctor Alessi nodded. 'There is evidence of historic drug

use so I'd say she's been using for a long time. She was also hallucinating on arrival but looking at her physical condition, I wasn't surprised. Your forensics person asked for a blood sample that could be analysed by toxicology. We're also running tests of our own so we know how to treat her.'

Gina was pleased that they were. The hospital would get much faster results than the lab. 'How long will it take for her to recover?'

The doctor leaned forward, clasping his long fingers together. 'I don't know if she will. We may have to intubate her to give her the best chance of recovery. We'll do our best to stabilise her here, then she'll be heading to ICU. After that, we'll constantly monitor her condition and see where we are in a while.'

The whole situation seemed hopeless, especially if their Jane Doe was destined to end up in the Intensive Care Unit on a ventilator. Their victim could literally lead them to Darcie if only she was able to speak to them. 'Please, is there anything you can do? Whoever did this to her has taken another victim and we're racing against time to save her.'

Doctor Alessi frowned. 'I really can't think of a way. She's too poorly and we can only concentrate on her survival right now. We have no option but to take her recovery minute by minute. She's so ill she runs the risk of going into cardiac arrest, plus she is not making any sense at all. We've tried to find out what her name is and we will keep trying. I'm so sorry. I understand your frustration and I really wish I could help, but our patient is just too poorly to give you what you need.'

Gina passed him her card and Jacob looked away, disappointed that they couldn't speak to Jane Doe. 'Do you have any idea how her finger was severed?' She had her suspicions because of the coarse fibres that Bernard had mentioned. The lab results would take a while, but she thought it worth mentioning the finger as the doctor may be able to shed more light on it.

'I'd say a tourniquet had been applied to the digit, then it was tightened until it cut to the bone, then it looked like the bone was sawed.' Doctor Alessi removed his glasses, rubbed his eyes and sighed. 'Sorry, I see a lot of injuries but I've never seen such a horrific act of violence. Our patient has suffered a lot. There are also ligature marks on her wrists and ankles.'

Gina gulped to try and get rid of the nauseous feeling in her throat. Victim one had been bound, drugged, starved of food and water, had suffered the pain of her finger being severed and there was water in her lungs. She pictured her pleading for the pain to stop as she begged for her life, or had she begged for death?

'There is something but it might also be nothing because she was hallucinating, but a few of her words did make sense.'

Gina unclenched her fists in her lap, hoping the doctor was about to deliver something that would help with the case.

'She was so weak but as soon as we wheeled her into the treatment room, her stare fixed on the wall clock. As we passed it, she reached up and knocked it off the wall. I'm sure she kept repeating the words, tick-tock.'

The woman lying in the hospital bed was still alive and that gave Gina hope for Darcie. The sound of a ticking clock filled Gina's thoughts. All she could think about was the young mother who'd been taken, and that the kidnapper was about to start torturing her.

SEVENTEEN

Jacob furrowed his brows as he walked alongside Gina through the police station car park.

'How are you feeling? Your first day back and you're battling a hangover.' Being arrested and held for a crime he didn't commit had made him wary and quiet. She could see that. It could take a long time for her to get the old Jacob back again.

'Better than I thought. Thanks for being there.' He paused. 'I know I could have taken more time off, and it was suggested, but like I told you last night, I want things to go back to normal.' He almost bumped into a journalist who was directing a photographer. 'This case is disturbing. I've never seen anyone in such a bad state who's still alive.' Jacob bowed his head as they entered the station, ready for the briefing.

'Me neither.' She wondered if Darcie was tough enough to live through what their latest victim had been through. 'The sight of that poor woman is going to stay with me for life. Someone out there must miss her. I hope Wyre has had time to look into missing persons. Did you manage to message her about checking mispers before we left the hospital?'

Jacob nodded. 'Yes, she was going to look into it after interviewing Kyle Fletcher. If Jane Doe has a family out there, they must wonder where she is right now?'

'I hope so.' Gina wondered if their first victim did have a drug problem. Had she had a falling out with her family? If so, they might never have reported her missing.

As they entered the incident room, Gina inhaled the smell of ramen noodles. Chopsticks and containers of food were spread across the table, inviting Gina to take one and give in to her growling stomach. 'Who bought these?'

O'Connor slurped a noodle and wiped a bit of gravy from his round chin. 'Briggs. He said we'd all had a long day and it was his treat.'

She grabbed a box and some chopsticks before heading to the front of the room while she waited for Wyre and Jacob to sit. Briggs entered with a mini spring roll clasped between his finger and thumb. 'Gina, great to have you and Jacob back. I've just issued an updated press release seeking witnesses in the Darcie Fletcher kidnapping and for Jane Doe. The team are in for a busy night and I know the press are going to be constantly loitering outside soon.'

'They're already there.' Gina held the noodle container in one hand and pincered a wilting spring onion between the chopsticks, filling her mouth before placing the container on the large table.

'Right, can we have some hush,' Briggs called out, after finishing his spring roll. 'Gina, can you bring us up to date? I know you haven't had a chance to update the system yet.'

'Of course, sir. Jacob and I will sort that out when we've finished here.' She waited for the room to quieten. Now was her time to show Briggs that she was doing things by the book, not like the last case. She glanced at the boards. One was centred around Darcie, the other marked up Jane Doe. The windows clattered and a burst of rain hammered against them. 'Jacob and

I have visited the address of registered sex offender, Mitchell Varley, and we followed that by going to the hospital to see if we could speak to Jane Doe.

'I'll start with Varley. He hasn't been at his address for a few days. He shares a room with a friend and that friend showed us a balaclava that belonged to Mitchell Varley. As we know, this fits his modus operandi. Varley likes to assault women while wearing a balaclava. We also know that Darcie's little girl, Cleo, said that she saw a man in a white mask. It's not a balaclava but our perp is still hiding his face from his victims behind a mask. Varley is currently our prime suspect, but we should still investigate all other options, especially Darcie's ex-partner, Corey Lowe. We don't know of any connection between him and Jane Doe but I don't want him ruled out, especially as we haven't identified Jane. Going back to Varley, he is also local. He would know the Broadwas Mews Flats and Hutton Village.' She wiped a bit of noodle grease off her hand and continued. 'We need to identify our Jane Doe. Wyre, have you come up with any missing persons' matches?'

Wyre read her notes. 'We have got some matches, some local. As it stands, we have almost fifty women that match her description and age, but they are spread throughout the country.'

'How about the locals?'

'We have fifteen within a ten-mile radius.'

'Can we start with those closest and work our way outwards? Are you okay running with that and double-checking descriptions? Speak to the families if needs be.'

'Yes, guv. I have made a start but I can't get hold of anyone yet.'

Kapoor hurried through the door shaking an umbrella. 'Sorry, guv. A PC only just arrived to relieve me of sentry duty at the back of Varley's bedsit.' She took a seat at the back of the room.

Gina updated Kapoor before continuing. 'Right, onto our Jane Doe. I have a feeling she might be intubated soon. We don't know if she was left at Broadwas Mews or if she got there of her own accord. It wasn't possible to talk to her. The doctor said that she'd been starved, dehydrated and possibly drugged. There is also evidence of long-standing drug abuse so Wyre, while you're investigating our missing persons, can you also check to see if any of our local drug teams recognise her description? You could check with social services and local drug counsellors. Maybe she's stopped attending sessions recently, or hasn't been contactable. Also, samples were taken at the hospital. Do we have any results yet from the lab or the hospital? Is she on our system?'

Wyre scribbled a note on her pad and then checked the messages on her phone. 'Actually, guv, that info has just come in and the answer is no. She's never been on our radar as her fingerprints haven't come back with a match.'

'The doctor also said that Jane Doe kept saying the words "tick-tock" and she smashed the wall clock on her way into a consulting room. I don't know if that little nugget of information means anything but it was going through our victim's mind while she was being wheeled into the examination room. She also used what little bit of strength she had left to break that clock, so I don't want to dismiss that she may have been trying to communicate something important.'

Gina bit the inside of her cheek before continuing. 'I don't need to tell you that time is against us. The perp left Jane Doe's finger behind when he kidnapped Darcie Fletcher. Jane Doe might not make it.' She pressed her lips together before carrying on. 'Not being able to identify Jane Doe is making this all the harder. We don't know if there is a personal link between the two victims. What we do know is that both women are in their thirties, that is all. Jane Doe more than likely has a drug problem. Darcie has a little girl and a job and there is no mention of any involvement in drugs for her. Their lives are polar opposites and they more than likely mix in different circles.' Gina needed to check out Darcie's house. She made a mental note to ask her brother, Kyle Fletcher, if he had a key and to give his consent for them to search Darcie's house if he did.

O'Connor pushed his empty food container aside. The smell of grease and garlic lingered in the air. 'Kyle Fletcher and Anna Heard came in earlier to make formal statements. Wyre and I interviewed them.'

'And?' Gina raised her brows. 'Did Anna mention that she'd been arguing with Darcie last night? Cleo said that her mother and Anna had been shouting and Anna had cried, but when I asked Anna about it, she said they hadn't.'

'No, guv. She said Darcie left and had called an Uber.'

'Do we have Darcie's phone records yet?'

O'Connor picked up his notepad. 'As we know, her phone lost signal before she'd even left Hutton Village and it hasn't come back on since. There are a lot of calls but hardly any messages. She mostly called her brother – Kyle – but those calls reduced in number about a month ago. She also called her work colleague – Shannon, and her friend – Anna. She'd also received some calls from an unknown number. Not many, just a couple. The last call was on Sunday.'

Gina opened WhatsApp on her phone and read Corey Lowe's number out. 'Is this the number?'

'Yep.'

'That's Corey Lowe's number. After he smashed Monica Bell's window and left, he must have called Darcie. Have we located him yet?'

'No, sorry, guv.'

'Okay, what else have you got?'

O'Connor continued. 'During his interview, Kyle told us that their parents were no longer alive. Darcie is in several WhatsApp groups; mostly parenting groups and they all just talk about their kids. It's a shame we don't have many messages but it appears that Darcie was more a talker than a texter. There is a message to her colleague, Joel, and Darcie asks him if he's sure he doesn't mind going out with Mitchell Varley on any future test drives, which backs up what her colleague said about Varley assaulting her and her not wanting to go out with him again. Darcie replies, saying that Varley gives her the creeps. Joel then writes *no problem*. So, not much there either.'

'How about social media?' Gina knew that a woman in her mid-thirties probably used some form of social media.

'She mostly Instagrams. There are photos on her profile of her and her daughter doing all sorts of fun things. Mostly painting, walking and dressing up. She shares a lot of her life online.'

'Do any of the people who engage stand out?'

'We found an account who likes every single one of her photos and I think it's Varley. The username is VarMitchCar-Man. The weird thing is, he's been liking her posts for around four months. She must have known it was him from that name. It's not like she gets lots of likes either. With every post, the average likes are ten and one of them is nearly always him. Her profile isn't set to private either.'

Gina furrowed her brows as she continued addressing O'Connor. 'We need to contact the social media providers, see if we can get access to her messages. I know that won't happen immediately so we'll work with what we have. We know that Varley had been visiting Shoreford's for two months and asking specifically for her. We know he told his roommate that Darcie was his girlfriend and we now know that he'd been tracking her online for four months at least. Her colleague, Shannon, also told us that Varley assaulted her recently. She may have tolerated him following her on social media for the sake of a sale. Now he's missing and so is Darcie. Is there a car registered to him?'

'No. I checked with the DVLA.'

'Can you check with the local car hire companies to see if he's been in. We know he has a driver's licence so maybe he hired a car.'

O'Connor made a note.

'We need all units on alert. I want officers to keep up the surveillance of Varley's unofficial address. Keep them hidden though. We don't want to alert him to our presence if he comes back. We know he doesn't have access to a lot of cash or resources, so he will more than likely have to come back at some point. Does he have any family?'

'We have an old address for his father but he no longer lives there. We'll continue looking.' O'Connor pressed one of his temples with his index finger.

'Thank you.' Gina looked over at Kapoor. 'Jhanvi?'

Kapoor sat up, eyes wide and ready for instruction. 'Yes.'

'Have you had any feedback from the door to doors in Hutton Village?'

She began speaking in her thick Brummie accent. 'No one else saw anything. Forensics came and took a few samples from the back of Anna Heard's gate and the neighbour whose mother saw the man outside on the night Darcie was kidnapped couldn't add any more to his earlier statement.'

A message flashed on Gina's phone. It was the doctor.

Hi DI Harte,

We've just had to intubate the patient. Her vitals were getting worse by the second and it was either that or lose her. We still don't know if she'll make it through the night but at least we're giving her the best chance possible. I'll keep you updated.

Dr Alessi

'That was Jane Doe's doctor. She's now in a medically

induced coma. Keep clocks in your mind, or ticking. Tick-tock might be the last two words she ever spoke. We have someone who tortures, someone who starves and drugs. As far as we know, there are no ransoms involved. Let's not beat about the bush. Jane Doe was left for dead. If we don't act fast, the same will happen to Darcie, if it hasn't already happened. Hopefully, we will know what drugs were used soon—'

Another message from the doctor flashed up.

I ordered blood tests earlier and there were a few I suspected might be in her system. We have the results back. Jane Doe tested positive for ketamine.

'I suspect he's drugging them with ketamine. Check with vets or local medical facilities to see if any of their stock is missing. As we know, it's a commonly used animal anaesthetic. It's also widely sold by dealers. As we're linking Darcie Fletcher's kidnap with Jane Doe's attempted murder, we have to delve deeper into Varley's life. We need his father's address. I know I don't need to say this but I will. We need to work this out and fast. We have to save Darcie and reunite her with Cleo. The alternative is unthinkable.'

EIGHTEEN

SHANNON

'I'm sorry, I'm sorry, I'm sorry,' Kyle repeated as he hurried over and placed his arms around Shannon's shoulders. That in itself felt odd as she barely knew him. Yes, he'd turned up at the showroom a few times to speak to Darcie and yes, he'd dropped Darcie at hers a couple of times before they'd gone on a night out, but right now, he was scaring the life out of her.

Shivering, she pushed him away and leaned on the wall alongside the house to try and steady herself. 'What are you doing in my garden and why have you broken my security light?' She let Barney's lead slip from her hands.

'I didn't smash your light. It was broken when I got here.' She stared at the plastic on the slabs and kicked as much as she could out of the way so Barney wouldn't cut his paws on it. 'I came around the back because I was worried about you. With what happened to Darcie, I panicked and I'm sorry. The gate was already open.'

She took a few deep breaths and hurried the rest of the way into her garden where she glanced up and down the lawn in the dark. Her shed was still locked and she couldn't see any broken or moved pots. The back door was locked. Barney sniffed the stone mushroom before peeing up it. She turned back to Kyle. His watery eyes told her that he was telling the truth. He was worried about Darcie, like she was. 'Look, I'm sorry too. You made me jump, that's all. Any news about Darcie? Is that why you're here? Have the police called you?'

'No, yes, and no.'

Deflated, she pulled her keys out and unlocked the back door, letting Barney and Kyle in before she flicked the kitchen light on. No news wasn't good news. The longer Darcie was held by some psycho, the worse it all was. The dirty crocks from the past two nights still festered in the sink, not a scene she was proud of. She grabbed some disinfectant and squirted it in the drainer sink to take away the eggy smell. 'Come in.' She slammed the door shut. Still shaken from the voice coming from behind the trees earlier and those messages from Finn, she opened the fridge and placed the half bottle of cheap rosé wine on the worktop. She needed something to settle her nerves. 'Do you want some?'

He hesitated and looked away. 'No, thank you.'

'How's poor Cleo? I can't stop thinking about her?' Shannon brought the wine glass to her lips and took a sip. She grimaced. It had soured or maybe it was just cheap. Whatever, she didn't care.

'Not good. She's with Rich at the moment. He's trying to distract her with the TV but she keeps asking about Darcie. Is the scary man going to hurt Mummy? Where is she? When can I see her? Then she cries. I don't know what to do because all I want to do is cry with her. I feel so helpless. I thought I'd come here to see if you knew anything, or if she said anything to you. I need my sister. Someone took her and they had to have been stalking her. Maybe you saw someone hanging around, or had she had a falling out with anyone?'

'When did you last see her?' Maybe it would be okay to fill Kyle in with what she'd told the police. After all, they both wanted Darcie back, safe and sound.

'A month ago. She said she never wanted to see me again. I didn't mean to turn up when I did in that state and I know I scared Cleo when I fell over. Darcie called an ambulance for me when I hit my head and bled all over her carpet, then told me not to come over again until I'd sorted my life out. It was the wake-up call I needed. I love my little niece more than anything and me and Darcie have always been close. I made an effort to be a better uncle for Cleo. Falling like that will always be the most shameful moment of my life.' His cheeks reddened. 'I've quit binge drinking and Rich paid back all the money I owed her. I'm fixing myself; I really am and she might never know that...' His lower jaw trembled. 'I stuffed things up with her and I need to tell her how sorry I am.'

Shannon grabbed the bottle of wine and placed it back in the fridge so that it was out of view for Kyle. She knew that Darcie had had a little tiff with her brother but she had no idea what it was over. Darcie had just described Kyle as draining the life out of her with his problems. What she saw was a man who was trying. 'She will get to hear you say sorry and you will do everything in your power to make it up to her, do you hear me? We are going to get Darcie back. It's been one day. The police are going to find her.' Shannon knew she had her own regrets when it came to Darcie and she blamed Finn. It was all his fault and never again would she let any man come between her and a friend. As soon as Darcie was found, she was going to grovel for her friendship like her life depended on it.

'But someone has her and they've probably killed her. I don't know what I'm going to do without her.' Kyle rubbed his stubble and his lower jaw wobbled.

'We can't think like that. Darcie is strong, she's clever and she loves Cleo more than anything. She'll fight with all she has to get back to that little girl.' Shannon didn't believe that for one second, but she couldn't bear to think that Darcie was dead.

Kyle leaned against the worktop. 'The police aren't telling me much. Did she mention anything she was worried about?'

'A customer assaulted her but I told the police that already.'

Furrowing his brows, Kyle grunted. 'She didn't tell me she was assaulted.'

'You weren't speaking to each other. It was only a few days ago.'

'But this is big. Despite our falling out, I thought she'd tell me something so important. What happened?'

'Some man on a test drive sexually assaulted her. It scared her so she jumped out of the car at the traffic lights.'

'No way? What's the bastard's name?'

Shannon didn't know if she should tell him. After all, the police were already onto Varley and she didn't want to jeopardise the case. She shrugged and rubbed her tired eyes.

'Shannon, who assaulted my sister? I need to know.'

Silence hung in the air as she remained tight-lipped. Something didn't feel right about her house but she couldn't work out what it was. Yes, she could. It was probably Kyle and this whole situation.

'Shannon.'

'He's called Mitchell Varley.'

Kyle looked down at his boots, then he pulled his phone out of his pocket and began tapping. 'Have you googled him?'

'No.' Shannon had never had a reason to.

'Oh, my goodness, he's a perv and he's done time.' He kept reading. 'Indecent exposure and sexual assault in a park, all while wearing a balaclava. This was years ago. He took my sister. I feel so bloody helpless.' He sniffed and flung his head back. 'How could I have not been there for her? I wasn't there for her when she had all those problems with Corey and I regret that. It's my fault. I'm her big brother and I've let her down again, now someone out there is hurting her.' Kyle stormed out of the back door, leaving it bouncing on its hinges.

Barney whined and tilted his head at her. She hurried over and locked the door, before taking the wine back out of the fridge where she took a long swig from the bottle. The house was silent and that silence unnerved her. It wasn't natural. Was her kitchen usually this silent? She snatched a lasagne from the fridge, pierced the film and popped it in the microwave.

A knock coming from the other side of the house startled her. She plonked the wine down and crept through the living room. Reaching out, she tentatively opened the lounge door to expose the front door and stairs but there was nothing there. The sound of teenagers laughing outside the door echoed through the hallway. It must have been them making the noise she'd heard. She headed back to her wine in the kitchen. The scent of melting cheese caught her nostrils but her stomach turned at the thought of eating. How could she eat when her friend had been kidnapped?

Her phone flashed with another message from Finn.

I love it when we play this game. How long until you're not angry at me? Maybe I should come over anyway. You need someone to fix your security light...

She knew it. Finn had been to her house and smashed it in a fit of anger because she wouldn't forgive him. He'd been using her and now she could see it. Brushing her fingers over her phone, it would be easy to press 999 and deal with Finn. She threw the phone down. Gordon loved Finn. He'd never forgive her for getting his favourite mechanic and friend into trouble with the police. It's not like sleeping with someone else and trying to get her back was a crime. She blew out a breath. Were the messages a crime? Maybe they could be classed as harassment. He'd broken her light, that was criminal damage. She shook that thought away. The police had better things to do like finding Darcie and she didn't want to take up their time. Finn would get the message sooner or later.

Her back gate was still unlocked. She pocketed her phone and hurried out of the back door, leaving the door open so that Barney could have a sniff of the garden. She padlocked the gate and hurried back in with her dog. Then she locked the door and waited for her food to cook. As soon as it pinged, she glanced up at the wall. Something was missing, but what? Her shelf was full of pots and pans. Standing in silence, she knew exactly what was missing and she knew why the kitchen was silent. Her wall clock had gone. She was missing the gentle ticking sound. She glanced along the skirting board and the floor. It hadn't fallen off and smashed. Only Kyle had been in her house. The clock had been there this morning. Why would Kyle want her clock and when did he take it? She didn't see him holding it but he was wearing a large coat and she hadn't been watching him when she opened the fridge to get the wine. Or had Finn made a copy of the key she took back from him? That was the more likely scenario. She messaged him.

How dare you come into my house when I'm not here and when did I give you permission to make a copy of my key?

He replied with three laughing emojis and another message.

Are you scared? Maybe I should come over to protect you?

He was getting off on scaring her. She yawned. Her muscles were beyond relaxed but it had been a horrible day. She needed to get to bed. Maybe she was coming down with a bug. Or maybe it was all the stress catching up. Her eyelids started to feel heavy.

Finn had only ever had one key. She ran to the front door and pulled the chain across. She was safe now. He couldn't come in and scare her again, not while she was in the house.

NINETEEN
UNKNOWN

She sees me, she sees me not? She might do if she comes up the stairs but I doubt she's got the energy to hurry. I place the meaty dog treat on the landing before heading into the loft, my feet keeping me steady on the banister as I pull my body up with ease and do a couple of press-ups to wake myself up. That's the beauty of working out so often. I carefully slide the hatch back in place. With my ears to the wood, I hear the dog chomping away. In a few minutes, Barney will be fast asleep but for now, he's going to do the same as he does every time I'm here. He starts to whine again. The good thing is, Shannon just thinks he's attention seeking because she leaves him in doggy day care all day.

I listen as she staggers up the stairs after him. 'Barney, there's nothing there,' she slurs. 'Why do you do this all the time? You know it scares Mummy.' She swears as she bangs into the doors. After checking all the rooms for intruders, she heads into her bedroom. 'Come on, Barney.' The dog continues to whine but I can tell he's getting tired. 'Barney. Bed. Now.' The dog patters across the landing and Shannon slams her bedroom door.

I silently slither like a worm, my elbows acting as paddles as I glide along the boarded loft. I glance through the hole I made within the intricate pattern of her ceiling rose. She struggles to remove her bra but after some wrangling, she drops it onto the carpet just before she falls into bed wearing nothing but her underpants. She grabs her phone with her eyes half closed. 'Come on, Darcie, answer me.' She turns the phone onto speaker and I hear the dead tone.

'Tick-tock, tick-tock,' I whisper as I watch both her and Barney drift into a deep sleep. I get a stir in my underpants as I watch her and it disgusts me. My thoughts wander away from her body and back to her. She worries that she's not well. I hear her telling her mother on the phone. When she has time, she'll get a blood test, she says, but she never does. She just keeps going and she blames the same wine she can't stop drinking. She fears being judged by the doctor for the few glasses she enjoys each night. I hear it all.

There was, of course, something a little sleep inducing in her wine that wasn't there last night. Five minutes and she's all mine. I reach for her clock and place it in my satchel, next to Darcie's phone.

TWENTY

Gina turned her key in the lock. After a long day, all she wanted to do was curl up with a book in bed followed by sleep, but she had too much to do. She had to take a closer look at Darcie's social media herself.

After catching up with the news and taking a shower, she sat up in bed and turned her laptop on while drinking a large glass of lemon in water. Her hangover had finally cleared and Jacob had seemed enthused to be back at work. Tomorrow was another day and she was determined to get further on the Darcie Fletcher and Jane Doe case.

She pointed the cursor at the Instagram app and clicked on it. Glancing across at the other side of the bed, where the case file lay open, she studied Darcie's photo again. The app opened so she typed in Darcie's username. The first photo had been posted a week ago. Darcie was lying on the living room floor with Cleo. She had held her phone above them and taken a snap to post. Her locket lay neatly on her chest. Underneath it she had written, 'I love this little girl so much. She is my world and my best friend.' She looked at the next one. It was of Cleo holding a wooden spoon dripping with chocolate icing. The caption read, 'Mother and daughter time is so precious. I never want her to grow up.'

A lump in Gina's throat began to form as she read post after post. She thought back to when Hannah was little. She'd missed out on so much of her daughter's early years while climbing the police ranks. Did she have regrets? Yes and no. She would have loved to have spent more time with Hannah as a young child, but she also needed to be able to provide and she knew she had to make the world a better place for when Hannah grew up.

She checked her phone and looked at the last message Hannah had sent. It was a photo of Gracie at her gymnastics club mid forward roll. They hadn't been on speaking terms for a while but Hannah had started to message her with the occasional photo. Hopefully time would heal their rift.

Gina's phone rang. It was Briggs. 'Hello.' She sniffed away the emotion that was making her eyes water and her nose start to fill. Silly, she knew, but like any mother she would always wonder if she'd failed.

'Are you okay?'

'Yes. Of course.' She forced a smile so that it would come through in her voice. Briggs had been a bit stifling since the last case. Yes, she had put herself in danger but she had no choice. Briggs hadn't criticised her to begin with, but he seemed to be going on about her keeping safe all the time. They did a dangerous job and he had to accept sometimes she would end up in dangerous situations. It was the nature of the beast. Their rift was hurting her too and not being able to talk with him about it the previous night weighed heavily on her now. 'Is everything alright?'

'We have a little breakthrough. Don't get too excited but I thought you needed to know as I'd like you to go with Jacob to see Varley's father tomorrow.'

'I don't need a male chaperone.'

He sighed. 'I didn't mean it like that. I just thought you'd want to go with Jacob now he's on the case.'

Maybe she had jumped to the conclusion that he was suggesting she take Jacob because he's a man. 'Sorry, I know. I didn't mean to snap but you have to trust that I can look after myself.'

'I can't stop thinking about how the last case could have taken a much worse turn. Bad scenarios keep playing in my head...'

'You need to stop doing this. I'm not some delicate little flower,' she replied. She'd tolerated his over-worrying over the past few weeks but it had to stop. 'Tell me about the break-through.'

'We have an address.'

'That's great news.'

'O'Connor found his phone provider and his account has led us to an address different to the one we had for him. It's not his registered address. It belongs to a woman, but we hope he might be staying with her. O'Connor also managed to speak to the council. Eric Varley rented a flat off them in the past. He was evicted for anti-social behaviour, mostly caused by Mitchell Varley's drug problem.'

'Varley had a drug problem?'

'Yes, which as we know provides a link to Jane Doe. And there's more.'

'There's more?' She raised her brows.

'Yes, we have got Darcie's social media messages from the providers.'

'That was quick.' She hadn't expected them to come back for another day at least but she wasn't complaining. 'And?'

'Varley has been messaging her on and off for months. Mostly he asked her about some of the cars that must have been for sale. Normally he asked about performance and condition. Then he tried to engage her in conversation. It's the last message that's the most disturbing. I'll ping them over so you can read them.'

'Great.'

He hesitated. She wondered if he was going to ask if he could come over but he ended the call instead. She'd barely paid him any attention since she started being there for Jacob and she hadn't had a chance to speak to him about the last case and how she had to do what she did. Going off radar with no backup had been a risk but it had paid off. She'd have to work things out with him after the case.

The email flashed up. She opened it up and clicked on the document and read. Up until the last couple of weeks, the subject matter was all cars then something more personal began.

VarMitchCarMan: You and your little girl look so cute together. She's so much like you.

Darcie: Thank you. Which car did you want to take out tomorrow? I know you asked about it last week, but I can't remember.

Gina could see that Darcie had tried to bring the messages back to cars but Varley hadn't replied for a couple of days.

VarMitchCarMan: You are so pretty but you know that, don't you?

Darcie: Aww, thanks. I don't think that's an appropriate comment though. Can we get back to cars?

VarMitchCarMan: So sorry. My bad. It's true though. Right, cars. I really like the Hyundai that you showed me.

Gina read on. Darcie went on to go through the car specifications with him.

VarMitchCarMan: I might pop by later. Is that okay? Maybe you'd like to go for lunch.

Darcie: I bring my own sandwiches.

VarMitchCarMan: Sandwiches are dull. Would you rather go get a latte or something?

Darcie: Mitch, I'm not looking to date. If you want to buy a car you know where I am.

They got to the date of the assault. Gina noticed that Darcie hadn't posted anything since which meant she wouldn't have seen Varley's messages.

VarMitchCarMan: I think we shared something special today. You really like me, don't you? I want you so badly. I've been making a home for us. Cleo can come too. We can all be a happy family.

VarMitchCarMan: Darcie. Why are you ignoring me?????

VarMitchCarMan: You know, this is such a bitch move. Why are you ghosting me?

VarMitchCarMan: How dare you! You can't lead me on then ditch me like this. I won't take it. You'll see.

VarMitchCarMan: Bitch! Talk to me!!!!!!!!!!

The message dated the previous evening around six made Gina shudder. She held her breath as she read it several times.

VarMitchCarMan: You made me do this! You. All you!

Gina exhaled and looked away from her screen, sickened by the messages. Those words, *you made me do this,* whirled through her mind.

TWENTY-ONE

SHANNON

Saturday, 2 March

With a fuzzy head Shannon stared at the fog through her bedroom window. She tried to pull up her tights again but she got tangled in them and she fell back onto her bed. Staring at the ceiling rose was making her nauseous as she thought of it spinning around so she turned to face her bedside table, taking a moment for the sickly feeling to pass. She grabbed her phone, needing to know what the time was. It was already eight and even though she didn't need to be at the showroom until ten, she had to drop Barney off and she wanted to be early just in case the police visited again with some news about Darcie. Again, she felt the tug at her heart when she thought of Cleo.

Barney jumped on the bed and licked her face. 'Okay, I'm coming.'

Finally, she managed to get dressed. Her hair wasn't its usual pristine self and her make-up was a bit shoddy but it was the best she could do. She grabbed her eyeliner and tried again but her fingers kept shaking. All she'd achieved was an errant line under her eye. The more she tried to scrub it away, the more it then looked like she had a black eye, which was worse. She threw her make-up into a bag, promising herself she'd do it when she got to work.

She opened the fridge door and poured the horrible wine down the sink.

Barney jumped up her and barked. 'Okay, Mamma's big baby.' She ruffled his head and went to unlock the back door but it was already open. She was sure she'd locked it last night. But... she tried to remember getting to bed. Everything was blurry. At one point, she crashed into the lock on the front door. Lifting the sleeve of her smart black jumper, she could see the slight bruise where the catch had dug into her flesh. What else had happened? Kyle had been there. She'd been fine when she was talking to him. Finn had been horrible but that was nothing new. After she discovered he'd been cheating, she'd seen another side of him. While running out into the garden and alongside the house, she saw that her gate was unlocked. She remembered the click of the padlock as she pushed it together. Or did she? She ran back into the house and opened the cutlery drawer where she kept her keys. The padlock key was there.

She held a hand to her sticky forehead. Maybe she was running a fever. A tear slid down her cheek as she forced the bile in her oesophagus back down. 'Pull yourself together, Shannon. It's just some bizarre reaction to the stress of Darcie being kidnapped and the hideous wine.' She hoped speaking that sentence out loud would rationalise how she felt.

She scrunched her brow and found her gaze flitting all over the room. The silence that had plagued her last night remained. She glanced up and stared at her wall clock, which was exactly where it should be. She could see that it had stopped at eleven last night. Maybe she needed to replace the battery.

Had it even vanished? She was losing her mind. It wasn't

the first time she'd had a funny moment recently. She'd been in denial but now she had to face the truth. Something was really wrong with her.

TWENTY-TWO

'Here it is.' Jacob pointed at the property hidden behind the larger house in front of them. The wide triple garage at the end of the driveway was topped with what looked to be a small flat leading out to a balcony. All the curtains were shut but it was only eight in the morning and it was a Saturday. Jacob had been as shocked as she had when she showed him the messages that Varley had sent to Darcie.

'It's more like an annexe,' Gina said.

A man wearing a milk-stained T-shirt came out of the large house. 'Can I help you?'

Gina stepped forward. 'We're looking for Mr Varley.'

'Oh him, he's my tenant's partner. Who are you? Celia doesn't get many visitors, especially not official-looking people.'

Gina held up her identification. 'I'm DI Harte and this is DS Driscoll.'

'Is there some sort of trouble? I don't know Mr Varley, but he does stay with her most of the time. Actually, I think he lives there. Asking Celia is on my to-do list but I haven't got around to it.' The man scratched the back of his neck. 'Why are you here? Should I be worried about him?'

Gina had checked out Varley's dad and he had no record of any offences as far as she could see. 'Not as far as I'm aware. He's not in any trouble. We are actually looking for his son.'

A baby started crying. 'That's a relief. Anyway, I have to go see to the little one. Looks like it's feed time, again. Just head over and knock at the flat door. I know someone is in as her car's there.'

Gina smiled. 'Thank you.' They walked down the path as the man closed his door. Gina could still hear the baby from the other end of the drive. They stopped on reaching the huge garage door. Gina peered into the side window and could see that it was a games room. Jacob rang the bell and they stepped back. Gina glanced up at the windows. A curtain twitched and a woman with mussed-up grey hair dropped the curtain and vanished from view. A minute later she opened the door.

'Hello. Do I know you?'

'No.' Jacob introduced them this time.

'So, you need to speak to Eric. Come in.' She led the way up the dark carpeted staircase. A terrier yapped from the top of the stairs before turning around and going back into the property. Celia pulled her pyjama bottoms up and began to try to tame her huge mass of tangled hair. 'Sorry, I look a mess. I wasn't exactly expecting you. He's in the living room watching crap on YouTube. Eric, make sure you're decent. The cops are here to see you.'

'What?' Eric called back with a raspy voice.

Celia pushed the door open to reveal a large kitchen and living space, combined with a walk out balcony next to the settee. The balcony was adorned with pots full of dead flowers but the view of a distant farm was pretty. Eric leaned back into a stack of cushions on the end seat of the settee. His bare feet rested on a pouffe while he balanced a bowl of cereal under his chin. 'This is Eric.' She smiled. 'I think I'll just go and get dressed. Will you be alright, love?'

''Course. You get yourself up so we can head out. How can I help you, officers?' The lines etched into his face had a warmth about them. 'Actually, don't tell me. It's Mitchell, isn't it?'

Gina nodded. 'May we sit down?'

'Of course. Make yourselves at home.' The terrier licked Gina's hand as she sat in the chair. Jacob sat at the other end of the settee and took his notepad out of his satchel. 'What's he done now?'

'Have you seen Mitchell lately?'

'No, I haven't seen him for a couple of years, not since he got me thrown out of my council flat. Good job I had Celia or I'd have ended up on the streets. She's been my saviour. She knows all about Mitch so there are no secrets here.' He placed his bowl on the floor and the dog began to lick it.

Gina had hoped that Mitchell had been to see his father. She wondered if Eric could be covering for him.

'Do you keep in touch at all?'

'He calls me out of the blue now and again but I don't want anything to do with him.' A look of sorrow passed through the man's face and he looked out of the balcony windows. 'I don't have the heart to change my number. I tried and got one of those pay-as-you-go phones but I caved in the end and messaged him my number. I know he did some unforgivable things but I can't cut him out completely.'

'Can you tell us a bit more about the calls and what happened between you?' Any little detail might help them to find Varley.

'Well, you know what he did. He went to prison but rather than get rehabilitated, he came out with a drug problem. You know, I don't know where I went wrong. I brought that lad up on my own and I did everything I could for him. He had a happy childhood and all the things he ever wanted, but then he met this girl in his early twenties. She left him for one of his friends and he turned into a hermit. He got angrier and angrier at her and women in general. He started spending more time online in these chat rooms, that's what they communicated through back then. One day when he was out, he left his computer running. He'd been spending all his time in chat rooms being brainwashed by misogynists. Made me sick to the stomach, they did. If his mother had been alive to see that and to know what he did after, it would have broken her heart.' Eric inhaled and closed his eyes for a few seconds.

'I'm sorry to hear that.' Gina could see how painful it was for Eric to relive the past.

'Thank you. It still upsets me. Anyway, fast forward many years, he got out of prison and came to see me. We'd argue and he was so violent. I told him that I didn't want him at my flat but that didn't stop him. I hate to say it but I was my own worst enemy because some days I'd feel sorry for him, move him in for a bit so I could try to help him kick the habit. I know what he did but he's still my son. I kept thinking of Rosalie and what she would've wanted me to do. She wouldn't have wanted me to give up on him. Things got worse. He started taking harder drugs.' Eric hesitated. 'He'd bash my door in, upset my neighbours, shout and take my money. He'd come in high and play loud music in the middle of the night and when I tried to stop him, he'd threaten me. I didn't know what to do. I didn't want to call the police on him again because it was the drugs doing the talking. Well, things went from bad to worse. The neighbours had recorded all the noise and kept diaries. That's when the council got involved and I got evicted. I mean, Mitchell even knocked the neighbour's door down one night, thinking it was mine and that I wasn't letting him in. That's how bad it got.'

Gina's heart was breaking for the man in front of her. 'When did he call you last?'

Eric pulled his phone out from the gap between the settee cushions. He put his glasses on and scrolled. 'Two weeks ago, almost exactly.'

'Can I take his number?' They had no phones registered for Mitchell Varley. Gina could only make the assumption that he was using a burner phone.

'I'll note it down for you.' He reached for a pad on the coffee table next to him and began to scrawl the numbers down. 'Here you go.'

Gina passed it to Jacob knowing that he'd message the number straight to the team. With any luck they'd be able to track his movements. 'How did he seem when he spoke to you?'

'Clean. By that I mean off the drugs. He said he'd met someone and she'd changed his life, but then again, that's what he said about the other girl a couple of months ago but apparently that went pear-shaped.'

Gina felt adrenaline coursing its way through her body. Could the first girl Eric referred to be Jane Doe? 'Can you tell us about the woman he was seeing before?'

Eric shrugged. 'I don't know much, not even her name. I think they were getting clean together at the time. He was angry as he stayed off the drugs and she went back on them. That's why it ended.'

Jacob gave Gina a glance. 'Did he say anything at all about her?'

'No, I wish he did. I hate to ask. Has he done something to her?'

'We can't discuss the case as it's ongoing but we do need to speak to your son and I really appreciate how much you're helping us. Can you tell us anything about his new relationship?'

'He said the woman had a little girl and this time he did give me a name. He said she was called Darcie and she sold cars for a living. Me being me, I got worried for her. I know what Mitchell is like and I didn't want Darcie to get hurt. He can get a bit deluded and carried away so I never know what to believe. He sees interest sometimes where there isn't any. Even at school, there was a couple of complaints from parents about him hassling their daughters but I hoped he'd grow out of it. I don't want anyone to get hurt.' Eric closed his eyes again. 'What the hell did I do wrong?'

Celia walked in, fully dressed in leggings and a jumper. 'Oh, Eric, come here.' She sat beside him and pulled him into a hug. 'Eric gets really upset when talking about his son.'

'I do. I always will, I think. Please find him and stop him if he's doing something bad.' Eric pulled away from Celia and dropped his feet from the pouffe. He scrunched his brow and tilted his head. 'It's the woman on the appeal, isn't it? I watched the news last night but it didn't click. I saw her name and she's missing. It's Darcie, isn't it? Mitchell did it, didn't he?'

Gina passed Eric a card. 'Unfortunately, we don't have any answers for you at the moment. We really need to speak to him with regards to the case. If you see him or hear from him will you please call me straight away?'

'Of course.'

Celia pulled away from him. 'Eric, I'm so sorry, love. I didn't want to upset you but I saw him about a week ago. He came here looking for you and I was scared. I didn't want trouble here and I didn't say anything to you because I know how upset you get when we talk about Mitchell. I also like living in this flat and I know how he got you evicted, so I had to get rid of him. He started demanding that he see you and I told him you didn't live here any more. I was going to tell you but you were a bit down. All week I worried, thinking he'd call you and tell you what I said. The truth is, I don't want him here, love. He scares me, so please don't hate me.'

Eric shook his head. 'It's okay, Celia. I understand but don't hide things like that from me in the future. Just because things upset me, doesn't mean to say they should be hidden from me. If I'd spoken to him, maybe he wouldn't have kidnapped that poor woman. This could have been prevented.'

Gina cleared her throat. 'Please don't blame yourselves. Whatever Mitchell might have done, it isn't the fault of either of you. Can you tell me when you saw him?'

'I can't remember. It might have been last Sunday or Monday. I'm retired so every day feels a bit samey. Sorry.' Celia pulled away from Eric. 'He gave me a message for you, just in case I saw you around.'

'He did?'

'Yes. He said he was sorry for everything he put you through but he was getting his life sorted. He said he had a new place and that when he'd tidied it up, he and Darcie were moving in together, but I didn't believe any of it. He was also so high he could barely stand which is why I was scared.'

Gina interjected. 'Did he say where this new place was?'

She shook her head. 'Not exactly, but he said it was local and that he could hear the church bells. He slurred out a joke about always knowing what time it was.'

Gina knew of only one church close by that had bells and it was the one on Cleevesford High Street. They were getting closer to finding him. A message from O'Connor pinged through her phone.

Guv. No one using Varley's name or matching his description has hired a car locally. I've called Kyle Fletcher and he said he's at Darcie's house. He said he wants to speak to you about something urgent that he needs you to take a look at. I asked him to come in but he was really upset and said that you really need to go to the house. DCI Briggs asked if you would go now and report back urgently.

TWENTY-THREE

Kyle Fletcher opened the front door of the old terraced house just as Gina was about to knock. 'Come through.' Kyle tapped his head as if thinking. 'You both have to see this.' He began hurrying up the narrow stairs.

Gina closed the front door as Jacob followed closely. In the hall she almost tripped over Cleo's wellies and book bag. She hurried up after Kyle, passing the grey tiled bathroom at the top of the stairs and stood outside Darcie's bedroom. The back wall was painted in a deep forest-green and the oak floor was littered with slippers, socks and a crumpled towel. Kyle lay on the bed amongst the scatter cushions.

'What is it you need to show us?' Gina asked. She knew she wanted to take a look around Darcie's house in order to see if they were missing a connection that could lead them to finding her kidnapper, but Kyle wanted them to see something specific.

He let out a manic laugh that slowly turned into a distressed roar. 'Sorry, I haven't slept all night.' He rubbed his eyes and yawned. 'I came here in the hope that I'd find anything that could help and I lay here for hours staring at the ceiling, wondering what the hell to do next. That's when I saw it.'

Gina glanced up at the artexed ceiling and tried to work out what Kyle was so transfixed with, then she squinted to see the tiny hole in the swirl.

'You see it, don't you? She was being watched.' He sat bolt upright and continued speaking at lightning speed. 'At first, I was like, what of it? In fact, I kept coming back to it after lying here for two whole hours, then I thought, what am I doing? I should look at it. Darcie's life depends on us finding her so what if it was nothing? At least I'd know.'

He jumped up and nudged past Jacob and Gina before standing on a bedside table that was already on the landing and pushing open the loft hatch. Carefully, he guided the ladders down. 'I didn't need the ladders to get into the loft but I guess you might.'

Gina decided not to take offence at him assuming she didn't have the upper body strength to pull herself up. Kyle was right. She'd definitely struggle with that manoeuvre.

'Go up and look.' He reached down and snatched a torch from the carpet before giving it to Gina.

After taking the torch, she passed Jacob her phone and bag before pulling a pair of latex gloves from her pocket and snapping them on. With each step the soles of her boots clanked on the metal ladder rungs until she reached the top. She flashed the torch but saw that there was a light. Placing the torch down, she flicked the switch but the light didn't come on.

'Bulb has gone,' Kyle shouted.

She eased herself onto the part-boarded floor and grabbed a strut to pull herself up.

'Head in a north-east direction until you're above the bedroom.'

She did as Kyle instructed.

'Are you okay up there?' Jacob called.

'Yes.' That's when she saw two empty biscuit wrappers and an empty pop can. She kneeled down and pointed the torch at the wrappers. Next to them was the other side of the hole. Someone had dug out a chunk of floorboard, pulled out the insulation and created the hole. She leaned down far enough to see that anyone lying on the floor would be able to see Darcie in her bedroom. 'We need to call this in and get forensics here, now.'

She hurried out of the loft, careful not to disturb anything. As she clambered back down, Jacob had already headed downstairs to make the call.

'He's been stalking her. That bastard who assaulted her has been in her house, watching her while she sleeps and gets changed.' Kyle began to pace up and down the landing. 'You know who he is, don't you? The tosser who assaulted her at work. Shannon told me.'

'Mr Fletcher, we are exploring a few avenues at the moment. It's important that you don't speculate and let us do our job.'

'Don't speculate. It's him. It's Mitchell Varley. There you go, you even have his name. Have you got him yet?'

Gina could tell that Kyle was getting het up and she couldn't blame him, but she also didn't need him hampering the investigation in anyway. 'I promise you; we are doing everything we can to find your sister. Right now, you need to be there for Cleo, she needs you.'

He let out a jagged sigh and folded his arms. 'I just can't sit on my hands doing nothing. Cleo needs her mother, not me.'

'That's not true. You're her uncle. She needs to know that she's safe and loved after what she saw. Right now, you're all she has.'

'Right now, I'm all Darcie has because from the way you're looking at me, you haven't got Varley. Why isn't his face plastered all over the news?'

Gina turned to the side, wondering how much to divulge. 'Because if he does have your sister, he might decide he has nothing to lose if he knows we're onto him. Also, we don't know for sure that he took her. We have to tread carefully as you can appreciate.'

Kyle hit the wall and roared. 'Why Darcie? Why?' He shook his head and turned away as he stifled his sadness. 'She's never hurt anyone.'

'I'm sorry, but forensics will be here soon and we will need to get out. I know this is hard for you but like I said, I will do everything I can to find Darcie and that's a promise. Is there anyone we can call to be with you?'

'No. I actually came over to take Cleo's hamster last night and then I stayed. Is it okay if I grab the cage?'

Gina smiled sympathetically. 'Of course. Before you go, may we take a swab from you?'

'Really?'

'I'm afraid so. It's only a cheek swab. As you went in the loft we need to eliminate your DNA from other items we find containing DNA in there. Forensics will take it when they arrive.'

Kyle nodded. He'd gone from hyped up to deflated and exhausted in a matter of minutes. He now resembled a man who was on the brink of exhaustion with his slumped shoulders and his sallow-looking skin.

'I best get the hamster.'

Gina followed him downstairs and Jacob ended the call he was on. 'Forensics are on their way, guv, along with uniform.'

'What happens next?' Kyle asked.

Gina stepped into the narrow hallway, almost brushing shoulders with Kyle as she opened the front door and led him outside. 'The house is now a crime scene. It will be cordoned off and officers will speak to the neighbours. Forensics will go through the house. Do you have a key that we can use?'

'I don't have another spare but you can have it.' He slid the silver key from his key ring and passed it to Gina. 'I only have her front door key.'

'Thank you. We'll go in and get the hamster and cage for you. What room is it in?'

'The kitchen. It's on the sideboard.'

Gina left Kyle on the doorstep and headed past the cosy lounge with its chunky loveseat at one end, and into the kitchen. Gina saw a greying pack of minced turkey on the side. She pictured Darcie leaving it out to thaw. A couple of plates covered in toast crumbs sat on the draining board. She glanced at Cleo's drawings on the fridge and saw one that sent a chill through her.

Jacob came up behind her and stopped. 'Is that a clock?' He grabbed the hamster cage.

The lines were all over the place and Cleo was only young, but it looked a little like the clock on the wall with its huge black dots for numbers. The little girl's wax crayon drawing was far from accurate but it looked like the clock was inside a square and two orange eyes were behind it. It was surrounded by other doodles such as flowers and a duck. 'I think so. It also looks like a loft hatch, or maybe I'm just thinking that because we've just come from the loft.'

Gina looked at the clock again with its huge single dots denoting the numbers. It wasn't straight. It was on a slant and one of the hands was bent on the number eleven. The sound of a ticking clock played in her mind and sent a chill down her. 'She saw him in the loft and he had a clock.' It sounded absurd but given what Jane Doe had tried to communicate to her, clocks meant something and Gina needed to work out what before Darcie was seriously hurt or killed. After taking a photo of the drawing, Gina bagged it up and ran outside.

Kyle stood on the path; mouth open as one of the forensics team swabbed his cheeks. She nodded to Keith who was pulling his toolbox from the back of his van while wincing as he held his back with his other hand.

'Has something happened?' Kyle moved away from the crime scene assistant and took the hamster cage from Jacob.

'Would you be able to come to the station with Cleo this afternoon?'

'I think Cleo has told you everything she knows.'

Gina held the clear evidence bag up to show Kyle the drawing and he stared with his mouth open. He almost toppled, then held his head. Gina reached for the hamster cage which he let her take before regaining his balance. 'I'll go straight home and get her.'

TWENTY-FOUR

SHANNON

'I'm just heading out to get some lunch, Shannon. Is that okay?'
Joel gave her a coffee and grabbed his coat.

'Yes, of course.'

'Can I get you anything? A can of Red Bull, maybe.'

'It's kind of you to ask but no, I'll be okay.'

Joel hesitated. 'I miss Darcie too. The police will find her, I
know they will.'

She slammed the coffee down. 'How? No one knows
anything so how do you know they'll find her? What if Varley
has hurt her because she rejected him? We could have done
something. I'm not only her friend, I'm her supervisor. I should
have said no to her going out alone with him. If she gets hurt, it's
my fault. What if he's...' Shannon shook that thought away. She
couldn't imagine a life without Darcie in it. Tears began to well
in the corners of her eyes. 'I shouldn't have been so hard on her.
It's all my fault. All this over Finn.'

Joel transferred his weight from one foot to the other. She
could tell she was making their trainee uncomfortable with her
tears but she didn't care that her oversharing was unprofes-
sional. 'Have you told the police about Finn?' he asked.

'No, Finn is a prize prick but it's not him.'

'Okay.' He grabbed a box of tissues from the front desk and passed them to her. 'I'm sorry, I don't know what to say but I like to stay hopeful. I was talking to my mum about it and we watched the news while eating our dinner last night. Mum said that we have to have hope.' Joel paused. 'I think we should tell the police about Finn. You might not think I notice but I see the way he is with people, women especially. He's not a nice person and I don't trust him.'

'If you value your job, you won't say anything against Finn. He's like a son to Gordon.' Shannon hated that Gordon thought the world of Finn. Besides it wasn't Finn, so there was no point any of them risking their jobs. Finn was bothering her, not Darcie. She thought back to a work pub night when she got jealous and accused Finn of flirting with Darcie. It wasn't anything Darcie had done; it was the way Finn casually touched her arms as she laughed and held her gaze. Maybe she had it wrong but it looked like he was flirting and it looked like Darcie had been okay with it. Little did she know back then. It wasn't even all about Darcie. 'It's not Finn.'

'Were you with Finn the night Darcie got kidnapped?'

'No, but I wasn't with anyone either so does that mean I could have kidnapped Darcie? Loads of people were home alone that night. Where were you?'

'Sitting with Mum watching telly. I'm happy to say where I was, Finn should be happy to do the same.'

'Can we drop it, Joel?'

'Okay.' He huffed out a breath.

She could tell Joel wasn't convinced about Finn and she felt horrible for snapping at him. Joel was right, Finn did have a nasty streak but he was all talk. He'd never been violent with her, maybe a little pushy and maybe he did break her security light but that was all. She thought back to her clock and the padlock on the gate, that had all been a weird fever dream from the wine. No more wine. She was fine and Finn was not a kidnapper. There were things that Joel didn't know and she wasn't about to tell him.

'I'll see you after lunch,' she said as she widened her damp eyes, hoping he would hurry up and leave. Joel turned and went out of the main door.

Less than a minute later Gordon pulled up in his black BMW. As he got out of the driver's seat he waved and smiled at Joel, before coming into the showroom. 'Shannon, any sales today? I've noticed the figures aren't looking great this week so we need to bolster up some energy. Convert those test drives into actual sales.'

She shook her head and clenched her fists. He could have asked if there was any news about Darcie first. It was all about the sales and nothing else with him. It was Finn this, cars that, and their new workshop.

'Are you ill?' He tucked in the shirt that just about stretched over his belly back into his trousers.

She almost wanted to laugh at that question. If Darcie wasn't missing, she might have. She was having one bad day but Gordon quite often came in looking worse for wear. She knew that he and Finn met up a lot and got hammered together. 'I've been up all night worrying about Darcie.' She didn't want to discuss her episode so she went with 'up all night' instead.

'Oh yes, poor Darcie. I got your message. I'm going to call the police in a bit but I don't have anything to tell them. You and Joel are the only other people to have seen Mr Varley. I wasn't here at the times he came. It's made me think a little more about staff safety and from now, I don't think anyone should do test drives alone with a customer. Shut the showroom for a few minutes if needed. Staff safety is my main concern.' Gordon began walking to his office. 'Come through.'

He slumped into his executive chair and let out a huge

breath as he flicked through the post. 'You know I think a lot of Darcie and I hope she's okay. For now, though, we need to trust the police to do their job while we get on with ours.'

Gordon had always been harsh as an employer. If they were ever sick, he expected them to still come in. Darcie had been called to Cleo's school as Cleo had a bad tummy and as usual Gordon thought that Darcie should have just left her. Shannon remembered how she was so tense while Darcie was answering him back. Gordon had then issued Darcie with a warning for insubordination.

He picked up the detective's card. 'Is this the person I need to call?'

'Yes. DI Harte.' She paused. 'You know, you were really unfair on Darcie the other week and now she's been kidnapped. As she's sitting wherever, probably trapped by some psycho, she's more than likely thinking of how horrible you were to her. That's if she's still alive.'

'Shannon, that's a nasty thing to say. How long have you worked for me?'

She wanted to say too long. Instead, she remained silent. She'd worked for Gordon for years but she really needed to keep her job.

'I was not horrible to her, I just need my staff to do the work I pay them to do and not swan off when they feel like it, or when they have boyfriend trouble, or when they take too long getting a sandwich. That boy is taking the pee. Where's Joel?'

'He's on his lunch break.'

'Whatever. He's always at that coffee machine and messaging on his phone. Don't think I don't see and we know it's your job to manage him.' He turned his computer on and sat back, waiting for it to settle.

It might be the hugest mistake of her life but maybe Joel was right. She only saw the Finn she wanted to see, but Joel was a newbie, an outsider. 'You know, Finn was acting a bit odd yesterday.' She wouldn't mention the messages or her security light to Gordon but she wanted him to see that Finn had caused a fair bit of trouble around the place. She was sick of never being able to say anything about him just in case it upset Gordon.

'He wasn't.'

'You weren't around. You didn't see him.' Gordon wasn't there when Finn overpowered her in the kitchen and was mean after.

He scrunched his thick brows. 'That's right. I was busy all day. It must have been the day before.'

'But—'

Gordon held a shovel-like hand up. 'But nothing. There's a customer. By the way, please can you back off Finn a little. He said you're harassing him and the last thing I need right now is to have accusations like that on my plate. Leave him alone.'

A woman pointed at a hatchback and smiled. Feeling like she might explode with rage, Shannon stomped out of Gordon's office. Was she angry at Gordon or was she still angry at Darcie, despite what had happened? If Darcie hadn't brought Anna along to one of their nights out, Finn would never have met her. Shannon saw Finn sneaking his number into Anna's phone when he thought she wasn't looking. He wasn't even meant to gate-crash their girls' night out but he couldn't help himself. Darcie didn't exactly discourage Anna and Finn, which had caused the huge wedge between Shannon and her. But none of that mattered now. If only she could take back all the horrible words she'd hurled at Darcie. All that over a man who didn't deserve any of them. Her phone beeped and it was a message from an unknown number.

Tick-tock. What's the time?

'Hi, can I test drive the Mitsubishi?' The woman waited for her to answer. Shannon would have to deal with the prankster later. She glanced through all the showroom windows. What a strange message to send. Her mind flashed back to her kitchen clock but that thought was broken by the customer clearing her throat.

TWENTY-FIVE
ENID

She shuffled to the end of the path while puffing away on her last cigarette. As soon as her son came home, she needed to ask him if he'd take her to the garage to get some more. She inhaled the cold air as she paced up and down the front garden. The wind whistled and a flapping noise caught her attention.

Glancing to her left at the fenced off row of houses, she wondered if they were full of rats. Derelict places soon turned to ruin. There were ten altogether. A terrace of slums. She knew her son was thrilled that they were coming down soon. He'd gone on about how much they'd devalued his house and he even said that as they were building flats, she should use the money from her bungalow to buy one. She knew he was trying to get rid of her, that she cramped his style, but she hadn't liked living so far away from him.

She opened the waist-height back gate and walked out onto the damp path. The one and only streetlamp barely reached where she was. After a few more steps, she threw her nub end on the ground and stamped on it. Pressing her nose against the flimsy metal fence, she tried to peer in. The boarded-up front window looked to be leaning against the frame, rather than fixed to it like all the others. She knew the council had boarded the place up a few times so she wouldn't be surprised if a homeless person was sleeping there. As another gust brewed, she heard the banging again. It was coming from inside the end house.

Her hand rested on the fence and as she leaned into it, the chain fell to the ground. Someone had cut it. She shivered and zipped her chunky cardigan up. She knew that her son and the other residents found the people who broke into the derelict houses a nuisance, but not Enid. She hated the thought of someone with no one to love them and nowhere to live. She'd fed the last man who had snuck in, much to her son's dismay. He'd been worried that she'd get hurt but no one had ever hurt her when she'd been kind to them.

'Hello,' she called out.

There was no answer. That didn't surprise her. Most people hid, thinking they were going to get reported. Until the houses were demolished, she didn't see why people couldn't use them to seek shelter. She reached the window and gave the wood a nudge. 'I just wondered if you were okay in there. I thought you might want a cuppa and a sandwich.' She let out a slight laugh. 'Don't tell my son, though.'

In the far corner, she could see a dark lump. She fished her phone from her pocket and used the torch on it to light up the room. As the body came into full view, she stumbled back into the stingers, catching her tailbone on the edge of a slab. Blood thrummed through her ears as she called for help. The phone had landed on the other side of the patio and had smashed into pieces. Then she felt a large gloved hand on her shoulder.

TWENTY-SIX

Gina rushed through the station like a whirlwind, getting the family room prepared to make it as comfortable as she could for Cleo. She'd bought a carton of chocolate milk from the vending machine and placed it on the table.

Jacob turned the heater on. 'Kyle Fletcher is on his way down with Cleo. Wyre has just met them at the front desk.'

'Great. We need to get this right. I don't want to scare her.' Gina's hands trembled at the thought of speaking to a five-year-old about such a disturbing picture. Her gaze fell on the turned over copy of the picture on the table. 'I think the room's as comfortable as we're going to get it.' She noticed that some of the yellow paint was really scuffed and the small box of old toys in the corner looked tired.

As Kyle and Cleo approached, the sound of Cleo's voice telling her uncle Kyle that Uncle Richard had been playing Connect Four with her filled the corridor. Jacob sat on the nearest seat to the wall. Cleo looked up and Gina noticed how large her dark eyes seemed. She stopped talking and placed her thumb in her mouth, before shrinking behind Kyle.

'Cleo, you know we said that the police wanted to talk to you?'

Cleo peered from behind him and nodded at her uncle.

Gina smiled. 'I'm Gina. We met yesterday.' Her knee cracked slightly as she crouched to greet the little one. 'You were really helpful and I wondered if it was okay to speak to you again.'

The little girl came out from behind Kyle and gripped his hand. 'It's okay, lovely. Shall we go and sit down on that comfy couch?' Kyle pointed at the grey sofa and Jacob waved them over.

'Okay.' She walked towards it and sat, her stare flitting between Gina and Jacob. Kyle sat next to her. 'Can I have that?' She pointed to the milkshake.

'Of course, you can, chicken.' Gina pulled out the straw and pierced the carton, before passing it to Cleo.

'Chicken.' She giggled. 'Am I a chicken?'

Gina laughed as she sat. 'You are definitely not a chicken. I call my lovely granddaughter chicken and we laugh about it too.' Gina felt a lump appearing in her throat. Gracie was a little older than Cleo but she did miss hugging her, especially at times like this. She wanted nothing more than to wrap Cleo in her arms and make her mother reappear, but she couldn't. All she could do was her job and asking Cleo about the drawing might just be what helps them nail the kidnapper and bring Darcie home.

Cleo put the carton on the table and leaned into her uncle. He placed his arm around her.

'Cleo, I went to your house earlier and I saw some of your amazing drawings on the fridge. Your mummy is obviously very proud of all your hard work.'

A smile spread across Cleo's face and, in contrast, Kyle had to turn away. 'I like making pictures for Mummy.' Gina turned over the piece of paper on the table and Cleo glanced at it. 'That's my picture.'

'It is. Those flowers are beautiful and is that a duck?'

Giggles spilled from Cleo's mouth. 'It's a mongoose, silly.'

Gina leaned in a little. 'I am so sorry, of course it is and you're right, I am silly. It isn't a duck at all.' She pointed at what looked like a clock. 'Because I am so silly, can you tell me what this is?'

'That's Mummy's clock.'

'And what is the square?'

Cleo quickly buried her face under Kyle's arm so that Gina could no longer see her face.

'Are you okay, Cleo?'

'I'm not allowed to say.' She peered out and shook her head.

'Who said?'

'The bogeyman in my bad dream. And Mummy said if I forget about it, it will go away. When I was scared, she let me sleep in her bed but we didn't talk about the bogeyman.'

Gina could see from Kyle's quivering jaw that he was struggling to contain himself, but he took a deep breath and spoke. 'You know what Mummy always says about secrets. We have no secrets. If anyone ever tells you to hide something from Mummy, then you should tell straight away because they are doing a bad thing.'

'I know, Uncle Kyle.'

The room fell silent. Jacob stopped writing and Cleo picked up her milkshake and drank a little more.

'Cleo, where is the clock in your picture?'

'The bogeyman takes it into the loft where he lives.' She puffed out a breath. 'It is a bad dream because the next day I told Mummy and she showed me the clock in the kitchen.'

Gina felt a shiver run through her body and perspiration beads began to form at her hairline. She leaned over and turned the heater off. 'How many times have you had the bad dream?'

'Two times.'

Gina's heart was breaking for the little girl. Cleo had seen her mother's kidnapper and right now, she thought it was nothing more than a dream. One day she would know the truth and that was going to be harder still.

'Can you tell me more about him?' Gina pointed to the orange eyes. 'The bogeyman.'

'He said if I tell anyone, no one will believe me because the bogeyman isn't real.'

Kyle hugged her. 'I believe you. We all believe you.'

'It was dark and I was on the landing. Mummy said I walked there in my sleep but I wasn't asleep. I needed a wee.'

'Did you see the rest of him?'

She shook her head. 'I only saw his eyes because it was dark.'

'Did you see what colour they were, or did you see his skin?'

'No.'

'Do you know who he was?' Gina wondered for a moment if it was her father, Corey, Cleo would recognise him.

'No, but he gave me something and said I had to keep it a secret. I tried to tell Mummy that the bogeyman was real because I still have the gift.'

'What did he give you?'

'A toy boat. I gave it to Hammy Hamster to make his house nice. Mummy said I could.'

Gina leaned back and Kyle raised his brows. 'There's a small wooden boat in the hamster cage at my place.'

Cleo began to rub her eyes. 'Has the bogeyman got Mummy?'

Kyle gripped his niece and hugged her closely. Gina stood and turned away. Jacob placed his pad down.

Hands clenched to the point her nails were piercing her skin, Gina turned around. 'Kyle, we're going to arrange for a family liaison officer to be with you for the time being. Her name is Ellyn and she's very experienced. I feel like you shouldn't be alone at a time like this and if you and Cleo need extra support, she can help you with that.'

Gina opened the door and caught Wyre walking by. She flagged her down to come in. 'Kyle,' Gina said in a hushed voice. 'Would Cleo be allowed an iced bun?'

He nodded.

'Cleo, this is Paula and she knows where we keep some lovely home-made iced buns. Would you like to go with her to get one while I speak to your uncle Kyle?'

'Yay,' the little girl shouted as she grabbed Wyre's hand and headed up the corridor.

Kyle immediately doubled over. He gasped and began to hyperventilate. Gina could relate to how he felt. The conversation with Cleo had her heart racing, too.

'He's been in my sister's house. He's been watching her and scaring my niece. Now he has her.' Kyle gasped again. 'Where is she?' he stuttered. 'Where's Darcie?' he repeated louder as he slammed his closed fist on the coffee table. The carton of chocolate milk bounced off and began to spill from the straw onto the floor.

That's the question they all wanted answering and they were no closer to finding out where Varley or Lowe were. The sound of bells kept going through Gina's thoughts. Varley had moved somewhere where the church bells could be heard. It was time to start door-to-door enquiries around the high street, asking people if they'd seen him. They were also going to need the toy boat from Kyle. Boats, clocks – what next?

She poured a glass of water for Kyle and passed it to him. Slowly his breathing returned to normal. 'I don't know what to do. I just want my sister back and I'm scared that I'll never see her again.'

Someone knocked at the door. She opened it and stepped out to hear whatever O'Connor was bursting to tell her.

'I've found a report of a break-in at a local veterinary practice. It happened two weeks ago and there was some ketamine taken. The vet who owns the business said that she can speak to you about it if you pop by. Forensics examined the scene but all the samples remain unprocessed at the lab. She came face to face with the intruder and was terrified.'

'I'm on my way.'

TWENTY-SEVEN

A dog's bark boomed continuously as Gina entered Cleevesford Veterinary Practice. Jacob sidestepped the St Bernard as its owner pulled the lead before comforting the dog. A cat peered out from behind its basket bars from the other side of the room. The smell of disinfectant reached Gina's nostrils as a young woman mopped around her.

'Can I help you?' the man on reception asked.

'I'm DI Harte, this is DS Driscoll. We're here to speak to Christy Everly about the break-in.'

He smiled. 'Of course, come through. She's in her office and she's expecting you.'

A vet peered out from behind a door to call the man with the St Bernard. Gina followed the receptionist behind the counter, where the sound of distressed animals began to fade as they continued walking along a corridor with several doors leading off it.

Every wall was painted in bright white. Gina spotted the dispensary door to her left, marked with a sign. A keypad had been fixed to the wall next to the door so only authorised staff were able to enter. The disinfectant was soon replaced by the smell of fresh wood. The dispensary door was definitely new. The report said that whoever broke in had completely smashed the door in.

The receptionist knocked on the door marked office at the farthest end of the building.

'Come in,' the person behind the door called.

'The police are here.'

'Great, I'll see them now. Thanks, Pete.'

He stepped aside to let Gina and Jacob through the door. Gina spotted an open bag of red jelly sweets on Christy Everly's desk, amongst a pile of purchase invoices and notebooks. Her crisp white medical tunic, finished off with a name badge, looked ultra-bright against the stark light in the room. Her round face and clear skin made her appear quite youthful but her tired eyes told another story, that of long hours and overwork.

'Take a seat and thank you for coming. I was meaning to call to see if there had been any updates. Have you caught him?'

Gina tilted her head as she sat in one of the seats opposite Christy. 'Sorry, no news on your intruder but I can confirm that forensics are working hard on all the samples taken at the scene.'

Christy slumped back in her chair and pulled a sweet from her bag. 'You'll have to excuse me. I haven't even stopped for lunch today. So, what is it you're here to speak about?'

'We're investigating another crime and there is a possibility that the two could be linked. We know that you had some ketamine stolen during the break-in.'

Christy sighed. 'You know, I thought that room was completely intruder proof. I had the best locks put on it and it was a sturdy wooden door, but he still managed to smash through it. The ketamine was also kept in a lockable cabinet and he managed to get the lock off by hitting it with something like a hammer. It came clean off. If some desperate drug user wants in, they'll find a way, that's all I can say.'

'You said in your statement that the CCTV caught nothing.'

'Yes, he cut the internet cable from outside so there is no camera footage. He also smashed the window to the downstairs toilet which is at the back of the building, so we didn't see him approaching. Our cameras do cover the back, just not that area. We have now rectified that by getting a new camera that covers the blind spot. We originally had, and still have, two cameras at the front and one along the side of the building.'

'You say he.'

She nodded, her mousy-brown straight hair brushing her shoulders. 'He was taller than me and I'm five eight. I'd say he was quite straight figured but strong looking. Big biceps. It was definitely a man. I couldn't see his face as you've probably read in the report. He was wearing a balaclava, a black jacket and dark joggers. He had gloves on too, so I don't think the forensics officer got any prints.'

Gina waited for Jacob to catch up with the notes, then she continued. 'Can you talk me through that evening? I know you've told the officers who attended the scene but I'd like to hear it from you.'

'Yes, certainly.' She picked up a pencil and began twiddling it as she spoke. 'This practice is my baby. It's my absolute life. I'm also a mother so as you can appreciate, when I go home, I have to make dinner and get some washing on. What always happens is that I end up having half jobs strewn all over the place and that day I'd been really busy. I not only run this business, but I also treat and operate on the animals that are admitted, so quite often, paperwork is left to do once we close. That night, after catching up with jobs at home, I came back to do my bookkeeping. It was stressing me out as I'd barely touched it for three weeks and I had suppliers calling every five minutes for payment and I hadn't even loaded their invoices onto the system. I guess I work hard. We do what we can for our children, don't we?' She stared off into the distance.

Gina gave her a verbal nudge. 'This was on Friday the ninth of February?'

She dropped the pencil and flinched. 'Yes, sorry. The whole encounter still terrifies me.'

'That's okay. Please take your time.' Coming face to face with an intruder was scary for anyone and Gina could tell that Christy was still shaken by the experience.

'I sorted everything out at home and came back around ten that evening.'

'Where did you park?'

'Around the front. I unlocked the door—'

Jacob interjected. 'When we came in, I noticed that there was an alarm box on the wall.' Gina hadn't spotted that. Christy had mentioned the CCTV but not the alarm.

'Oh, that,' Christy replied. 'The alarm hasn't worked for a few months. It needs replacing but I just haven't got around to it yet. I've had to budget so much for new equipment and staff wage increases, I've let that one slip. I thought the box in itself would be a deterrent. How foolish was I?'

'You unlocked the door, then what happened?'

Christy shuffled in her seat and looked up in thought as she recalled what had happened. 'I came in and turned the main light on. Nothing was out of place so I continued past reception and along the corridor. I felt a breeze. That was my first thought and then it clicked. I knew there had to be an open window or door and I was certain that I hadn't left any open as I checked them all before leaving. I don't know how I missed the state of the door when I entered that corridor, maybe it was tiredness. There were chunks of wood all over the place. I remember freezing with fear. It was like my feet were glued to the floor. I didn't know whether to shout, run, grab my phone, or check to see how bad the damage was. Anyway, I held my breath and listened for what felt like ages but I didn't hear a sound.' She reached for the drink on her desk with shaky hands and took a sip from the cup.

'I know it's hard to relive that night. You're doing really well.'

She pressed her lips together and looked up for a second before continuing to speak. 'I can't sleep at night and I haven't been back here after hours since the incident.' Christy bit her bottom lip and continued. 'With my phone in my hand, I decided that because I couldn't hear anyone, whoever had broken in had left. It's not like I confidently walked up to the smashed door, my legs were shaking so I reluctantly crept up to it. I stepped in and as soon as my body passed the doorframe, these strong arms hurled me at all the debris on the floor. The light was off in the dispensary but there was a bit of light seeping in from the corridor. That's when I saw him in his dark clothes with his face covered.' She grabbed a tissue and held it, almost like she was anticipating getting upset at any moment. Her eyes began to water. 'I thought he was going to kill me and all I could think of was my boy and if I'd see him again. It all happened so fast but it felt like a lifetime in that moment. He threw a gilet that had been left on a chair at my head before scarpering. I've never been so relieved in my life. I then called the police straight away. In hindsight, I should have run out of that building and called them from the car park. I still don't know what I was thinking. I've heard of drug takers breaking in for ketamine and other drugs, but it's never been a worry for me. My practice has never been targeted before. The intruder took all the ketamine I had. The officer that came took a copy of all the records so he has the exact amount recorded. There was enough to anaesthetise a lot of animals.'

'Thank you for going over that with me.'

'When I first saw him, I thought he was probably an addict but his arms were like iron and there was no shakiness about him when I approached him. I keep mulling that night over in my mind and my thoughts keep coming back to the same thing. Maybe he's a dealer. Who knows?'

Gina held her head up as she mulled that thought over. Her mind was telling her that he was stealing it to pump it into Jane Doe's and Darcie Fletcher's bodies.

'Well, I hope I helped with your other incident and I have everything crossed that your forensics team will find something soon. I'll definitely be able to sleep better when he's been caught.' She paused. 'Do you think he'll come back?'

There was no answer to that question. Gina knew that he found it easy enough to take what he came for but would he strike the same place twice? She made a mental note to ask one of the team to warn the other vets in the area to look out for suspicious people. 'All I can say is make sure you get your alarm fixed. I'd like to hope he won't come back here.'

'Me too. There's something I didn't mention to the officers because I thought it was stupid. You have to appreciate I work long hours and I'm always tired so I put it down to that.'

Gina's interest was piqued. 'Of course. It can often be the smallest detail that helps us to catch these people.'

'Normally, I park around the back. The frontage has limited spaces and I know the staff and customers need them. I don't like it around the back as I feel alone out there. If you look out of my office window.' She stood and pulled the cord to open the blind. 'You can see that just past my car, there is a line of bushes. Behind those bushes is a lane that leads to a convenience shop. For three nights before the burglary, as I left, I just had this feeling someone was there, watching. I heard sounds I don't normally hear, like footsteps cracking on branches, but the person didn't walk away. It sounded like they were loitering. I heard a phone beep too. I think the intruder had this place under surveillance. I hadn't come back later on those three nights so whoever was watching me leave must have thought the place would be empty until morning. Me coming in at ten on the Friday was obviously a surprise for them too. Then again, I've mulled this over, was it just someone walking to the shop and pausing to check their phone, or was it some drunken person waiting for me to go so they could pee up a tree? I just don't know.'

Jacob filled his notebook page and turned over to a fresh one.

'Do you think I'm safe?'

Gina smiled sympathetically. 'I think the intruder got what they came for.' She passed Christy a card. 'If you can think of anything at all when we're gone, or you think the intruder is back, even if it is just a rustle in the bushes, call us.'

She took the card and placed it next to her bag of sweets. 'Thank you.'

The phone in Gina's pocket began to vibrate. 'Excuse me, I have to take this.' She left Jacob in the room to finish off with Christy. 'O'Connor. What do you have for me?'

'Guv, I've been looking into where Varley could be staying near the church and I have a list of vacant properties close to it and get this, there are a whole row of old houses that have been fenced off for demolition. They are set to make way for a new block of apartments later this year. I was just about to call you to let you know we were going to check them out when a man called, there has been an incident outside one of those houses.'

As O'Connor told her more, she knew she had to check out the scene. She waved to Jacob. 'We have to go. Emergency.'

TWENTY-EIGHT

SHANNON

'Bye, Joel.' She waved at him as he crossed the road and walked into the shop.

Shannon set the alarm at the showroom and made sure the whole place was locked up. Several minutes later, she arrived at the bus stop and stepped onto her usual bus. It was deathly quiet but then again, she had finished late – again. She was thankful that Joel had stayed to help her get everything done, otherwise she'd still be there now. Most people finished work around five or six, and after that it got quieter on the bus.

A man stepped onto the bus and sat right behind her, despite the bus being empty. He was so close his breath tickled the nape of her neck. Standing, she got up and headed nearer the front so that she could see the driver. Why did that always happen to her? She glanced down the aisle at the man and was grateful that he had his earphones in and was watching something on his phone.

The bus snaked around the estate, taking forever as it stopped every couple of minutes to let no one off and no one on. Just as the driver approached her stop, she hit the bell and stood at the front of the bus. As the doors opened, she jumped off and glanced back to see if the man was still seated, and he was. Yes, she was scared and yes, she was paranoid. Darcie had been taken so as far as Shannon was concerned, a dangerous person was still out there. The man on the bus could be the kidnapper. Anyone could be the kidnapper.

Turning around, she couldn't help but look into all the dark places that she couldn't quite see into. The clump of bushes next to the dark-coloured bin – did she see a shadow just then? The road ahead and behind – the bus had gone and there wasn't a car in sight. The whistling breeze caught her hair and she felt goosebumps prickling on her arms under her coat. Without another thought, she ran on her heels through the trees and straight to Barney's doggy day care, almost stumbling on the rough concrete more than once.

Before she knew it, she was home and safe. With her back against the front door, she watched as Barney darted through the living room, then into the kitchen, no doubt waiting for his food bowl to be filled. The sound of him nudging it across the kitchen floor told Shannon she needed to get her act together and feed her dog. She flinched as the fridge made a cracking sound and then her heating whooshed as it came on. Why didn't she feel safe? The night before had all been a bit odd and feverish but her clock hadn't vanished. It had been there all along. She was losing her mind like her poor nanna did towards the end of her life. Maybe she needed to go to the doctor and get some tests. Did she want to know if she was losing it? She gasped, overwhelmed at her every thought. Her skewered vision made the hallway look like it was swaying. 'Stop,' she yelled, wanting the panic to stop.

Her buzzing phone caused her to flinch and bash her hand on the door handle. She raised it and shook the pain away as she read what was on the screen. The burglar alarm had gone off in the showroom and the app was letting her know. Then her phone rang. 'Gordon?'

'The alarm has gone off at the showroom. I've just checked the camera in my office and the one covering the main door and there's no break-in. Did you close and lock all the doors and windows? It wouldn't be the first time you've left one of them open.'

He was right. Shannon had been back to the office twice last month. She even thought that Darcie or Joel might have left the offending windows open but they had both denied it. Both times it happened after she'd had a really weird night's sleep. In the end she had to own her mistake, which is why Gordon was easily blaming her now.

'I locked everything.' She swallowed, hoping that he wouldn't have a go at her. She couldn't deal with that right now. Her mind wandered back to earlier. She'd opened the toilet windows after a customer had changed her baby's nappy in there. 'I'll go back and check.' It was her job after all. She always dealt with the alarm and it was always nothing. She had opened that window but she also thought she'd closed it. She shook her head to see if it still ached, and it did. It had to be her fault the alarm had gone off but at least no one had broken in.

'I know you've probably just got home. Grab a taxi and I'll reimburse you tomorrow. Make sure you get a receipt.'

'Thanks, Gordon.'

She called a taxi as she hurried to the kitchen. Barney snuffled in his empty bowl before he let out a whimper. 'Okay.' She opened the cupboard and reached in for his food but her fingers felt nothing there. 'What?'

Barney replied with a whine. She kneeled down to take a better look into the bottom cupboard, the one she kept Barney's food in, but the two tins she knew were there seemed to be missing. She pulled the dog biscuits out and the pack of chews and there were the tins of food, right against the back wall. She scrunched her brows, wondering how she'd pushed them so far back. Her gaze flitted up to the wall clock. She hadn't been right this morning. Had she nudged the tins of food all the way back there?

'Mummy has to pop out, Barney.' She emptied a tin into his bowl and grabbed her keys to leave the house. She knew Barney would whine which is why she didn't like to leave him on his own for long. Outside she glanced back at the house while waiting for the taxi to arrive, her attention fell on her second bedroom window. Her curtain was ruffled. Had she left it like that? The taxi driver tooted his horn, almost scaring the life out of her. She got in and as he drove off, she tried to look back but they were already halfway down the stretch of road. Had her curtain been tampered with? Could someone have really been in her house? A nervous flutter in her stomach made her wonder if Finn was there now. Was he trying to drive her mad because he couldn't use her any more, or was she losing it? It had to be him.

TWENTY-NINE

SHANNON

The taxi pulled up and minutes later Shannon was fighting with the bunch of keys to find the one for the main door as the alarm screamed away. The glass frontage of the showroom only revealed darkness and the shine of car bonnets as the street-lamps along the road glistened off them. She gestured for the taxi driver to wait, then her phone rang again. 'Gordon. I've just got here.'

'Great. Can you hurry, I can't hear you over that racket.'

With the phone clutched between her ear and shoulder, she unlocked the main door and punched in the code, relieved when the alarm stopped. She could still hear the ringing in her ears. 'Done. I'll just give the place the once over and head back home.'

'Actually, can you hang on another fifteen minutes. Finn is on his way to collect a car. I know he wanted to collect it earlier so I called him when I knew you were going back. The keys for it are on my desk. He also just wants to check something in the new workshop. The fitters need some measurements.'

'Really? The taxi is waiting. It's going to clock up a fortune.'

'Just let the driver go and wait for Finn. He won't be long.'

'Great,' she mumbled. She walked back to the driver and pulled a ten-pound note from her purse and gave it to him. After he drove off, she headed into the showroom. Damn, she'd forgotten to ask for the receipt. Her footsteps echoed through the large room. All the cars looked to be intact and nothing had been tampered with. She pushed the toilet door open to reveal the window on the catch.

'Have you found out why the alarm went off?'

'No,' she lied, not wanting to admit she'd left the window open. 'It must have been a technical fault.' It pained her to say that. It was her fault and with it being a bit breezy as soon as a gust had howled through, it had set the alarm off. 'Everything is okay here.' She gently pulled the window closed and pulled a face as it locked into a closed position.

Her body tensed but all was okay. Gordon hadn't heard her closing the window.

'Right, I'm going to go then. Wait for Finn and I'll see you tomorrow.'

She went to reply but Gordon had already hung up. She was not getting in a car with Finn. She'd had enough of his games and she'd pay for her own taxi home, but Gordon didn't need to know that. She could imagine his response. He'd tell her to stop acting so unprofessionally. Snatching the keys off Gordon's desk, she set the alarm off again and it roared angrily. Her phone rang and she answered to Gordon again.

'What's going on there?'

'Sorry, I accidentally set the alarm off again,' she shouted over the noise. She glanced out of the back window. The new workshop looked to be locked. Everything was fine.

'Have you checked the back?'

'Yes. The new workshop is padlocked and I am just about to leave.' She ran to reset the alarm before locking up again. 'I'm outside waiting for Finn now.'

'Okay, see you tomorrow.' He ended the call.

As far as Finn was concerned, his fifteen minutes could be half an hour. She sat on the wall that enclosed the showroom car park and began scrolling through Facebook. She clicked onto the 'What's Up Cleevesford' Facebook page and saw all the comments about Darcie. So many people were scared that an ordinary mum could be snatched from the side of the road. Everyone sent thoughts and prayers for her safe return. A lump formed in Shannon's throat. She thought of her friend and all their memories. Their childhoods were filled with laughter and fun. They'd both been on the netball team at school and she remembered Darcie telling her first when she'd lost her virginity to a boy name Will. All those precious memories. How could she have fallen out with Darcie like that? She pictured Darcie with psycho Varley in a dark room and all the time she wondered if Darcie hated her still.

Shannon clicked onto Darcie's Facebook profile. She didn't use it much but Shannon just wanted to look at her friend's happy face. A tear drizzled down her cheek. She replayed their last argument where Shannon had accused her of being the worst friend ever. Darcie had actually cried, explaining that she'd been caught in the middle, that she was sorry she'd lied. If only they could go back to that moment. Shannon would hold her friend close and tell her it didn't matter at all. Huge sobs escaped her mouth as she hugged herself in the dark corner of the car park, hidden from the main road and all the dangers that came with it. Damp from the wall had started to seep through her nylon trousers. She wiped the wetness from her face with the sleeve of her coat. Where was Finn? She checked the time on her phone, she'd been waiting for twenty minutes now. Then again, Finn had always been late and when confronted about it, he'd laugh. She pressed his name in her phone, wondering if she should text and ask him to hurry but then thought better of it. If she asked him to hurry, he might take even longer.

She furrowed her brows as car lights came up behind her

from around the back of the building. As she turned the head-lights almost blinded her. Grabbing her bag, she ran towards the light, wondering why Finn had parked back there and angry that he had his main beam on. All she could see were green blobs now. The overall-cladded man stomped towards her but instead of a face, all she could see were green blobs while her vision adjusted. She fished in her pockets for the car keys that she'd happily throw at Finn. As she went to slam them into his chest, she could see that the man in front of her was wearing a smooth white mask. He clasped his hand over her mouth to stop the scream that was just about to escape. Arms flailing, she tried to hit out, to catch any part of this person who now had his arm around her neck as he dragged her backwards. In the distance, she saw a bent over man with a stick making his way past the closed shop and she wanted to scream and call to him for help, but she couldn't.

Then she felt the fine prick in her neck and she knew she'd been injected with something. Her body weakened before flop-ping as her attacker held her close to his chest. It was as if he were hugging her from behind, not in a nice way but like he was trying to squeeze the life out of her. She tried to push him away but whatever he'd given her was weakening her by the second and now her head was swimming in a sickening way.

Silent tears continued to fall as he flung her in the boot, smashing her head on the side panel as he forced every part of her into the confined space. With the little bit of strength, she had left, she began to kick at the lights and the back seat but the fight in her was oozing out of her body as she succumbed to the drug. 'I don't want to die,' she half whimpered, in the hope that her kidnapper would be merciful. She thought of Barney. He'd be all alone and he needed her. Then the man slammed the boot and it felt as though she was sinking into another world where hands were coming out to grab her as she fell into the unknown.

THIRTY

'This is Enid and her son Charles,' PC Ahmed said as Gina approached. 'They found the body. Enid is a bit shaken as her son came home and found her outside the derelict building next door to them. He said she just needs a few minutes before she can talk. She had a bit of a fall and refused to be treated by a paramedic. Another paramedic has been in the house though. They didn't know if the man was still alive but he's definitely dead.'

'Thanks, Shaf.'

Gina spotted Bernard placing several stepping plates on the ground. 'It doesn't rain around here, it pours,' he shouted from behind his face mask. He was right, two kidnappings and now a body.

'Do you have any information yet, Bernard?'

'Hold on. I'll be with you in a moment.' He tucked his beard into his face covering.

Two crime scene investigators passed, one carrying a large box and another holding a camera and floodlight. Another was already erecting a tent on a patch of grass within the metal barriers. The white forensics suits stood out, glowing like beacons in the darkness. Gina glanced back and saw mother and son sitting on a bench in the garden next door. He was passing her a hot drink and putting his arm around her.

Jacob strolled up. 'I just about managed to find somewhere to park. Have we identified the body yet?'

She shook her head. 'Bernard is just organising his team by the looks of it.'

Several clangs sounded as the stepping plates went down. Bernard called them over. Before going in, Gina grabbed two crime scene suit bags and threw one at Jacob. Once they'd togged up Gina headed past the metal fencing into the garden. The floodlight bathed the area in light just as she reached the window.

Bernard stepped in the way. 'We have a dead male and it looks like a drug overdose. He literally died with a needle in his arm and from the angles, it looks like he administered it himself. The paramedics have been in through the window. They were in there when we arrived and the man was declared dead straight away. There is something very strange about the scene, though.'

'Did you find any identification on him?'

'We haven't looked yet,' Bernard replied. Gina turned just as the door had been wrenched open and a CSI went in. 'Hopefully we might find something in a minute.'

'What is strange about the scene?' she asked.

He stepped aside, allowing Gina and Jacob to step forward to look in. The beam from one of the portable lights lit him up. She could see brown hair and a flannel shirt. The man faced away from them. His left arm had flopped down and an empty syringe dangled from him, just above a pink fluffy rug. The one corner of the room had been dressed to looked like a comfortable lounge. The man was sitting on a huge blow-up sofa covered in colourful cushions and on the fold-up coffee table next to him stood a framed photo. Gina recognised the woman in the photo. 'That's one of Darcie Fletcher's Instagram photos,' she said to Jacob. She shivered as she saw the pile of children's toys, perfect for a five-year-old; a mixture of teddies, dolls and board games.

Jacob peered in. 'That's weird. It looks like he's tried to make a home here. The other walls are dirty and damp, but that corner, it's even had a coat of paint.'

Gina stepped back from the window. The smell coming from the room was making her nauseous. She spied the trail of vomit down the far side of the sofa. Gina called over to the CSI who had just opened the door and stepped in. 'Can you estimate how long he's been dead?'

The CSI began to rummage for identification. 'There is loss of rigor, so I'd estimate his death to have been at least twenty-four hours ago.' Gina knew that rigor mortis kicked in quite soon after death, and that the muscles became fully stiff after around eight to twelve hours. After twenty-four hours, the stiffness began to weaken. 'Wait, I've found a wallet on the rug.'

'Can you open it and tell me who it belongs to?'

The CSI began trying to prise it apart in her gloved hands. 'There's a driver's licence.' She held it to the light and scrunched her eyes to read it in the limited light. 'It's Mitchell Varley and the photo matches the man I'm seeing here.'

'You need to check all the other rooms. He's the main suspect in the kidnapping case we're working on. The victim is called Darcie Fletcher and that's her in the photo.'

The CSI called over another one and they both left the room. Gina began to nervously tap her foot on the stepping plate as they waited for news. She only hoped that Varley hadn't killed Darcie before overdosing.

Gina stepped back into the garden and took a deep breath. Jacob came up beside her and they waited for what felt like an eternity. The CSI stepped out of the house and pulled her face mask under her chin to address Bernard, Gina and Jacob. 'There are no other people present in the house.'

Every muscle in Gina's body relaxed. 'If she's not here, where is she?'

'We'll find her, guv.' Jacob pressed his lips together and kept his gaze on the front door.

'I've found something.' The other CSI came out. 'It's a suicide note and it's addressed to Darcie.'

Gina took the envelope. 'We need to open it. Darcie's life might depend on whatever is in this envelope.'

With gloved hands, Gina pulled out the note and read it to Jacob. 'Darcie, I didn't mean to scare you when we were in the car together and those messages were unforgivable. Please forgive me. Realising what I did, sickened me to my core. I'm a predator, an animal, and the only way to deal with a biting dog is to euthanise it.

'I stuffed everything up and when you find out about my past, you'll be disgusted and that's something I can't face. I've come to realise I can't change and I can't be cured. I'm sick, really sick in the bloody head. I made this place for you because I thought you might want to spend time with me but I can see now. Why would you want this place and me? I love you and I know I can't have you. I don't have a life. Anyway, I'm signing out. I won't bother you again. Mitch.'

Jacob raised his eyebrows. 'Does this mean what I think it might?'

Gina nodded. 'I don't think he took Darcie. If he didn't, then who did?'

THIRTY-ONE
UNKNOWN

I stare into her eyes as she flits in and out of consciousness and I wonder if she's hallucinating something wonderful. If I hadn't gagged her, maybe she would try to murmur a few words but looking at her, I don't think she's going to make sense for a long time. My lips are dry. I pull my strawberry-scented lip gloss from my deep pocket and swipe a bit across my bottom lip and press the two together.

'It's lovely to see you again, Shannon.'

She doesn't respond through her drool-soaked rag, which suits me. With what he gave her, I have time to get on with my day. I shiver. It's so cold in here. Grabbing a thick blanket, I shake the dust out of it and place it over her body. I've secured her to the fixed metal bed and no one will hear her, so she'll be fine.

Tick, tick, tick. The clock is ticking and when eleven comes, we'll take a lovely trip down memory lane.

A rat scurries across the flagstone floor and I flinch. I never did get used to the rats. They make my heart sink and my head spin like I might pass out. My heart begins to bang, then I hear the snap of a trap. Phew, it has been eliminated.

My thoughts are with the one in hospital. I thought there was no way she could even walk but she proved me wrong when I removed the binds to swap them for something better. I only left her for a few minutes and she'd gone. She won't survive. I swallow. She escaped, so maybe she has more strength than I'm giving her credit for. No, I shake my head. She's in a coma and she'll never come out, I'm sure of it. I only have to remember the state she was in. Organ failure had started and when a person is as weak as she is, they don't bounce back. I clench my hands. She can't bounce back. I can't entertain that thought. What I need to do is believe and hope. Yes, that's what I'll do. There won't be any stuff ups this time. Not with Darcie or Shannon.

I glance down at the pathetic creature in front of me and I whisper. 'Beneath your kind eyes and your smile, you have no soul and you have no heart.' Just like the other bloody bitch. I want to say that, but I don't. Instead, I slap her but she doesn't respond.

All this isn't going to plan but then again, plans are made to be changed.

I hold back the sadness within. What the hell have I done? There's no going back now as it's not just my life I'm about to ruin. I should stop now and hope for the best that the other one doesn't recover, but I can't.

I glance at the clock that ticks and ticks. When it stops, we play. There are no winners or no losers in this game. She will lose but she has to play.

Tick, tick, tick. 'Your time is coming...' I will not let her escape. There will be no leaving her unattended. When I look at Shannon, I know I have to do this. She came back into our lives for a reason and this is it. She is dead.

THIRTY-TWO

JILL

Sunday, 3 March

Jill yawned as she pulled her front door closed. Shannon's dog had never barked so much in its life but last night wasn't on. Being an animal lover it pained Jill to have to say something, especially as last time she had to complain Shannon started putting Barney in doggy day care so that he didn't bark all day. He was just a dog that couldn't be left alone for long, not like her Pippy.

She walked up to the door, listening to the dog going crazy on the other side. It wasn't even a little yap, it boomed through the whole street.

Mr Smithe from across the way came out of his house and scrunched his wrinkled face up. 'That bloody dog.' He put his cap on and continued down the path to get his morning paper.

Jill wanted to yell at him and all the other neighbours for leaving it up to her to do this awful deed. Someone else could have said something, for once. Instead, Jill was looking like the whingy neighbour. Granted, it had only been one night but that one night had felt like forever.

As she went to knock, she paused and wondered if Shannon was okay. It was odd that she spent so much time shuffling around in her loft. At first Jill had thought she had a rat until she went up to investigate. There was no rat, just a scuffling sound coming from the neighbouring loft. Whatever Shannon was doing up there was none of her business. While she was at it, she'd mention Shannon's bizarre nocturnal activities too. She owed it to herself to get a good night's sleep. After taking a deep breath and psyching herself up, she knocked. Assertiveness wasn't exactly her middle name which is why her stomach started to churn. There was no answer.

She jerked back as Barney became entangled in the living room curtains and brought the whole rail down. Jill stepped onto the grass outside Shannon's lounge window and peered in, trying to see between all the leafy plants that adorned her neighbour's window ledge. That's when she saw the settee cushions shredded up on the floor and a mound of dog mess next to them. Something was wrong.

Jill swallowed, suddenly feeling mean for thinking the worst of Shannon. She tapped on the window and shouted. 'Shannon, are you okay?' All that did was cause the dog to jump up and drag a plant pot back with him, scattering soil all over the mess.

Maybe she should check out the back. Shannon might have had an accident. She could have fallen over and bumped her head on the worktop. With her hand gripping her phone, Jill hurried over to the side gate and went to push it but it was locked.

'What's with that dog? My mum said it's doing her nut in.'

The neighbour-but-one's teenage son stood there, his hood pulled up and his baggy joggers looking like they might fall down.

'I think something has happened to Shannon. I was going to check around the back but the gate is locked.'

He eyed it up and down. 'Shall I climb over and take a look?'

Jill nodded. 'Yes, I think we should. I could never forgive myself if she's hurt. Would you mind?'

'Nah.' With his grip on the top of the fence and his trainer-covered feet walking up the wall of the house like he was some sort of free runner, he was up and over in a few seconds.

She waited for him to come back. He peered over the fence. 'I can't see her but her kitchen cupboard is open, there are dog biscuits everywhere and the bin is all over the kitchen floor. It looks like the place has been ransacked.'

With that, Jill called the police. She knew something terrible had happened.

THIRTY-THREE

Gina sat at the head of the table in the incident room, Briggs pacing behind her. He glanced out of the window and pulled the blind down. 'The bloody press is everywhere. I need to write another press release. Can you take over, Gina?'

'Yes.'

Briggs stormed out of the room. She'd come in early to try and speak to him, but he'd coldly led her straight to the incident room as they discussed the next move. The decision they had made was the right one and Gina had to convey it to the team. Jacob, Wyre, O'Connor and Kapoor all nursed their mugs of coffee as they awaited further instructions.

Gina cleared her throat with a swig of her own drink. Her puffy eyes told the team that she'd barely slept and they didn't look much better either. 'I'm going to try to summarise this quickly. Jacob and I did update the system last night which is why we didn't leave till gone midnight, so have a look after this briefing.'

'I can't believe we found Varley dead, guv.' O'Connor leaned back and rubbed his chin.

'I know it's deflating but we were wrong and we have to

follow all the other leads. As for last night, Mitchell Varley was pronounced dead by suicide. There appears to be nothing found at the scene to suggest that anyone else was involved. I'm gathering you've all read the note?' Gina pointed to the copy that was in the middle of the main table.

A hum of yesses filled the air.

'PC Ahmed was instructed to inform Varley's father of the news last night and Mr Varley will be heading to the morgue to formally identify the body, but it was definitely Mitchell Varley. The identification is just a formality. We don't believe that he took Darcie which means that our perp is still out there.' Gina glanced at her notes. 'Jacob and I went to speak to Cleevesford Vets last night and Christy Everly gave us some information that hadn't been included in her initial statement.'

Wyre sat up straight and placed her cup down.

'For three nights before her practice was burgled, she thought someone was watching her leaving at the back of the surgery. Although she thought it might just be someone hanging around for other reasons, it seems too much of a coincidence. It could well have been someone studying her movements, clocking the times she left and pinpointing the CCTV cameras. She described the intruder as tall and stocky, like he worked out.'

'Guv.' O'Connor got her attention. 'Christy Everly called this morning and said that she remembered a car being parked up at the back on one of the nights. She said it was a black hatchback but that's all the detail she could give.'

'Great. We don't know if this vehicle is linked but we need to add it to what we have so far. Do we have a description of Corey Lowe, Darcie's ex?'

Wyre nodded. 'He has a Facebook profile but it seems dormant. It was last used a year ago but he does have a profile picture and it's of him pumping iron in the gym. Lean, not too bulky but strong.' Wyre tapped away on her phone and held up a photo of Lowe holding a huge weight above his head as he lay back on a padded bench.

'He fits Christy Everly's burglar description. Are we any closer to locating him?'

'No, guv.' Wyre puffed out a breath. 'He hasn't triggered any ANPR cameras or used his credit cards. It can only be a matter of time but it's also Sunday. Maybe he had the weekend off and he hasn't left his digs.'

Gina walked over to the window and poked a finger through one of the blind slats. A photographer looked up so she pulled her finger out quickly. 'I know this is a massive job but can you organise for a small team to call all the gyms in Bristol, see if he's registered with any. I don't want to put his face out there yet.' She shook her head. 'I get Lowe's link to Darcie but is there one to Jane Doe? Us not being able to identify her is really holding us back.' She glanced at the boards and pointed at them. 'We need to go back to basics and look at other potential suspects.'

'We could revisit her place of work,' Jacob suggested as he raised his eyebrows.

'I think we will. Have we heard anything from Darcie's boss, Gordon Shoreford?'

O'Connor shook his head. 'Nothing.'

'I left my card on his desk. He was meant to call me or pop into the station when he got to the showroom. We need to speak to him. Wyre, any luck with mispers? We need to identify Jane Doe and I was hoping missing persons would have the answer.'

'I'm still working through them, guv.'

'Actually, can you stay on mispers?'

'Yes.'

'O'Connor, can you and Kapoor organise the calls to the gyms in Bristol? Jacob and I will head to Shoreford's next. About the plan. DCI Briggs and I spoke before you all came in. Jane Doe is still in a critical condition and it is obvious that whoever dumped her left her for dead. We have decided to tell the press that she's in a permanent coma and that she won't come around – ever. It's important that the perp doesn't feel like all is lost so on the off-chance Darcie is still alive, we can protect her. If the kidnapper thinks for one minute that Jane is awake and can identify him, we have no idea what the consequences will be but we can't risk Darcie's life. We don't believe either woman was taken for a ransom as no demands have been made, not for Jane or for Darcie. All we have is that Jane was almost killed and we might still be looking at murder if she doesn't pull through. I'm also not ruling out the fact that Darcie could already be dead. Looking at Jane, it's likely.' Gina glanced at the board and wondered if the perp had slipped up with Jane.

Briggs hurried in and stared at Gina. 'I've just had a call from dispatch. A uniformed officer got called out to Shannon Calder's house to check out a possible incident. There is no sign of forced entry but the dog is distressed and the owner is not answering. The neighbour was concerned something had happened. As we were concerned for her welfare, police managed to break in but found no one there.'

Gina almost dropped the pen she was holding. Straight away, she knew that Shannon was now a part of the kidnapper's plan and she wondered if the modus operandi was the same. 'We need to check her loft. And any clocks.'

Briggs agreed and continued. 'There is more. Shannon's boss, Gordon Shoreford, has also just called. About twenty minutes ago he arrived at the showroom to open up at Shoreford's as Shannon didn't turn up to work and he noticed a small gift box in front of the door. It contains a finger.'

THIRTY-FOUR

Gina drove to Shoreford's and Jacob talked all the way. 'The kidnapper has definitely struck again, guv,' he continued. 'Where is Darcie? After Darcie was taken, Jane Doe turned up, but this time the pattern is different. This time, Darcie is still missing. Of course, she could still turn up, though I think we're waiting for a body this time.' He stared out of the windscreen, deep in thought about the case.

Gina pulled the handbrake on and put her phone in her pocket. A wave of nausea hit her. They both knew what the other was thinking. Jane Doe was on death's door. Maybe the kidnapper would succeed in murdering Darcie. Gina tried not to picture Kyle Fletcher's face as she told him the news of his sister's death. Worse, she pictured little Cleo's face as it dawned on the child that her mother was never coming home. Her chest tightened as she became anxious. She shook those morbid thoughts away. They had no body yet so, as far as she was concerned, Darcie was still alive and time was against them to find her. 'We can't think the worst.'

She stepped out onto the damp pavement and took in the scene before her. Bernard and four crime scene assistants were already at work. She weaved in and out of the cars on the fore-court with Jacob close behind until she reached PC Smith who was guarding the outer cordon. The end of the tape had been tied to a post and it flapped noisily as a breeze caught it. Cars began to slow down on the road in front of the showroom, each and every driver wondering what had happened to warrant the police cars and a forensics van.

'Morning, guv,' PC Smith said as he stood straight in his uniform brandishing a sympathetic smile.

'Morning. What do we have?' As first officer on site Gina hoped that he'd been updated by the forensics team. The clunk of a stepping plate made Gina flinch. Barely three days had passed and they already had too many scenes to handle.

'I got here about an hour ago and cordoned the area off as per Bernard's instructions. There are three other PCs with me. I instructed two to go on a door to door. They were going to start by asking someone at the shop opposite if they had any CCTV. They went in about ten minutes ago but they haven't come out yet.'

'That sounds promising. Where was the finger found?'

PC Smith pointed at the floor in front of the entrance doors. 'It was there, right in the middle of the path. Bernard has boxed it up but one of the CSIs did take photos first.' A yellow evidence marker remained where the boxed finger had been found.

Gina glanced around at the crowd forming on the path. People whispered to each other and some held their phones up. She took in each face, wondering if the perpetrator had come back to witness the aftermath of their handiwork. Not one face was recognisable to her.

'We probably need to move the public on otherwise this'll turn into a circus and I could do without that.' Gina had had her fill of wannabe crime vloggers and bloggers who interfered with their cases.

'When the other PC gets back, I'll ask him to sort it.'

'Where is he?'

'Looking around the back with a crime scene investigator.'

'Is this all of Shoreford's? The showroom.'

'As far as I'm aware.'

There were several units around the back. Gina made a mental note to check out who owned them. 'Do we have access to the CCTV from the showroom?'

'The business owner, Gordon Shoreford, can access it remotely.'

'And where is he?'

'He's sitting on the wall, behind all the cars. We spoke to him and he didn't have anything to say. He said he was going to check the CCTV. I said you'd want to speak to him when you arrived but he looked a bit sickened by the find so I thought it best we leave him for a while.'

'I think we'll go over and have a chat with him. We need to get him out of here.' She spotted a teen filming Gordon. One thing that caught her attention was that Gordon was portly but he was also broad shouldered, taller than five eight and looked strong.

Jacob nodded towards another door set in the brickwork of the showroom. 'Maybe we can use his office if we don't go through the front door.'

Gina called over to Bernard who was completely togged up. He walked over. 'I don't have anything yet. I need half an hour.'

'That's okay. We need to interview Gordon Shoreford. Can we use the side door to get into the building so that we can talk to Mr Shoreford in private?'

'No, he said the last time he spoke to Shannon Calder was around eight yesterday evening. The alarm had started sounding so she came back to reset it. We don't know what happened after that, but we need to go in first to make sure that there hadn't been a break-in. We could do with the keys and passes to enter the building. We have a lot of samples from outside, including freshly disposed of cigarette butts and the finger, obviously, but we really need to check inside before anyone else enters and contaminates the scene.'

Gina turned to address Jacob. 'Would you please ask Mr Shoreford for the keys, any passes and the alarm code?'

Jacob hurried over to the man, leaving Gina with Bernard.

'Is there anything else you can tell us?'

Bernard shook his head. 'I wish I could but there are no prints on the box containing the finger. It's a small blue gift box. Do you want to see it? Obviously, we sent the finger to the lab immediately.'

'Yes, thank you. About the finger. We're working on the theory that it could belong to our victim who was kidnapped on Friday, Darcie Fletcher. We have a DNA sample from her brother Kyle so we can confirm if it is hers or not.'

Bernard led her to the evidence tent and showed Gina a marked-up evidence bag inside. Through the clear plastic, Gina could see a small blue box with little boats printed on it. 'Can we have any crime scene photos emailed to the incident room as soon as you can?'

'One of our assistants has already transferred them from the camera onto the laptop. I'll ask her to email them to you in a short while when we've checked inside.'

'Thank you.' She saw Jacob in the car park, waving to get her attention. 'Coming,' she called.

'Guv, Mr Shoreford has the CCTV up on his phone. Did Bernard have anything to say yet?'

'The box that the finger was placed in had little boats on it. Cleo drew that picture of someone in her loft and she said that the intruder gave her a little toy boat. Do we have that yet?'

'Not as far as I know.'

'We'll head to Kyle Fletcher's after here. I want that boat

booked into evidence ASAP. Right, let's take a look at this CCTV.'

Gina and Jacob sat either side of Gordon Shoreford on the wall. She turned her head to see if anyone was behind them but what was left of the crowd were far enough out of the way from them. 'May I take a look?'

Gordon passed Gina his phone with the app open. 'You just select which camera and you can look at the footage. It constantly records to a hard drive but recent footage hasn't been overwritten. I'm afraid the cameras around the back are useless. I was meant to get all the spider's webs off them and I haven't. It's all very white and blurry.'

After taking Mr Shoreford's phone, she clicked onto the main camera recordings and saw a still picture of the forecourt. While watching last evening's footage she saw a cat passing, then a short while later Shannon entered the building. Several minutes after that, Shannon left the showroom with her phone pressed against her ear then she went out of view to her left.

'Do you know who she's speaking to?'

Gordon nodded. 'It was me. She was telling me that everything was fine and she'd just had to reset the alarm.'

'Do you know what set the alarm off?'

'No, she said it was nothing.'

'Who else has access to the building?'

'Only me and Shannon. Darcie never had a key and Joel is new and he's a trainee, definitely not ready for key holder duties yet. Shannon is Joel and Darcie's supervisor. She's worked for me since leaving school so I trust her totally with the keys. Well, I did until recently.' He pressed his thin lips together and loosened his tie underneath his buttoned-up overcoat. 'I often get a bit short with Shannon. She has developed a habit of leaving the toilet window open and although she said it was nothing last night, I suspect she left it open yet again. She doesn't seem herself some days and I don't know why. I know the alarm is working fine. It's new and it doesn't play up but I have to get it checked still. In fact, I came in a little fired up to discuss it with her this morning, then I found that box containing a finger. Is it hers? Has someone hurt her?'

Jacob began jotting down what Gordon had said.

'We don't know but forensics have it and we're going to find out.'

'I should have come here myself last night. I called Shannon because I was already in my dressing gown, watching the telly. Also, I live quite far away and she's local. I'm now ashamed to say that a part of me wanted to punish her for not closing a window properly. Although, I did tell her to get a taxi and I said I'd pay her back. I didn't want her catching the bus.'

'She got a taxi?'

Jacob stopped writing and they both waited for Gordon to continue speaking.

'Yes, well, I'm assuming so. I told her to get a taxi.'

'Do you know which firm she used?'

'No, sorry.'

Gina watched a little more of the footage and saw nothing but a shadow cast across the front door. 'That must be Shannon. It looks like she was waiting around.' Her shadow went after a minute and a half, just after the pavement was lit up. 'That must be headlamps. Would she have asked the taxi driver to wait for her?'

'I don't know,' Gordon replied. 'That would have been the most logical thing to do.' He placed his chunky fingers on his knees and shuffled back on the wall. 'Can I go into my office soon?'

Gina felt he was getting slightly nervous. 'You say you were at home last night, at the time Shannon was at the showroom?'

'Yes, it was Saturday night. Why are you asking me that? Do you think I did all this?'

'We just need to eliminate you. It's a routine question, Mr

Shoreford. We also have two missing women and they both work for you.'

He huffed out a breath and scratched the redness that crept up his neck. 'I, err, I ordered a curry. It came just before Shannon called.'

'Thank you.'

Jacob stopped writing. 'Where did you order that from, Mr Shoreford?'

'I don't know. My mind has gone blank. It's one of my favourite places, you'd think I'd be able to remember. I think it's the stress of what's happening.' He scrunched his brows and pointed to his phone that Gina was holding. 'Check my messages, the name comes up when they contact me. They confirmed that my order would be delivered within the next twenty minutes, that was around seven thirty.'

On his instruction, Gina opened up his messages and opened the most recent one. 'It's from the Taj Mahal,' she said. 'And it was received at seven thirty-six. Thank you.' She turned back to Gordon. 'How far away do you live from here?'

'I moved to just outside Cheltenham last year. It would take me forty-five minutes to an hour to get to Cleevesford.'

'Is the Taj Mahal in Cheltenham?' Gina waited for Jacob to jot the times down.

'Yes. It's on Butler Road. Call them up and they will confirm they delivered to me. I order from them about twice a week so the delivery person recognises me. I think his name is Raf.'

'Thank you.'

He cleared his throat. 'Do you think someone is targeting my employees?'

She thought of Jane Doe. So far, they couldn't link her to Darcie, Shannon, or the showroom but that didn't mean she hadn't worked for Shoreford's in the past. 'We're investigating all angles and that is one of them. Have you had any other employees over the past five years?'

'A couple. I don't have a high turnaround of staff.'

'Who are they?'

'One called Fredrick and another called Tracey. I know Fredrick is dead as I attended his funeral last year.'

'How old was Tracey?'

'Late fifties. She was really good but she retired to move to Cornwall to be nearer to her daughter.' He paused. 'You know that Darcie got assaulted by a man called Mitchell Varley, don't you? I think Shannon filled you in on the situation. Do you think it's him? Could he have targeted them?'

After seeing his body and the note, Gina was certain it wasn't. Shannon going missing had sealed that thought. Varley had been dead at the time. He wouldn't have been able to have taken Shannon, nor could he have left the finger in the box outside the main doors. 'We've eliminated him from our enquiries. Is there anything else you can tell us that might help? Has Shannon had any issues with anyone else that you know of?'

'No, we are a lovely team and we all get on. I don't know much about her personal life.'

'Hey, boss, what's going on?'

The young, slim man approaching them from behind made Gina jump.

'Morning, Joel. It's Shannon, she's gone missing too.'

His chirpy expression was soon replaced by a stark look. 'What? No way. Is there anything I can do?' He jumped over the wall, sandwich box in hand as he waved back at the car being driven away.

'We will need to speak to you at some point. Could you come to the station this afternoon?' Gina asked.

'Err, yes. I'll message my mum. She'll drop me off.' He

began tapping away. 'She's just driven off so she won't be able to answer for a few minutes.'

Gina stood. 'Thank you. If you can let the officer know when you've confirmed a time, that would be great.' His slightly round chin and dimpled face made him look so young but Gina guessed he was about twenty. 'How did Shannon seem yesterday?'

'Err, okay. Tired. I don't think she'd slept well. Her make-up was a bit all over the place and she seemed a bit hungover. She's not normally like that but occasionally, I think she has a bit of a drink.'

'Do either of you know if she's been seeing anyone?'

'No. She wasn't seeing anyone,' Gordon said, almost before Gina had finished her sentence.

She stared at Gordon. He looked into his lap. She turned to look at Joel. He smiled nervously and then he frowned. What weren't they telling her? She gripped Gordon's phone. 'We need to get the CCTV footage off your device. Is it okay if we borrow your phone?'

He shrugged and nodded. 'Go ahead.'

'Oh, Mum has just messaged back. She said she'll drop me off at the station at about twelve if that's okay.'

'We'll see you then.' She wanted to make sure they got back in time to interview Joel.

Gina walked away and gestured for Jacob to follow. 'They're not telling us everything. They're as shifty as hell, or is it that Joel feels he can't say anything with Mr Shoreford around. It'll be good to speak to him without his boss being there when he comes to the station. Can you message the details of the Taj Mahal and ask Wyre or O'Connor to check Mr Shoreford's alibi out?'

'Guv, the shopkeeper wants to speak to you,' PC Smith said just as she reached him. 'She'd already closed the shop up last night but she'd stayed behind to do a stock check. When she left, she saw someone suspicious. She's free to talk now.'

As she and Jacob waited to cross the road, Gina's phone pinged. It was O'Connor.

PCs and CSI have checked Shannon Calder's house. There are signs of someone being in the loft. We have a shoe scuff mark and a hole in the ceiling that would give the intruder a view of Shannon's bedroom. The CSI has found a drink's can so that is good news. One other thing. The kitchen clock had stopped on eleven o'clock and it wasn't on the wall straight. It's evident that someone was stalking Shannon from her own loft.

THIRTY-FIVE

Gina almost felt a wash of fear go through her as she imagined what it would feel like to find out that someone had been watching from the loft in her own home. As she relayed the update to Jacob, she had even less hope for Darcie. They were dealing with a calculated and dangerous person.

A ding at the door sounded as Gina and Jacob entered the tiny convenience store. Sidling along towards the till, trying not to knock the toilet roll mountain over, Gina spotted the white-haired woman smiling at her from behind the till. 'Hello, I'm DI Harte and this is DS Driscoll. Our colleague said that you saw someone acting suspiciously last night.'

'That's right.' She finished piling the chewing gum onto a shelf next to the till.

Jacob moved to the left of Gina and used the counter to rest his pad on.

'Can I take your name first?'

'Mavis Hargreaves.'

'Can you tell me what you saw?'

'Yes, I actually close at seven and as soon as those doors were shut, I started the stocktake in the hope that I'd be home for three in the morning. It's not a huge shop but I have what feels like a million low-value items. Just after closing, I thought I'd start with a ciggie to get myself warmed up so I went out the back and walked through the alleyway between me and the house next door. Just as I went to stub it out on the wall, I caught movement out of the corner of my eye. Actually, if you both come outside, I'll show you where it was.' She led the way back through the shop.

'Let me get this right, it was just after seven?' Gina stepped out and looked across at the forensics team through the glass windows of the showroom. The crowd had mostly dispersed, apart from two women.

Mavis continued. 'Yes. To the right of the building there's a road. Shoreford's car park is behind the forecourt but some-times people park on the road alongside it. Last night, I saw the shadowy outline of a person. It could have been a woman but I think it was a man. He was wearing dark colours. Had he stayed still, I wouldn't have noticed him at all. If you look where the nearest streetlamp is' – she pointed to the one on the main road that was opposite the entrance to Shoreford's – 'it doesn't light up the side or back. I wondered if he was scoping the place out, but then he walked away in the direction of the back of the building so I thought that maybe he was just carrying on to one of the other roads or units behind Shore-ford's. I went back in and worked for a while. Later I heard the alarm sounding.'

'Did you go out to see what was happening?' Gina stepped back to allow a man with a snuffling dog to pass.

'Yes, and I saw Shannon. I know who she is as she comes in now and again for a packet of mints. The alarm goes off quite a lot, not all the time, but more than most. Shannon seems to be the one who turns it off so I didn't think anything of her being there. That's when I saw a cigarette glowing alongside the building, then it vanished. I wondered if whoever had been lurking was back, but then I couldn't see anyone so I came back in. I wish I'd called the police now. I heard she's gone missing.'

Gina nodded. 'You weren't to know.'

Mavis raised her brows. 'She came in with a man once, a right unsavoury character and they were bickering. When I say she came in, I mean she came alone and he charged in after her. I didn't like him and I'm sure people think I can't hear things from the other side of the shelves but I heard them arguing. Shannon was angry at one of her friend's for lying to her and she was blaming him and maybe I've put two and two together and got five, but I'd say her friend was sleeping with him and Shannon and he were a couple.'

Heart pumping, Gina hoped this was the breakthrough they needed. 'Can you describe him?'

'He was a strong-looking fella. Tall and muscly. Wearing overalls. Quite handsome but he knew it. Square jaw, brown stubble and short black hair, quite shiny, or maybe he was wearing hair wax.'

'Would you have them on your CCTV?'

Mavis shook her head. 'No, it will be overwritten. One of your officers came in for it, but its field of vision doesn't reach Shoreford's so it's no good for last night, unfortunately. The officer had a look but there was nothing useful to be had.'

'Have you seen the man that Shannon was with before?'

'No.'

'Did you see any cars parked up last night that aren't normally there?'

'I think there was a car parked up alongside Shoreford's, right by where the shadowy figure had been hanging around but I couldn't see it. All I saw was an outline. It was a dark-coloured car as it blended in with the dark road behind it. I'd say it was a saloon or an estate but then again, it could have been bigger. Maybe it was an SUV. It looked to be grey from here. I'm not sure, sorry. As for a registration number, don't ask. I wasn't wearing my glasses and I've got no chance of reading anything without them, but then I don't think I could read a registration from here if I had them on.'

'Do you remember anything else that might help us?'

The woman coughed and pulled a cigarette from the packet in her cardigan pocket. 'When they were in the shop, the man and Shannon were talking about his other woman, the one I think he'd cheated on her with. They called her Anna.'

Gina's eyes widened. She only knew one Anna and now she knew what Anna Heard had been hiding. All she needed to know was why.

THIRTY-SIX

LAYLA

She knocked yet again, hoping that her mother would get up. It was lunchtime and her mother's habits were getting ridiculous but if Layla dared to say anything, she'd get an earful about the sacrifices her mother made for her and her sister. Oh, and those sacrifices were all for nothing as they were both a pair of failures. It was no good. She pushed the pushchair around the back of the house and parked little Sonny up on the broken paving slabs while he slept.

After hammering again for a few more minutes, the neighbour peered over the fence. 'She went out about half an hour ago. Now can you shut up with the banging.'

She had always hated that man so she gave him the middle finger before pushing Sonny's pushchair back to the front of the house. That's when she saw her mother, Carys, with her one shopping bag, its contents chinking with each step she took. Carys hadn't changed one bit.

'What are you doing here? I thought you'd died it's been so long.'

'We need to talk, Mum.'

On reaching the broken garden gate, Carys looked up with

dark rings under her eyes and cracked lips. Her poor sister, Jamie, had no chance. Jamie should have left when Layla had. Actually, Layla should have insisted that her sister go with her but she'd used all her energy saving herself. When she came back for Jamie, she'd already succumbed to heroin.

'I've got nothing to say, Layla. You walked out of here ten years ago and claimed I was the worst mother ever, that I had ruined your life.' She paused and looked in her bag. 'I have a busy day ahead so I think you should go.'

'A busy day doing what? Getting hammered and then trying to get through work hoping that no one will notice how drunk and incompetent you are before they sack you?'

'Work, what work?' Carys snorted. 'Look at you with your fancy dyed hair, all black and silky and all that make-up. Maybe you did do well. Does the baby have a father?'

Layla didn't want to discuss her newborn's father; it would fuel her mother's arsenal of drunken insults. She didn't need Carys's approval. Sonny had been an accident but one she and his dad were both happy about. That's all that mattered. 'I didn't come here to talk about me. The police have called and you need to hear what I have to say so I suggest you don't make this unpleasant. I don't want my son upset; do you hear me?'

It took a lot to stand up to Carys but Layla wasn't going to let her mother continue to put her down. She hid her shaking hands in her pockets, hoping that her mother couldn't sense her nervousness. For a moment, it felt like she was a child again, waiting for one of her mother's drunken outbursts, or a surprise slap around the head for coming home late.

'What's his name?' Carys bent over and peered into the pushchair.

'Irrelevant. I haven't come to talk about him. You haven't called me for years so I really didn't think you'd care that you had a grandson. Just let me in so we can get this over with.'

With a tremble her mother managed to get her key in the

lock and turn it, her long grey clump of hair flopping forward in rats tails. 'If I knew you were coming, I'd have baked you a cake...' Carys burst into a fit of laughter. 'Only joking. Mind the mess.'

Layla almost heaved as she walked through the door to the smell of rotting bin. She left Sonny sleeping in the hall. There was no reason to subject him to the stench by bringing him into the lounge. She checked her smartwatch. He was due a feed. Maybe it would be her lucky day and he'd oversleep.

'Sit.' Carys pulled a bottle of cheap red wine from the bag, unscrewed the lid and drank straight from the bottle. 'Right, you said something about the police. Are you in trouble? You always were up to no good.'

'I am not in trouble, Mum. As for being up to no good, I did normal teen things and, if you must know, I qualified as an architect but I don't expect you to be proud or care. Me and Sonny are doing fine.'

A giggle escaped Carys's mouth. 'So, there isn't a daddy in the picture. They all abandon us, just like your father abandoned me when I couldn't cope.'

'This is about Jamie.'

'Oh her.'

'Yes, her. Your other daughter. I thought you should know that a detective called me. They have a woman in hospital on life support. I didn't say anything there and then, but I took the detective's number. It's Jamie, I know it is. They said she had a mole on her thigh. She's at Cleevesford General.'

'Why would the police call you and not me?'

'Because it was me who filed the missing persons when she left here for the streets, when you threw her out.'

Carys shrugged and plonked the bottle of wine on a bookshelf and a tear fell down one of her cheeks. 'You two couldn't get far enough away from me, could you? I did everything I could to push you away because I'm toxic. I ruin everything and everyone. You see, I did what was best for you. Jamie should have left with you but things were bad. I had to get her out too before I made her worse.' Carys bit her chapped lips. 'Why did you come here? You could have just gone on your own to see if it was Jamie. Look at me. I can't cope.'

'You're still her mother.'

Her mother's sobs began to bang through her head. Now came the self-pity. Her mother had already been drunk before she swigged from that bottle of red wine. 'I'm sorry. I'm such a screw-up. I don't want you seeing me like this but you're here and it's not right. You shouldn't have brought him either.' She pointed to Sonny's pushchair in the hall.

'Look, Mum. This isn't about you. I've decided I'm going to call the detective back, or maybe I'll head to the hospital and they might let me see if the woman is Jamie. I need to know if it's her and I thought I should tell you first. That's all I came for but it looks like I'm on my own, like I always have been.'

Her mother moved her head back and scrunched up her nose. 'Go then. I'm not selfish, you are. Look at you. Miss Hoity-Toity.' She wiped her damp eyes. 'Think about yourself and not how I feel.'

'I have to think about my son.' Layla walked up to her mother and stared her in the eye. With a quiver in her voice, she spoke. 'I came here today after many years, in the hope that you'd changed but I can see you haven't. Don't expect to see me again.'

She hurried out of the smelly living room away from her mess of a mum and she opened the front door before pushing Sonny into the fresh air. As she walked him down the path, she pulled her mobile out and hit call on the last number received. 'Hello, can I speak to DC Wyre. It's about the woman in Cleevesford Hospital. I think she may be my sister.'

THIRTY-SEVEN

Gina held the cup of coffee that Kyle had made for her. The toy boat was in an evidence bag ready to go to the lab. Jacob placed his empty cup on the coffee table. Kyle's husband, Richard, came to take the cups, leaving them alone in the living room again.

Gina gave the man a few seconds to let what she said sink in. 'I'm sorry, I know this is hard for you.'

'No shit. The idea that someone was in my sister's house, watching her in her bedroom and now he's taken her.' He wiped his nose with the back of his hand. 'How long?'

'Sorry?'

He scrunched his brow. 'Until you have the DNA results on the...' He closed his eyes and swallowed. 'The finger?'

'We'll fast-track them but it could be a while.' Bernard and the team at the lab had so much to process it was unreal.

'So, it sits in a pile all the time my sister is being held by some lunatic who has cut off her finger. Or is she even still alive? We both know it's her finger and we know Shannon is next. Even I can see that a pattern is occurring and I'm no genius.'

Gina took a deep breath and proceeded. 'I'm sorry to have to ask you this, but where were you between eight and nine yesterday evening? It's just a matter of procedure that I ask and I know you want to help us find Darcie.'

'No way I could hurt my sister and you have to do what you have to do. I was here with Rich and Cleo.' He swallowed. 'I did pay Shannon a visit the night before though, just to try and find out if she knew anyone who had been upsetting Darcie. I thought I might be able to help, to do something. I feel so powerless and useless.'

'How did she seem?'

'Worried, obviously. Anyway, there is something I should tell you now Shannon has gone missing. Shannon was scared. I got to her house before she arrived home. I noticed that the back gate was open and her security light had been smashed to pieces. At this point, I didn't know she wasn't home so I went around the back to check if everything was okay. Then she arrived with her dog and by being in her garden in the dark, I spooked her. I didn't mean to and she was okay when she saw it was me. What I'm getting at is someone smashed her security light and left her gate open. I thought I should tell you that. Maybe it was the kidnapper.'

'Did Shannon have any idea who might have smashed it?'

'If she did, she didn't tell me.'

Gina felt her leg muscles tense up. They needed to be out of here and back at the station. 'Does Shannon have any relatives close by?'

'Not as far as I know. I think Darcie told me she was down as Shannon's next of kin as she joked about having to have Barney if something ever happened to her. Shannon had a boyfriend but I don't know his name. Sorry I can't be of any more help.'

'Can you describe him?'

'No, I only know because Darcie told me in passing. I didn't really listen but I know Darcie didn't approve of him.'

'Did Darcie say why?'

'Not to me.'

'Thank you for that.' Gina wondered if it was the tall, well-built man in overalls that had followed Shannon into the shop for an argument involving Anna Heard. The man that Cleo had described taking her mother had also worn overalls. She needed to find Shannon's ex. 'We're going to head back to the station. Myself or a colleague will let you know as soon as we have the results back.'

'Please do. Straight away. We're beside ourselves here and it's driving me crazy. The thought of her...' He turned away and gulped a few breaths in. 'I can't give Cleo bad news. I just can't.'

Gina wished she could offer him some hope but right now, she had none to give. The only hopeful thought was that Jane Doe hadn't quite been killed, but in her heart she knew the perp had made a slip up there. Her phone rang. 'I'm sorry, I have to take this. I'll keep you informed.' She let Jacob finish up while she stepped outside to take the call. 'O'Connor, what do you have?'

'Taxi firm, guv. A passer-by saw the sign writing on the taxi that dropped Shannon off. It's A-Zee Taxis, a local firm. We're delving a bit deeper to try and find which taxi driver dropped her off and we'll ask them to come in to make a statement and bring any dashcam footage. They said it could take a while as last night was a busy night, and they had quite a few drivers working.'

'Great, thank you. Jacob and I are heading back now.'

'There's something else.'

Jacob stepped out of Kyle Fletcher's house.

'I think we've found Jane Doe's sister. A woman called Layla Purvis said that Wyre had phoned her while delving into the mispers. She had reported her sister, Jamie Purvis, missing a year and a half ago after their mother threw her out. She said she was just arranging for someone to look after her baby and she could be at the hospital for four this afternoon.'

'That is the best news. We're on our way back and I'm hoping an interview with Joel will identify the man Shannon was seeing. I'll fill you in on the rest. Fingers crossed we can identify Jane and find a link between her, Darcie and Shannon.'

THIRTY-EIGHT

Back at the station Gina updated O'Connor with all they'd found out while she prepared interview room one for Joel's arrival. They'd hopefully confirm that Jane Doe was Jamie Purvis that afternoon and she was going to press Joel to tell her everything he knew about Shannon's boyfriend. She knew that Gordon Shoreford was trying to stop him talking earlier and she had to find out why.

'Guv.' Jacob almost made her jump as he stood in the interview room doorway.

She grabbed three glasses off the side and placed them next to a jug of water. Joel was a witness and she wanted him to feel at ease. 'Yes, is he here yet?'

'He's just being brought through. That's what I came to say.'

A uniformed officer knocked and showed Joel into the interview room.

'Joel, come in and please take a seat.' She gestured to the chair the other side of the table, opposite to where she and Jacob would sit. Jacob sat and headed up a page, ready for the interview.

The young man pressed his lips together in a worried smile and gently sat.

'We're going to be recording the interview,' Jacob began. He continued explaining the process to Joel. 'Can you tell me your surname?'

'It's Summers. Joel Summers.' He sat up in his pristine white shirt and baby-blue checked waistcoat and jacket. His hair had been neatly brushed across one side of his head and seemed to be gelled so stiffly into place that it didn't budge at all when he moved.

Jacob asked a few more basic questions and introduced everyone in the room for the tape. After clarifying all his details and noting the date and time, Jacob continued. 'You're almost twenty-one.'

'That's right. At the end of the month, Shannon and Darcie were meant to be taking me to a rave bingo night for my big one and now...' He shook his head and a sad look spread across his face. He hunched over and stared into his lap.

Gina allowed Joel to have a moment then she began. 'Mr Summers—'

'Can you call me Joel?'

'Joel, how long have you worked at Shoreford's?' she continued.

'Erm,' he began counting on his fingers. 'Six weeks, maybe seven now.'

'What are Darcie Fletcher and Shannon Calder to you?'

'Shannon is my supervisor and Darcie is a car salesperson. I started as a trainee on a twelve-month apprenticeship, but Gordon has already said he loves having me there and I'll be given a salesperson role when the twelve months is up.'

'And how do you get on with Mr Shoreford?'

'I enjoy working for him and I love working at the show-room. He said when I make salesperson, he'll pay for me to take my driving test so I'm grateful for the opportunity. I like Mr

Shoreford. I don't know him that well as he shuts himself in his office most days. He leaves Shannon in charge.' He bit the inside of his cheek and sniffed. 'He tends to come in for longer when he has to get paperwork together for the bookkeeper. Most times he pops in for a couple of hours to give us all a bit of a motivational speech in the hope that we'll sell more cars.'

'So, you don't drive?'

'No.'

'Do you smoke?'

'I vape sometimes.'

'How well do you know Shannon?'

He bit his bottom lip. 'Quite well. She's always nice to me. I always make coffees for everyone and she tells me I shouldn't be making coffee all the time, that we should all take it in turns. I like that she makes me feel like I'm part of the team. She's funny and caring.'

'What was she like yesterday?'

He shrugged and sighed. 'Not herself, to be honest. She came into work with smudged make-up, looking really tired and hungover. She's not like that every day but she has been like it a couple of other times over the past month. I think she has some personal problems.'

Now they were getting somewhere. Gina needed to know the nature of Shannon's problems. 'Is she seeing anyone?'

'No.'

'Had she been seeing someone?'

Joel nodded slowly.

'For the tape, Mr Summers is nodding,' Jacob said.

'I love working at Shoreford's and I don't want to get into trouble.'

'Joel, Shannon and Darcie are missing and I'm really worried for them. If you know anything, you need to tell us.'

He let out a long breath through his full lips. 'She was seeing Finn. I don't know his surname but he's a mechanic. If we get any trade-ins or second-hand cars, he takes them and does the work on them. The MOTs and such. He valets them too. He's not directly employed by Gordon but he gets a lot of work from him.'

'Do you know the name of Finn's business or where it's located?'

'No.'

'You said she *was* seeing Finn. What happened?'

'They broke up after I started at Shoreford's but I can't remember when.'

'Do you know why?'

Joel leaned forward and linked his fingers on the table. 'I'm sorry, I really will get into trouble if I talk. Gordon thinks a lot of Finn. They get on really well and he's done the MOTs for Gordon for years from what Shannon told me. If I say anything bad about Finn, Gordon will probably hate me and I don't want him to hate me. Besides, Finn is a horrible man but it's probably not him.'

'Horrible, in what way?'

'The way he treats women. He's a misogynist. Like the other day, he came in to see Shannon and she didn't want him all over her but he got her alone in the kitchen. When I walked past, it looked like he was getting heavy with her, trying to touch her from what I saw. I know why Shannon dumped him. She found out he was sleeping with someone else and it's someone Darcie is good friends with, which is why they fell out.' He hesitated. 'Do you think I'll lose my job?'

Gina scrunched her brow. 'It would be very unfair of Mr Shoreford to let you go for helping us with the case. You've done the right thing.'

'You don't have to tell him I told you. Just get Finn, he'll have to come clean. People saw them together all over the place. It was no secret and anyone could have told you about Finn. If you could keep me out of it, I'd be really grateful. Please, I love my job.'

'We'll do everything we can.' Gina thought about Mavis and her description of the man who followed Shannon into her shop. That might be all she needed to bring Finn up with Gordon. 'Can you describe Finn?'

'Muscular but lean, he goes to the gym. Really short and shiny dark hair. Tall. Brown eyes. Slim.'

'It's just routine but can I ask where you were last night between seven and nine?'

'I was at home with my mum. I still live at home. I'll give you her number. Her name is Tina.'

'That would be helpful, thank you.'

He nodded. 'Is there anything else you need to know?'

'Did Shannon drive as we know she got a taxi to Shoreford's last night?'

'She said she used to have a car but she had to sell it to pay some bills. I don't know what bills. She seemed okay with getting the bus home. Mum told me she'd be happy to give her a lift. I mentioned that to Shannon but she declined Mum's offer, not wanting to put her out. I think she liked to do her own thing and she worked late a lot.'

'Lastly, have you seen anyone hanging around? Anyone who looks suspicious, or out of place? Or even a parked-up car that you're not familiar with?'

He scrunched his brow. 'I heard Shannon arguing with someone outside when I left Shoreford's to pop to the shop. She must have been standing along the side of the building as I couldn't see her. I could only hear her. It was last week, Wednesday, I think.'

'Did you see the person she was arguing with?'

'No, I didn't want her to think I was eavesdropping so I went back in and waited for her to finish.'

'Did you recognise the other person's voice?'

'I'm sure it was Finn but I didn't see him.'

'How did she seem when she came back in?'

'She told me to go for lunch and take my time. It was like she wanted me out the way.'

'Did you hear what they were arguing about?'

'She told him to stop harassing her. I saw a white SUV parked up and when Shannon came in, it left the car park.' Gina saw Jacob make a note about the white SUV. They'd need to know whether Finn had access to one of those. After finishing up and stopping the tape, Joel stood. 'What happens next?'

'If you think of anything else, please call us.' She passed him her card.

After he'd left, she leaned back on the wall while Jacob closed the pad and stood. 'I think we really need to speak to Finn.'

She had to agree. Finn had just made it to the top of their suspect list. 'We should go and pay a visit to Anna Heard. She seems to have known Finn well and I'm not happy that she didn't mention him when we spoke to her or during her interview. Right now, I don't trust her. She purposely hid him from us and I want to know why. We've got time to speak to her before we meet Miss Purvis at the hospital.'

THIRTY-NINE

Anna looked a little confused at seeing Gina and Jacob at her door again. 'May we come in?' Gina asked.

'I was just about to go out for lunch.'

As Anna flicked her hair, Gina almost sneezed at the smell of her strong perfume. Anna's burgundy lips, leopard print skirt and knee-length heeled boots looked quite glamorous. 'Where are you going?'

Anna drew her head back and frowned. 'Why are you asking me that?'

'It's just routine.' Gina didn't want to come straight out with the fact that she knew Anna had held back on something crucial to the case and that Gina thought she was about to meet Finn, the very man they needed to find. She sighed. 'If you must know, I'm meeting my little sister for lunch at The Hare. Look.' She held out her phone and brought up a text from someone she'd named in her phone as "Little Sis".

Gina read the text and it simply said that they were booked to eat at The Hare for two thirty. 'Thank you for confirming that.'

'I guess I best message her to tell her I'll be late.' She

punched a message out and hit send. 'Do you have news about Darcie? Come in. I've been worried sick.'

They stepped into Anna's lounge for the second time that week. Anna gestured for them to sit on the settee, which they did. She sat in the bucket chair under the window.

'I'm sorry but we still have no news on Darcie. Something has happened, though,' Gina said.

'What?' There was a quiver in Anna's voice, one that told Gina she was worried about her friend. 'Is it Cleo, is she okay?'

'Cleo is safe. It's her work colleague, Shannon. She's gone missing too and we suspect she's been taken by the same person who took Darcie.' Gina didn't want to mention finding a finger outside Shoreford's but that was their biggest clue to link the cases.

Anna brought her hand to her mouth and frowned. She then placed it in her lap and a worry line spread across her forehead. 'How... she can't. Maybe she's just gone somewhere... or to see a friend.'

'I wish that were the case,' Gina replied.

A hiccupped sob came from Anna's throat. She took a couple of breaths and exhaled for a few seconds.

'Tell us more about you, Darcie, and Shannon. I know you are friends with Darcie and I know that Darcie visited you on the night she disappeared.'

'I know them both, but I'm closer to Darcie. We've kept in touch regularly over the years. I moved back to the area three years ago after working as a holiday rep. I'd been placed in Dubai. When I returned home, Darcie was so sweet. She wanted to spend time with me and called me a lot, but Corey was so controlling. We kept in touch, called each other often.'

'How did you meet?'

'We both went to school together and we just clicked. Corey went to Cleevesford High School with us too.'

'What about Shannon?'

'She went there as well but...'

'But what?'

Tears slid down Anna's cheeks. 'I guess as Darcie and I had become so close over these past few months, when Shannon came onto the scene, I found her a threat. I didn't have much of a home life back at school when we were all friends. I'd been abused as a young child and I ended up having to move in with my nanna. I tended to cling onto anyone who cared and at that time, Darcie was my rock. She was my bestie and my absolute world but Shannon was slowly taking her from me. I did things I didn't want to do to stay in with them, such as drinking and taking the odd party pill but it was never enough. We drifted apart. In the end I left school, went into holiday repping and left that life behind. When I moved back here, I picked up with Darcie, which was lovely as we rekindled our friendship. I was happy until Darcie started working with Shannon. They became really close again and I felt left out. It was just like being back at school.' She let out a laugh and wiped her eyes. 'It sounds so stupid. I'm thirty-five and these childish emotions make me feel like I'm a teen reject again.'

'Tell me a little about your recent relationship.'

Anna rubbed her neck and pulled a pained face as if it ached. Gina knew the truth was hurting her and she could sympathise. If what Anna was saying was true, her abusive past may have led to her leaning on her friend more and if she felt that Darcie had abandoned her, it would have upset her. 'Darcie and I regularly went out together after she left Corey last year. We've had a lot of good times where we've danced the night away. Since starting work at Shoreford's last June, Darcie mentioned that she felt bad that Shannon didn't get out much. She said that Shannon had become a bit of a hermit, just her staying in all the time with her dog and not having many friends. Apparently, her and her on-off boyfriend weren't mega close and the relationship was rocky. I wasn't too pleased about

Shannon joining us on our nights out but I began to relax a bit. We were now all in our thirties and I thought things would feel different and more relaxed. After all, I was the party girl, the one with all the exciting stories and the travels abroad. So many people back then probably thought I'd amount to nothing.'

'And did things work out between the three of you?' Gina was happy for Anna to keep talking. It was important that she felt secure and relaxed, ready for when Gina asked about Finn. Also, it seemed that Anna wanted to get a lot off her chest.

'To begin with, yes. Then I found out that they'd been to mine and Darcie's favourite places and left me out on nights that Darcie had said she couldn't meet me. It sounds ridiculous, I know, but I felt like that rejected teenager again. Anyway, one night, Shannon had tagged herself at one of our regular pubs. She'd taken a photo of her and Darcie and uploaded it to her Instagram and in my silly mind, it felt like she was having a pop at me. I could have ignored it and carried on watching whatever rubbish I was watching on TV that night but no, I put on my best going-out clothes and I gate-crashed them. I wasn't going to lose Darcie again to Shannon.'

'And when you got there?'

'They said hi and invited me over, like I was meant to meet them there. Darcie never said sorry for excluding me, or anything like it. I ordered a large stiff drink with the aim of getting hammered. I'd planned to talk to Darcie about it on her own the next day, but I never did and that's probably because of the shame.'

Gina tilted her head. 'The shame?'

Anna slowly nodded. 'Shannon's boyfriend turned up and I don't know what came over me. It was like an instant attraction and I knew he was feeling it too. I've met a lot of men in my last job. Horny tourists, other travel reps, bar staff, hotel porters, and I've had a lot of flings but I've never felt anything like this. Before the night was over he'd slipped his number in my phone when Shannon wasn't looking.' She wiped a stray tear away. 'I'm not normally that kind of person. Attraction or not, I've never been involved with anyone who is already in a relationship, but I saw Darcie and Shannon huddled together, whispering and laughing. They were doing that without me so I thought what the hell. He'd only left a few minutes before. I sent him a text and he picked me up down the road and one thing led to another. For once, I had got one over Shannon. I wanted her to know how it felt to lose someone who was precious to you.'

'When did she find out?'

'We've been seeing each other for weeks but she found out about a month ago.'

'Who is he?'

'Finn Sampson. He has a garage and he does a lot of work for Shoreford's. I didn't plan this, but I love him.'

Gina felt for her and Shannon. From what Joel had told her, Finn wasn't worth their time. 'Is that why you were arguing with Darcie on the night she was here?'

Anna nodded twice, slowly. 'Darcie told me that I'd put her in a horrible position with Shannon. She felt I'd betrayed her as I'd also hidden my affair from her. She saw him leaving my house one day when she popped by unannounced. Shannon had already split up with Finn by then. Very soon, Shannon knew about us and that news had come between her and Darcie. I thought it would feel good to take something of Shannon's but I feel disgusting and horrible, but I can't go back. Finn and Shannon weren't meant to be. He loves me. Darcie kept trying to tell me I should dump him, that he was mean to Shannon, but I think she was just saying that as it was ruining her friendship and it would be easier for her if I wasn't with Finn.' Tears began to land on her skirt. 'After, she said something that really hurt. She said that Finn had tried it on with her only a couple of weeks ago, but I didn't believe her. All I know is she was trying to split us up. She kept going on, telling me he was nothing but a player but I don't see that in him. The Finn I know is a sweetheart.'

Gina waited for her to compose herself.

Hugging a cushion, Anna continued. 'On the night Darcie was taken, I told her to get out and that I never wanted to see her again. I didn't even give her a chance to call an Uber but things had got so bad, I needed to be on my own before I said even more things I'd regret. I literally slammed the door on her. The last thing I remember was seeing Cleo's sleepy eyes having a quick peek at me as Darcie carried her away.' She sobbed loudly into the cushion. 'Darcie was taken because of me and she's probably been killed by some maniac. I sent her out there all because of a stupid argument. She had Cleo with her and I slammed the door as she left.'

'Anna, can we call anyone to be with you? Your sister, maybe?'

She shook her head and used a rolled-up tissue to blow her stuffy nose. 'I can't let her see me like this. I'll be okay.'

'Where was Finn Sampson on the night that Darcie was taken?'

'He texted me to say he was nearly at mine. He'd just stopped off at a garage for a bottle of wine. I had to cancel him as Darcie had just arrived and him turning up while she was here was the last thing I needed. I had told him she was coming but he must have forgotten. As far as I know, he turned around and went home.'

Gina wondered if he'd hung around to watch them. They had cigarette butts left by the Hutton Village sign and another from the back of Anna's garden gate. All they needed was Finn. If his DNA matched the saliva on any butts at both locations, they'd be able to place him at the scenes. Gina exhaled. It could be a while before those results came back.

'Can I see the text?'

Anna scrolled through her phone and passed it to Gina. The message chain was exactly as Anna had described. Gina read a few after which were from Anna to Finn, all asking where he was and why he wasn't answering when she called. She had told him that Darcie was there on the Friday at seven forty that evening. That would give Finn plenty of time to turn up at Anna's back gate and watch her before sitting around and waiting for Darcie to leave her house.

'Were you with him yesterday?' Gina asked her.

'No, I haven't heard from him since I told him to turn around and go home. It's been driving me crazy, which is why I asked my sister if she wanted to meet for lunch. I don't know if he's hurt, or if he's upset with me. Do you think something has happened to Finn, too?' Her eyes widened.

Gina thought that Finn could be behind the kidnappings, but she was going to reserve judgement until she'd spoken to Layla Purvis about her sister, Jamie. It wouldn't be the first time she thought someone was the perpetrator, only to find out later that they were a victim. 'Do you know a woman called Jamie Purvis?'

Anna scrunched her brows. 'No, the name isn't ringing a bell.' She hesitated. 'You think Finn is behind all this, don't you?'

'We are following several lines of enquiry and we do need to speak to him. Do you have his address or the address of his garage?'

'No to the garage address. I know he lives with his dad and cares for him. His dad has Parkinson's so Finn has to help him a lot. It gets too much for him sometimes, even though he never complains. We haven't been introduced yet but from what he says, life is hard for them. That was why he was angry when he came over to see me the other night. His free time is precious and I wasn't there for him. Finn is lovely but he has this hard exterior. Anyway, he lives on Brickford

Close. It's number seven. I saw a letter addressed to him in his car.'

'Thank you. What does he drive?'

'He has a really old car, a classic. Erm, I think it's a Ford Capri and when I referred to it as blue, he corrected me and said it was marine blue.'

'Does he have another car?'

'He has a work van, it's a white transit. I guess he may drive other cars that he's been working on.' Anna's phone began to ring. 'Is it okay if I go and meet my sister now? I need to be with her.'

Gina nodded and stood. 'If you hear from Finn Sampson, can you call me immediately?' Gina passed her a card while Jacob gathered his things.

'Of course. If you have any news about Darcie or Shannon, can you please let me know. I need to tell them I'm sorry and I hope they can forgive me. I mean Finn has ignored me for days. Maybe Darcie was telling the truth about him. We'll see.' She scrunched her brow. 'Have you looked into her ex, Corey, yet?'

'We are trying to locate him.'

'You know that he and Darcie were childhood sweethearts? They were a thing in high school. I know when we left school, they broke up and I think they met a few years later. Anyway, back then, he was always in trouble or being excluded, mostly for fighting and vandalism.' She shrugged. 'I always felt that he, Darcie and Shannon were keeping something from me but I don't know what. Actually, Darcie and Shannon were quite secretive. Maybe it had nothing to do with Corey, maybe it was me reading something into nothing because Darcie had dumped me for Shannon.'

Gina made a mental note of the friends' history and a thought flashed through her mind. What if their school friendship was the connection? That theory would be more stable if Jamie Purvis was a part of their clique.

A text from O'Connor flashed up on her phone. She opened it while Jacob said their goodbyes and explained what would happen next.

We have the taxi driver's name, guv. He's due in at seven so I'll interview him if you're not back. His boss said that the driver came back a bit worried about a woman he'd left outside Shoreford's last night. Also, Layla Purvis is on her way to the hospital now. She's getting there a little earlier.

FORTY

LAYLA

The smell of cleaning chemicals sent Layla's stomach turning. Hospitals weren't her favourite place and she was glad not to have to bring Sonny with her. If only she hadn't received that phone call. In her mind, Jamie had followed her dreams of becoming an artist by the seaside and she was living with some hippy mates. It was easy to paint the illusion in her mind but deep down, she always knew that Jamie was the sensitive one. She knew their mother's drink problems were slowly becoming Jamie's too and she had left her. After passing the vending machine, she saw a sign for the Intensive Care Unit. This time, she wasn't going to leave. She was going to do what she should have done all those years ago, which was to be there for her big sister. If Jamie came around, she would help her through rehab and she would see her sister realise her dream of becoming an artist by the sea.

Layla rang the bell and peered through the glass panel in the door as she tried to attract the attention of a nurse who was on the phone. The nurse looked up and he smiled before pressing the buzzer to let her in. He placed the phone down as she approached the desk. 'Are you looking for someone?'

'I think my sister is here. Jamie Purvis. The police told me to come.'

'Ah, yes. Bear with me. You're a few minutes early. The detectives have arrived to see you but they're just in the canteen. Take a seat.'

She sat on the blue plastic chair watching people holding the hands of their loved ones in ICU. It hurt to see such close families and Layla wished that she'd experienced that closeness. She really hated her mum sometimes even though she knew without the alcohol, her mother could be a good person. A machine beeped away as a nurse pressed a button on one of the monitors.

She checked her phone. On any other day, she'd smile at the message that had just pinged into her inbox.

I love you and miss you both so much. Can I come over later or maybe I can take you somewhere romantic before we pick Sonny up?

He was Sonny's dad and she was close to telling him she loved him too. Sonny had been their accident and they'd decided they were going to do their best while they still dated and got to know each other better. He brought around money and gifts and showered them with love, but Layla wasn't sure. They were so mismatched and she wondered if society would judge her, but then again, why should she care? Maybe she needed to grasp the things she loved in life instead of worrying what people might think. She thought back to the day they met. She'd been drawing plans for a chapel conversion on the Welsh border before deciding to pop to the café on Cleevesford High Street to get the team a coffee. Just as she'd walked through the door, a pigeon had messed on her head and he had come up behind her with a tissue, smiling. He'd just come from a job interview. Later that night, they were rolling around in her bed.

She replied, knowing that she needed him right now.

I'd love to see you tonight but it may be later. I miss you too. X

And she did miss him and the last thing she wanted later was to be alone. She knew Sonny would be okay where he was until morning and she needed space to process everything that was happening. She read the message again and a warmth filled her tummy. She craved him in the neediest kind of way and that scared her. Was he really up to the job of being a life partner and father? She had so many doubts but she had to give him a chance.

'Miss Purvis?'

The brown-haired woman in the long dark coat looked like she'd been caught in a hurricane and the smart man standing next to her smiled. 'Yes.' She popped her phone in her bag and stood. She knew she was waiting for someone called Detective Inspector Harte. 'Are you DI Harte?' She waited for the man to answer.

He shook his head. 'No, I'm DS Driscoll. This is DI Harte.'

Whoops, she'd made a mistake and she could see the DI frowning like that had happened a million times to her. 'Sorry.' She was genuinely mortified.

The DI moved closer to the corridor. 'Shall we go and see if our patient is your sister?'

'Yes. I need to get this over with.' Although, if it wasn't Jamie, she made a promise to herself that she was going to actively start looking for her sister.

'Do you have anyone with you?'

Layla shook her head. She wished her life had been different and that her mother was beside her right now.

'I will warn you,' DI Harte said as she stopped, 'she isn't at all well and she's also on a breathing machine.'

Layla swallowed, wondering if she had the strength to see

her sister in that state then she remembered, if it was Jamie, she had no one else but Layla. She nodded and kept quiet, not knowing what to say. As they took the walk towards the side rooms, Layla felt her heartbeat speeding up. The smell, the strip lights and the thought of a tube keeping her sister alive – all those things were making her nauseous.

The DI nodded to a uniformed officer who was sitting outside the door, reading a spy thriller. She pressed the handle down and went in first. As Layla entered, she saw the thin, pale strip of a woman covered in a white sheet and she knew instantly that it was Jamie. Her sunken eyes made her look like a skeleton covered in overstretched flesh. The bruises and scratches on her big sister's face and chest almost made her recoil. A tube had been fed up her nose and the monitor next to her beeped away. Layla turned away when she saw the lung drain; that was too much for her to take in. What had her poor sister been subjected to? She had no idea how someone could be so cruel.

'It's her. It's Jamie.' She stepped over and gently held her sister's hand, careful not to knock the cannula that dripped clear liquid into her body. Sitting, she used her other hand to move Jamie's lank hair from her forehead.

The nurse who had spoken to her on reception, knocked and walked in. 'There has been some progress and we're happy to be able to say that we've removed the breathing tube. Our patient is breathing on her own. That's not to say all is okay, she has a long way to go, but she can breathe for herself now. Her stats are still poor but there are small improvements.'

'That's good news,' DI Harte said. 'Do you know when we'll be able to speak with her?'

'I don't,' the nurse replied. 'The doctor will be coming around sometime this evening but I think she'll be like this for a while. It's not going to be a fast process.'

The DI sighed and Layla's shoulders slumped. She wanted

to speak to Jamie more than anything. She knew that only her sister could tell them what had happened and who had hurt her.

'Can we step outside to talk?' the DI asked.

Layla nodded. She lifted her hand off her sister's and wiped a tear away.

The DI closed the door, leaving the nurse and the DS speaking.

'I'm sorry, this must be really hard for you.' The DI tilted her head. 'Can you confirm that she is your sister, Jamie Purvis?'

'Yes, it's definitely Jamie.' She showed DI Harte a photo of her and Jamie. Although the photo was sixteen years old, anyone could see that the woman in that hospital bed was her sister.

'That's a lovely photo of you both,' the DI said.

'It is. We'd been on a camping trip together. The weather was awful but Jamie had laughed all the way through it. I hated it but now, I wish we could go back.' Layla tried to hold back her tears. If only it were that simple. 'What happened to her?'

'We think she was kidnapped. She was found like this at the back of a block of flats. If the girl who found her was any later on the scene, we believe that Jamie wouldn't have survived.' The detective paused and looked down as if she were contemplating what to divulge. 'We fear that the perpetrator has two more victims. Do you recognise the names Shannon Calder and Darcie Fletcher?'

Layla's stomach clenched and she clammed up. 'I recognise one of them. I know the name Darcie but not that surname. I mean, I never knew Darcie's surname. Jamie was in the same class as a Darcie in high school as she brought Darcie to our house one day. Darcie ignored her after that because my mother was, and still is, an embarrassing raving alcoholic.' Her hands were shaking. She wasn't just speaking for Jamie right now. Carys Purvis had turned all her friends away too and then there was the promise, the thing that Jamie told her she should never mention. She went to speak but closed her mouth instead. No way was she getting Jamie into any trouble. Jamie was a victim here.

'Do you know anyone who would want to hurt your sister?'

'She was on heroin and I know she was living on the streets. I guess many people may have wanted to hurt her.'

'When did you last see or hear from her?'

'I haven't seen her for years. Our mother told Jamie to leave eighteen months ago but Jamie had called me on the phone a couple of times on different numbers, not hers. We haven't seen each other much really for a long time. When I turned eighteen, I left home. Jamie stayed with Mum. I was going to wait for her to leave with me but she was never ready so I had to go.' She burst into tears. Layla had left her behind and if she hadn't, Jamie wouldn't have had over a decade's worth of misery. 'It's all my fault. I should have come back for her.' DI Harte led her to a chair.

'It's not your fault and we're going to do all we can to find whoever did this to her.' The DI's phone beeped and her tired-looking eyes suddenly widened. She pulled a card from her pocket. 'If you need to speak to me, ask me anything, or you think of something that may help the case, please call me. One other thing, I know this will be hard to do but can you not tell anyone that your sister is improving. We want to keep that information under wraps for her safety.'

'Yes, I mean I won't say anything.' A flush of fear went through her. Was someone still after Jamie? Did they want to finish the job?

Moments later, the two detectives had left in a hurry, leaving the officer outside the door in charge.

'Can I sit with her for a bit?'

He nodded. 'Sure. I'll have to come in with you but that's

fine.' He stood, grabbed his book and followed Layla into her sister's room.

She sat back by her sister's side, knowing that Jamie wouldn't wake up that night. She fired a quick text off to Sonny's dad explaining about her sister and hoping that he'd pick her up later. Self-blame oozed from every pore. It was her fault, she knew it. She lay her head on Jamie's pillow and whispered in her ear. 'What happened to you, Jamie?'

FORTY-ONE

'What is it, guv,' Jacob yelled as he fed his arm into his coat and ran at the same time.

Gina kept jogging towards the car. 'I've just informed uniform to get over to Monica Bell's house immediately. Corey Lowe has trapped her in the bedroom. She managed to message me, asking for help.' Gina felt like her heart might explode as she thought about the young woman and her baby, scared and trapped by her violent, jealous partner. She pressed the central locking on the car and got in.

Jacob was already seated and doing his belt up. 'Is he a suspect for Shannon and Jamie?'

'You heard what Anna said. Corey and Darcie were an item at high school. Corey would know Darcie and Shannon and I'm also guessing that if Darcie knew Jamie, he would have come across her too. Why them? I have no idea but I want to find out. First, we have to bring him in.'

After a minute, Gina found herself behind a police car and pulling up outside Monica's house. She hurried out of the car and checked up and down the road for Corey Lowe's vehicle. It was nowhere to be seen.

'He can't have been driving his van as he would have shown up on ANPR,' she said to Jacob. She spotted a man waiting in a van a short way down the road. PC Ahmed stood on the path, waiting for her. 'Shaf, can you ask one of the other officers to make sure that van doesn't get away? Get each end of the road blocked in case he tries to drive off. I think Lowe got someone to bring him here.'

PC Ahmed nodded and ran over to instruct another officer before coming back.

Gina addressed the female officer next to her. 'You go around the back. I have a feeling he'll try to run.' She nodded and hurried away with another uniformed officer. 'Shaf, we're going to knock and if there's no answer, we're going in. The victim's name is Monica Bell and her partner, Corey Lowe, has her trapped in the bedroom. There is a baby in there so we have to try to knock and maybe talk to him first. But let's be prepared to knock the door down should we need to.'

PC Ahmed reached into his boot and pulled out the battering ram, in readiness. 'Ready, guv?'

Gina nodded and walked up to Monica's door. Jacob stood by her side and PC Ahmed waited behind them. She knocked but there was no answer. She opened the letter box and tried to listen but the bristles in the box were getting in the way. Then she heard the baby crying. 'Monica, are you okay?' She was reluctant to announce she was police, scared that it would easily turn into a hostage situation. Again, there was no answer and the baby's cries became louder. She was going have to make the call on whether they bash the door in and it was making her tetchy. The baby's cries turned into pained shrieks. She nodded at PC Ahmed.

PC Ahmed pulled the battering ram back and just as it came close to impact, someone nudged the upstairs window open.

Gina looked up and saw a tear drenched Monica leaning out. 'Are you okay?'

She nodded. 'He's gone. Just as you pulled up, he ran out the back.'

Damn, she wanted to kick a wall. They had come that close to catching him. In fact, she wasn't giving up that easily. 'I'm going after him.' She turned to Jacob. 'I didn't see anyone coming out the front and I know behind this house there's a path. I'm going to take a guess that he ran in the direction his friend's van was pointing.'

She glanced over at a PC. 'Bring the driver in. Jacob, you head along the front and keep going. Meet me at the end of the row. Check all gardens and alleyways. He has to come back onto this road or he will reach the end of the path. It eventually leads to a small shopping area but he can't have reached that yet. Get a car there now and if I estimate right, he could be there within the next couple of minutes.' Jacob nodded to one of the officers who left immediately. 'I'm going to head around the back.' She thought of Briggs and what he might say if she went alone. He was right in what he'd said. She had put herself in danger during the last case and she didn't need him to be any more upset with her. 'Shaf, you can come with me. Let's go.'

Just as the officer reached the stationary van, the driver turned on the engine and revved it up. It dodged the officer and sped up the road. Gina hoped that the police cars were in place to catch him. As she ran down an alleyway that led to the path at the back, PC Ahmed slightly ahead of her, she heard a sickening crash. Along the back, trees rustled in the wind and puddles filled the churned-up tarmac, making each step treacherous. Darkness had completely fallen and barely any streetlamps worked.

After several minutes, they reached the shops. Gina could see blue lights flashing. She gasped several times to get her breath back. PC Ahmed took his police hat off and wiped his sweaty forehead. 'Do you think he got away, guv?'

'No, I think he's veered off.' She began backtracking, looking for any way through the trees onto the fields. She knew the land was private and most of it was fenced off. Behind it was several acres and an old fishing lake. She pushed her way through the foliage, her coat getting caught on thorns as she did so. PC Ahmed followed and made updates as to their location through his radio. She followed the fence, squeezed between bushes and the wood. That's when she saw a nail sticking up. She turned her torch on and directed the light towards a red glistening smear. Fresh blood. 'We're going over. Call it in and tell the others where we are.'

'Will do.' Once again, he spoke into his radio, updating the team.

Gina stepped onto the rotten wood and threw a trousered leg over. She followed that with the other before dropping into a muddy puddle. 'Corey, police, stop,' she shouted. 'You're injured and every officer we have is looking for you and a drone is searching for you. You can't get away. The whole area is surrounded.' Gina wanted him to feel trapped. The team was currently small and as far as she knew a drone operator had not arrived on the scene.

They heard a twig snapping ahead and Gina sprinted towards it. The dark figure ahead of her, half ran and half stumbled until he fell into a mound of earth. PC Ahmed hurried ahead of Gina with his handcuffs ready. As he kneeled, Gina pointed her torch at the man.

He glanced over his shoulder, eyes stark and teeth clenched. 'Fucking touch me and I will kill the pair of you.' He rolled over and just before PC Ahmed got the cuffs on him, he struck the officer in the throat, taking his breath away.

Forget safety, she wasn't going to let him get away. As Gina darted towards him alone, he managed to get up on his feet and started to leap over tufts in the grass, towards another fence. If he got over that one, she could lose him. It was no good, she had to check on Shaf. He might need medical help. 'Shaf, are you okay?' She walked over to him and grabbed his radio. 'Officer down, hurry, we need back up and a paramedic.'

'I'm okay.' He coughed and choked. 'Go and get him before it's too late.'

Corey Lowe hopped and hobbled closer to the fence so Gina sprinted with all she had, pointing her torch at him. Blood had seeped through the leg of his light-coloured jeans. She had him. 'Stop, you are under arrest for assaulting a police officer.' There were many more things she needed to arrest him for but his attack on PC Ahmed was just a start. 'You do not have to say anything,' she puffed out as she struggled to keep running, 'but, it may harm your defence if you do not mention when questioned something which you later rely on in court. Anything you do say...' She grabbed the hood of his sweater and yanked him back. He turned and punched her cheek. At that moment, all she saw was her dead, violent ex, Terry, and right then, her rage filled fists wanted nothing more than to pulverise his face. She pulled out her cuffs. 'Anything you do say may be given in evidence... make that two, two assaults. Kidnapping and attempted murder of Jamie Purvis, kidnapping of Darcie Fletcher and Shannon Calder.' She had no idea what had happened with Monica Bell but she would get to that later.

He stared at her and roared. Just as he went to charge at her, she dodged out of his way and placed a foot out. He tripped flat on his face onto the grass. She straddled his back, fighting as he wriggled to escape. 'Get off me, you bitch. You're hurting me. I'm going to sue you for assault. I didn't do all that. Those bitches lie. I'm injured.'

She clicked the cuffs on. 'Whatever. We'll take it to the station then, shall we? You can have your say there.'

PC Ahmed came up behind her, holding his throat, and two other officers ran towards them. 'Great tackle, guv.'

Her heart was beating ten to the dozen. Last thing she wanted was to show the team how scared she was. Now the moment was over, her hands shook and she felt a bit woozy. Briggs was definitely going to be concerned and angry when she turned up back at the station with a bruised face but had she waited for more officers to arrive, they'd have lost him. 'I, err...'

'Guv, you okay?' Jacob ran up to her.

'Yes, it hurts.' She opened and closed her jaw and it clicked. She swore a man would never get the chance to hit her again. The fact that Corey Lowe had punched her hurt far more than the actual punch. She stared at him as he swore and fought the PCs that took him away and she knew he was on something. He was like a rabid dog.

Jacob's phone rang. He answered and spoke a few words, but not enough for Gina to work out who he was speaking to. 'The ambulance has arrived. We need to get your face checked out.' He held a hand out and she grabbed it and allowed him to help her.

'Thanks, Jacob.' As she hobbled back to the front of Monica's house, she could see the young mother standing on the doorstep with her baby.

One of the PCs ran towards her. 'Monica Bell wants to speak to you. She said she's worried about Darcie and that it's urgent.'

Gina turned to Jacob. 'My face will have to wait.'

FORTY-TWO

Monica sat on her sofa nursing a hot drink while her baby slept in the Moses basket. 'What happened, Monica?'

She sniffed and blew her nose. 'I'd just got back from Dad's and when I opened the door, I knew Corey was here. I could smell his aftershave. I called out to him but he didn't answer so I thought that maybe he'd come for more of his things and left. My mind has literally been playing tricks on me. I then thought I could smell him because one of his coats was still hanging on a peg by the door. I pushed the pram into the hallway and started climbing the stairs to transfer Patsy to her cot. As I reached half-way, he appeared from the living room. I've never seen such rage in him. I mean I've seen him lose it but this time, it was like he was enjoying seeing me scared. He was toying with me.' Monica stared into her drink.

'That must have been really scary for you.'

'Honestly, it was petrifying. I thought he might kill us. He muttered something about taking cocaine with his friend. He then said our relationship problems were all my fault and that I had turned him to drugs, that any man would have been pushed to that if they were with me. I thought he would have gone back to Bristol but he said he was staying at his friend Tyler's house, as Tyler stays with his girlfriend most of the time. All that time, he was only two roads away from us.'

'Is Tyler the man in the van outside?'

She nodded. 'Yes, Corey said his van had broken down. He said he'd been borrowing Tyler's car but they were just passing in the van.' Gina bit her lip and held a cold hand over her throbbing cheek. She knew that Corey Lowe had access to a vehicle now, one in which he could have transported Shannon Calder in.

'Do you know his friend's full name?'

'No. He didn't say. He just called him Tyler. They work together.'

'Do you know what car Corey has been driving?'

'No.'

'So, he followed you up the stairs. What happened next?'

'He nudged me in the nursery and slammed the door closed. He refused to let me leave. He snatched Patsy from me, saying I was trying to take her from him. I don't understand him. When I had her, he resented her, saying that all my attention went on her and he got none. I just don't get him.' She burst into tears. 'I don't think it's safe for Patsy to be around him. I didn't say anything before but he's hit me a few times.' She opened her mouth to speak, but held her head in her hands for a few seconds before coming back up. 'I haven't told my dad any of this. I've just said that I was leaving Corey because of his anger outbursts. People don't understand. I hear them saying those words, why didn't she leave him? How could she put up with that? It's not like I couldn't have gone to my dad's at any time.' She shook her head and sniffed. 'They don't understand how the control works, that I lived for those moments when he was kind and sweet, that I blamed myself when he was horrible and promised to be a better girlfriend. No, people have no sympathy for the likes of me. No wonder I couldn't talk to anyone about it. I'm sorry for going on...'

Gina swallowed the lump in her throat. She knew exactly how Monica was feeling and she knew how it felt to be a prisoner who could open the door at any time. Those judgemental people would never understand how coercive control worked. They'd continue to mock and judge despite how much better-informed society was, because, of course, it could never happen to them. She felt a burning anger on Monica's behalf.

'You are doing amazingly and I promise you, now that you see what he was doing, he will never have that power over you again. There are always people that judge but they know nothing. He took your kindness and your love and he abused it. It was his fault, all of it.' Dammit, she wished she could do so much more than offer a few words but she hoped she'd helped a little. 'Are you okay to continue?'

Jacob was aware of her past as a domestic abuse victim although they never really spoke about it. He gave them a sympathetic look.

'Thank you. It means a lot to hear that. I'm good to continue, in fact I want to.' Monica cleared her throat. 'Anyway, I said everything I could to try and soothe him and eventually he put her back in her cot after shouting at her to shut up when she started screaming. I then ran towards the door, hoping to just get enough distance between us to call you but he slammed my fingers in it and dragged me back and flung me to the floor.' She held her red knuckles up.

Gina's heart began to palpitate and when she swallowed, it felt like it might beat its way up her gullet. So many people shared her own personal story or were living it and they too lived beneath this veil of shame when they were the victims. Why? Because they were still being blamed by an uneducated, emotionally deficient society. She was so glad she'd left Terry to die at the bottom of her stairs all those years ago. He had abused her for years, until she'd finally found the strength to stand up to him.

'He left me and picked her up. I managed to send you that message while he was looking out the window with her. I thought he was going to kill me.' She burst into tears. 'I'm going to pack my things and go to my dad's. It's time to tell him what's been going on. I don't want to be here any more.'

'I think that's for the best. You need to stay somewhere you feel safe. You mentioned Darcie too.'

'While he was pacing, he kept saying Darcie was as bad. How she treated him badly and then dumped him and wouldn't let him see his kid. He said he was going to kill her and if I left him, he would kill me too. I mean, he doesn't even want Patsy and he's treated me like shit. He just wants to own me. I asked him if he'd hurt Darcie and I told him that you'd been asking about her, and he laughed at me. It wasn't a funny laugh. He had this manic look in his eye and a sickening grin across his face. Oh, I have these.' Monica fumbled with her phone and showed Gina a photo of her bruised chest. 'There are four altogether. He has hit me four times and I didn't know what to do so I took selfies.'

'You did really good taking those. Can you send them to me?'

'Of course.'

Gina glanced over to see PC Ahmed peering around the door. 'Bear with me one moment.' She left Monica with Jacob and went into the hall with PC Ahmed. 'Shaf, are you okay?'

He nodded. 'Paramedic gave me the all clear. He didn't hit me that hard, it just took my breath away for a few seconds. I'm still on duty.'

'Would you mind taking a statement off Miss Bell? Also, get all the information you can from the photos on her phone. I'll be adding Monica's assault to his arrest list when I get back to the station so make sure you get a thorough statement detailing all of the assaults on her too.' Her phone beeped. Monica had sent the photos through.

'Of course.' They both stepped into the room.

Gina introduced her colleague to Monica. 'PC Ahmed is going to take your statement, if that's okay.' She paused. 'I'm glad you messaged me and we were able to catch Mr Lowe. Please keep my number. If you can think of anything else that might help us, don't hesitate to contact me again.' Gina smiled.

'Thank you, and I'm sorry he hit you.'

'You have nothing to be sorry about. He has, but you haven't. Just look after yourself and your baby and I'm glad you have your dad.'

As she turned to leave, she saw a set of transparent plastic drawers filled with children's craft supplies next to the shoe rack. Glittery pipe cleaners stuck out and a bottle of PVA glue had been left on top. Gina scrunched her brow and peered through the bottom drawer and she almost gasped at what she saw; a white paper craft mask just begging to be decorated. It was exactly like the one Cleo had described when she spoke of the man who took Darcie. He was wearing one exactly the same. 'Monica?'

'Huh,' she called back as she placed her drink on the floor.

'May I look in these drawers?'

'Er, of course. My niece loves doing a bit of crafting when I babysit for her. I've been saving things up for when Patsy's older.'

Gina slid the drawer open and counted two masks. 'How many of these do you have?' She held one up.

'I don't know. Two or three.'

Gina hoped that Monica would agree to her next request. 'I know this is not a nice thing for me to ask you but it will really help with the case. Can we search your house?'

As they'd arrested Corey Lowe, she could arrange a search of the house but Monica didn't need them going in heavy-handed. Besides, she sensed that Monica was on their side in wanting to get Lowe charged so that she could have some breathing space.

'Why?'

Gina swallowed, knowing that she had to divulge what she knew about the mask to Monica. 'The man who took Darcie was described by a witness as wearing one of these masks and if you had three and now there's two... you can see where this is going?'

Monica remained silent with her mouth open for a few seconds and she shivered. 'Yes. Do it. Although I may have only had two. I can't remember. Can you do it when I've gone to my dad's? I don't think I can be here.'

Gina took a photo of the masks and stepped outside, leaving Monica with Shaf. She knew he'd be able to organise the search while she did the best thing she could do right now, which was to go back to the station and interview Corey Lowe. He had a lot of explaining to do.

FORTY-THREE

LAYLA

She paced up and down outside the hospital. Ambulances lined up along the road that led to A&E. Her sister had remained sedated but it had felt nice to be there for her and hold her hand for a couple of hours. Where was he? It was almost nine and it was so cold. He promised he'd pick her up and he'd mentioned something romantic but then again, she wasn't in the mood for anything like that right now. In fact, all she wanted to do was to pick Sonny up and give him the biggest cuddle ever. She checked her phone again. Nothing. She pinged a message to him through Messenger this time. At least she could see if he'd read it.

> I thought you were picking me up. I'm getting cold here and I'm worried. Are you okay?

The two blue ticks didn't transpire. She tried to call him instead but his phone went straight to voicemail. She hung up and began walking towards the end of the road until she reached the island. The bus stop was only about a five-to-ten-minute walk. It was best that she made her own way home if he wasn't even answering. To think that earlier she was telling herself that she should let go of her doubts and be with him, live with him and embrace a life together. Right now, she was furious that he'd let her down in her hour of need.

Another thought ran through her mind. What if he'd been hurt or been in an accident?

Her phone rang. It was an unknown number. That was it. Something had happened and he'd lost his phone so he'd bought a new one. 'Hello.'

The other person was silent.

'Is it you?' Why would he not say anything?

'Hi,' a woman said.

'Who's this?'

'I, err, I just made it to the flats on Broadwas Mews as they took Jamie in an ambulance. I knew it was Jamie and she told me all about you. I thought I should call and see if you've heard anything.' The woman sounded a bit broken up and hesitant with every word she spoke. 'We lived on the street together just down the road from there. I heard the sirens going and I just knew.'

'How do you have my number?'

'She gave it to me just in case there was ever an emergency. I just hoped it was the same number and you hadn't changed it. Is she okay? I need to know.'

Layla remembered what DI Harte had said to her. She wasn't to tell anyone that her sister had slightly improved.

'Please, I love your sister to bits and I'm beside myself with worry. I need to know if she's okay.'

'What's your name?'

'Elle.'

'Elle who?'

'It doesn't matter. I saw the news and they said the woman they brought in is in a coma. Please just tell me how she is. Is she awake?'

Something seemed totally off but then again, Elle could be genuine. If she was one of Jamie's drug addicted friends, maybe she would be a bit defensive.

'You're right. She's in a coma and it's not looking likely that she'll come around. I'm really sorry.'

With that the caller hung up.

FORTY-FOUR

It was almost ten in the evening and Gina was wasting her time trying to get Corey Lowe to speak. He slunk back in his chair after saying no comment in response to every single question. His solicitor sat next to him, twiddling a Biro between his fingers and Jacob yawned.

'I'll ask you again. You said that you were going to kill Darcie. Is that what you've done to her?' Gina observed the slight twitch at his cheek and she wondered if he was clenching his teeth.

'No comment.' His navy-blue sweatshirt had been streaked with mud from the tumble in the field. His stone-coloured jogging bottoms were smeared with blood from his now treated leg that had caught on the fence.

'You know Darcie Fletcher, Shannon Calder and Jamie Purvis. You all went to high school together. Isn't that right?'

'No comment,' he mumbled. He kicked the leg of the desk and began nervously tapping his feet. 'Are you going to charge me or what?'

'Oh, we will be charging you alright.' She leaned across the desk, not letting him intimidate her. The assaults against her and PC Ahmed were indisputable. Corey Lowe wasn't going anywhere that night and if she had it her way, he wouldn't be making bail when his twenty-four hours were up either. If needs be, she'd apply for an extension to keep him in custody while they investigated the kidnappings further. She felt a jitteriness brewing inside the pit of her stomach. If he had Darcie and Shannon hidden and trapped somewhere, things could go from bad to worse. On being admitted to the police station, Lowe had his DNA and fingerprints taken but Gina knew that there was no way they'd receive the results back that night. It was possibly going to be days, even on a fast track. She wouldn't know if his DNA matched any cigarette stubs forensics had sent to the lab.

'Great. Just get on with it, then. I have nowt more to say.' He sniffed hard and rubbed his nose.

Gina wondered if he still had any trace of cocaine left in him now. The drug test that they'd taken after booking him in showed that Monica Bell was right about him using that day, but they had found no drugs on him or his friend, Tyler. 'Where's Darcie Fletcher?'

'No comment.' He folded his arms and leaned back.

'Where is Shannon Calder?'

'No comment.'

'Look, Mr Lowe. This could get a lot worse for you. So far, no one has died which means I won't be arresting you for murder. You can end this, now. Do the right thing. Where are they?'

The solicitor placed his folder on the desk. 'My client has nothing more to say. The burden of proof is on you and you repeating the questions and accusing him of attempted murder and kidnap without evidence is getting you nowhere, Detective Inspector. Either you actually charge him or you leave him in a cell until his twenty-four hours are up and then you let him go.'

Corey Lowe held his hand up. 'I didn't do anything to

Darcie, Shannon or Jamie. I don't know what the hell all that is about.'

'But you threatened Darcie?'

He roared and ran his fingers through his sticking out hair, dislodging a dried clump of mud that landed in his lap. 'I didn't. Monica is just a drama queen. That bitch is out to get me and take my daughter from me, just like Darcie did. Those photos of her bruises are her doing because she fell over in the garden and she left the window open when I was there this evening. The wind blew the bedroom door shut on her hand. I didn't hurt her and you have no proof I did.'

'I have proof that you're a violent man who is willing to use your fists. For the tape, I am pointing to the bruising on my own face where Mr Lowe punched me earlier this evening. Also, Mr Lowe has a prior conviction for assault.'

'You caught me by surprise. I thought you were trying to jump me,' Lowe shouted as his solicitor whispered into his ear. 'I've got this, okay. Stop telling me what to do.'

The solicitor shrugged and threw his pen on the desk.

'We disclosed that we were police.'

'Well, I didn't hear you.'

Gina brought up another photo on her phone. 'Tell me about this? For the tape, I am showing Mr Lowe a photo of a set of plastic drawers full of craft supplies that was taken at his house. One drawer is open and he can see a pair of white craft masks.'

He frowned and his dark brows looked like they'd almost knitted together. 'Is this some sort of joke? Why are you asking me about a drawer full of kids' stuff?'

'The person who took Darcie was wearing one of these masks and we found some in your house.'

'Those things are nothing to do with me. I've had enough of this bullshit. No comment, no comment, no comment.'

Gina exhaled. 'You've not once asked about your daughter, Cleo.'

'Because I know where she'll be. She'll be with Darcie's dickhead of a brother. In fact, I wouldn't be surprised if Darcie is behind all this. She was always attention seeking.'

'What about Shannon?'

'Her too. Stupid pair of witches and Jamie is nothing but an idiot junkie.'

'How do you know that? Have you seen Jamie recently?'

'I spoke to her sister, Layla, about a year ago. As you know, we all went to school together. I saw her on the high street in Cleevesford.'

'Do you have access to a car?' Gina knew he only had his van insurance.

He let out a laugh. 'No.'

'Did you drive Tyler Job's car to Shoreford's last night and take Shannon Calder? Your friend said that you borrowed his car last night and that you told him you were insured to drive any car. We know you're not.'

The solicitor loosened his tie and whispered in Lowe's ear again and this time he listened. 'No comment.'

'My client has nothing more to say.'

'You said that before, but it's clear that Mr Lowe has lots to say. You do have something to tell us, don't you, Mr Lowe?'

'No comment.' He placed his fingers in his ears and stared down at the table and started humming an unrecognisable tune while occasionally stopping to sing the words, no comment. He stopped for a second and laughed after the tape had been stopped. 'You lot have no idea where they are, do you?' He clicked his tongue and winked. 'Take me back to my cell.'

He was playing games with them. Gina's fists were that tight, she really wished she had Lowe's neck in her grip rather than pressing her nails into her own skin.

FORTY-FIVE

After wrapping up the interview and placing Lowe back in his cell, Gina and Jacob headed to the incident room. O'Connor, Wyre and Kapoor were waiting to hear what had been said.

Gina wasted no time in stepping up to the head of the table. She placed each hand, palm down, on the wood as she leaned over and addressed the room. 'We have Lowe for the assaults but we don't have enough to go for him when it comes to the kidnappings. He's mouthy and we have the mask link. All we know is, when it comes to the kidnappings, the link to Lowe is circumstantial. We need more to present a case for him to the CPS. Take him borrowing his friend's car last night, for example. Did he use it to take Shannon or was he merely driving around without insurance? We need the car booked into evidence. What we do know is that he's violent. He has the strength to overpower his victims. He has the means but if he did take them, where did he take them to? We still don't know where Jamie Purvis was taken from and when she was taken. Did the kidnapper have her for a week or longer? All we have to go on at the moment is how much her fingernails have grown since she last painted her nails. Bernard estimated that to be a maximum of a month ago.'

She took in all that she was saying and she hoped that a piece of evidence tying everything together would be found in the search. Maybe in Corey Lowe's trade, he had access to partly finished buildings that weren't being occupied and some of his paperwork might uncover what he'd been working on. Maybe they'll find details of the contractor he works for. 'Shaf stayed at Monica Bell and Corey Lowe's house to organise a search. Has he or one of the team been in contact yet?'

Wyre raised her brows. 'He phoned to say he'd made a start but estimated that they could be there until midnight. He said that Miss Bell had left the house and gone to stay with her father.'

'Great, I'm glad she didn't have to remain there while the search was going on. Keep me updated if he calls in with anything that might help us to locate Shannon and Darcie.' She paused. 'O'Connor?' He swigged from a mug of black coffee. She knew he preferred it milky but the long day was getting to them all. Running on caffeine was all they had left. 'Do we have any witnesses from the news appeals?'

'Nothing helpful, guv.' He placed his cup down. 'No one saw anyone suspicious hanging around where Jamie Purvis was found at the back of the flats. It's good news that she's off the ventilator.'

'It is. It's just a shame she's still sedated. Any more updates that I should know about?'

O'Connor referred to his notes. 'Nothing further on the search of Shannon Calder's house. Her laptop has been sent to tech but that will take a while to process. We know that someone was watching her from her attic. Samples have gone to the lab but we're not likely to get much in the way of forensics back fast, so we get on with good old-fashioned detecting. Her kitchen clock had stopped at eleven o'clock which was noted.

Given that Cleo drew the picture of the intruder with the clock, I'm certain it's relevant. The CCTV from both Shoreford's and the newsagent on the other side of the road have given us nothing more. Wyre and I interviewed the taxi driver.'

'And?'

'He said he dropped Shannon off at Shoreford's and after waiting outside for a few minutes, she came out, paid him, and told him he could leave. He didn't really have much to add although he thought he heard some of what she was saying on her phone and he was under the impression someone was coming to pick her up.'

Gina raised her brows. 'That leads me onto Finn Sampson. We ended up in an emergency situation tonight with Lowe. Given that we have two kidnap victims, it wasn't ideal but we were alerted that Monica Bell was in immediate danger. We had no option but to intervene. Regardless of what we think of the kidnapper, they might be the only person keeping our two victims alive right now and if it is Lowe, it saddens me to say that there's a chance we might have blown it. There is definitely a chance that both Shannon and Darcie are dead.' She stood up straight and combed her fingers through her tangled hair, wanting to scrape through the knots in frustration and pull it out.

Wyre looked down. 'Even more so if he's running around desperate.'

'I want to believe they're still alive. We don't have any bodies. We know that the finger left at the garage probably belonged to Darcie so at the very least, she's injured and bleeding right now. If she's alive, she'll be vulnerable to infection and if we look at Jamie, she'd been starved and was dehydrated. If Lowe is our perp, then how long can his victims survive without him? Then we have Finn. He was in a relationship with Shannon.' Gina took a moment to try to unravel the mess of the case in her head. 'Anna turned up to one of

Shannon and Darcie's night's out uninvited, where she met Finn Sampson for the first time. They began a relationship which caused a lot of upset between Shannon and Darcie. We have Finn's address. Before we got the call from Monica Bell we were going to head over to his house but now, I'm glad we didn't. We need to tread carefully.'

Jacob opened his mouth. 'Do you think we could have two people working together, guv? We have a lot of victims in such a short space of time. I was just wondering how one person could handle it all.'

Gina nodded. 'We definitely need to keep that thought in our minds. We need to do some more digging into Finn Sampson. Also, O'Connor? Can you and Kapoor look into the pasts of Darcie, Jamie, Shannon and Corey. They all went to Cleevesford High. They are all thirty-five years old so would have been in the same year at school. I want to know about anything and everything that happened at that school, or to its pupils during the years they attended. I know it means a lot of research and as soon as the school opens, I'd like you to also contact the headteacher. See what they might still have on file. Or maybe some of the teachers from back then are still there.' She looked over at O'Connor and Kapoor. 'I know I'm asking a lot of you because it's late and you're tired, but can you both do that? Can you start looking into newspaper articles that link the school to any incidents back then?'

O'Connor drank the rest of his coffee down in one. 'Red Bull is on you, guv.'

She smiled. 'That's a deal. Thank you. In fact, thank you all for going above and beyond. We are going to have a lot of PCs available to help and some are being sourced from a neighbouring force. They should be with us soon. Shannon and Darcie need us right now.'

Gina stared at the board, casting her gaze over everything and it felt like a confused mess. Her gaze fell on Finn's name and the lines that had been drawn from Shannon, Anna and Darcie to him. 'For now, I want Finn Sampson's house kept under surveillance and his garage checked. I know we were going to interview him earlier but we need to hold that thought. If he is involved, I hope he will lead us to them before it's too late. Jacob, you and I will stake out his house until the other officers arrive to take over. O'Connor, can you send a couple of the PCs who are due soon over to Finn Sampson's residence when they arrive so Jacob and I can grab a few hours' sleep? Kapoor, Wyre and O'Connor, stay on research for the next couple of hours, then go home and sleep. Then I need you here fresh first thing, so that you can call Cleevesford High as soon as they open.'

Everyone nodded and mumbled a yes.

'I'm putting Gordon Shoreford on the potential suspect list, especially as we are now considering that there could be two perpetrators. I don't know why he would be involved, but without further investigation I can't rule him out. Also, if there are two, then they will all have alibis for at least one of the kidnappings, which makes our job harder.' She sighed. 'But Lowe went to school with them all and as far as we know, Gordon Shoreford has no connection to Jamie Purvis.' She flinched as she brushed her fingers over her cheek, feeling the bruise. 'Where is PC Smith?'

Wyre spoke up. 'He's sitting outside Jamie Purvis's room. He relieved the other officer about an hour ago and I think someone is set to take over his job in about an hour so he can go home.' Her phone rang. 'Actually, that's him now.' She pressed answer. 'Hello... oh my goodness, really?'

'What is it?' Gina asked.

'Bear with me a second,' she said to Smith, before addressing the room. 'They are reducing Jamie's sedation and they expect her to come around over the next two to three hours.'

'Yes!' Gina punched the air. 'Tell him to let me know as soon as she's able to talk with us.'

Briggs walked through the door and stared at her bruised face. Gina looked away. She couldn't deal with any kind of lecture right now. She had barely any backup when chasing Lowe but if she hadn't kept after him, they wouldn't have him in custody.

Wyre ended the call. 'Apparently, the staff said that Jamie might not be up to it until morning but Smith said he'd keep us updated.'

'Jamie has to know the person who took her. I don't believe for one minute there are strangers behind all this. We're going to nail them. I just hope we won't be too late for Shannon and Darcie.'

FORTY-SIX
SHANNON

All she could see was the white mask and the broad shoulders as the man standing next to the car injected her. The man began to grow and grow until the top of his head reached the dark stormy sky. Tick-tock. Tick-tock. The clock face emerged from his gaping white cardboard mouth and just as it hurtled towards her head, she screamed.

Heart pounding, she awoke to the sound of the ticking clock. What day was it? Was it still the same day? However hard she fought with her eyelids; her eyes began to close again as her mind dragged her deeper and deeper into the world she was trying so hard to escape.

She rose from her bed, floating towards the ceiling before turning over and seeing herself on a cold slab. An angel beckoned her to follow him towards the light.

No, it wasn't real. Her brain was fighting back and the truth was, she was still lying on her back on something hard and cold.

She stared into the darkness and the ship was being tossed in the storm and she was on it. Just as it was about to capsize...

No, wake up, she wanted to shout but the drug was powerful. Was she restrained in the dark or had she entered another realm? Maybe it was the latter. Maybe he'd already killed her.

The white mask floated through the darkness and rested just above her, its cardboard nose touching hers.

Her muscles stiffened.

Stop falling asleep. Fight the drug.

Shivering, she craved a blanket but there had been nothing. Her feet, did she still have them? Her hands, her fingers – nothing worked. She pictured her body with missing legs and arms and she imagined herself screaming. She prised open a crusty eye. Her dry throat begged for water. Her kidnapper hadn't even offered her a drink and the gag had slipped further back. The vivid dreams had been her weird reality but they were beginning to fade and all she could think about was the nausea welling up inside her. She was sure that if she wasn't lying in pitch blackness, the room would be spinning.

She gazed from side to side, wide-eyed as her senses started to come back. Whatever he'd drugged her with had taken her on a journey she never wanted to repeat but then again, she knew he was going to kill her. He'd gone on and on before the drug fully kicked in, saying how he'd made a mistake with Jamie and that he was in such big trouble because he'd screwed up.

Tick-tock, tick-tock. She couldn't stop thinking about those clock hands.

Her hearing sharpened as she hushed her inner voice. She tried to make out the fluorescent hands of the clock on the ceiling to see what the time was. Eleven o'clock stuck in her mind; he had repeated it. Not long to go. As soon as he removed the cloth from her mouth, she'd beg and plead for him to let her go. She wondered how Barney was and just the thought of his gorgeous chocolate dog eyes sent tears springing from her own. Without her, Barney would have no one. She had no close family and she knew he'd end up in some dog shelter and that broke her heart.

A thought came back to her. Had she heard a woman sobbing while she'd been out of it, or was it just another trippy dream? There was also some shrill crying. Maybe it was her own. A pain shot through her chest as more things came back to her. The kidnapper had said something when he left her in this horrible room but what was it? A loud alarm pierced her ears. She stared at the clock. It was dead on eleven.

Footsteps clonked above and the old door creaked open. A heavy-footed person headed towards her and removed the gag. 'It's eleven. Do you remember?'

She didn't recognise that voice. It wasn't him. It was someone with a gentler voice.

'Do you remember?'

Remember what? She'd remember anything her captor wanted her to if they'd let her go. She almost choked on a sob as she thought about Darcie.

The cold table she was lying on creaked as she was tilted back. As her eyes adjusted, she could just about make out the outline of the white mask in the dark but the eye area was black, like they had goggles on over the top. She inhaled the scent of strawberry.

'Do you?' the kidnapper shouted, their spit hitting her forehead. The voice no longer gentle.

Remember what? Think, think, she kept telling herself. What did this have to do with her and Darcie and the man who'd taken her? She wanted to cry and sob. If she knew, she would say. She nodded.

The kidnapper nudged the gag material onto her chest. 'Why are you here, Shannon?'

She let out the loudest sob. 'I don't know. Please let me go. Please. I beg of you.'

'Wrong answer, you selfish bitch.'

With that, the kidnapper replaced the gag. Then came the sloshing sound. Maybe they had a bucket of water or a watering can. She wriggled in her own wet trousers in the hope of loosening some of the binds but it was no good.

'Maybe this will help jog that bad memory of yours.'

Without warning, a cascade of water landed on her face. The icy liquid was soon absorbed by the cloth. She held her breath in the hope that it would stop but it didn't. Her mouth began to fill and it was no good, she kicked and fought against her binds but they were too strong. Against her wishes, she inhaled sharply and she knew that was her end as she began to choke.

She remembered what the other kidnapper had said when he left her in the room.

Darcie is dead and you're next.

FORTY-SEVEN

Monday, 4 March

The sweet smell of energy drink hung in the air of Gina's car. She grabbed the empty can off the dashboard and dropped it behind the passenger seat that Jacob was gently snoring in. The streetlamp above them was conveniently broken so no light had been cast over her car. With his head back and mouth open, Jacob blew out another breath just like he'd been doing for the past hour. She'd parked along the side of 7 Brickford Close in the hope that Finn Sampson would emerge and lead them to where Darcie and Shannon were being held. Her phone rang and Jacob stirred. 'Hello,' she said to O'Connor.

'Guv, the PCs that are taking over will be there in about half an hour. They are in plain-clothes and have an unmarked car, and they have your number should anything happen overnight.'

'Thank you.'

Jacob yawned. 'Sorry for falling asleep. What's happening?'

'We're being relieved soon so you'll be able to go to bed for a few hours.'

He pulled his phone out of his pocket and squinted to see the time. 'That went quick. It's past midnight.'

'You've got dribble down your chin.'

'What?' He wiped it away with the back of his hand. 'Anything happened?'

'No. The lights in the house went out about fifteen minutes ago and then nothing.' The porch light came on. 'Wait, scrap that.'

Finn opened the front door and walked out taking long strides towards his car. His overalls had been pulled down and tied at his waist and his T-shirt clung to his ripped torso. Gina sunk back as Finn glanced in their direction. Jacob pulled his hood over his face. Finn opened the driver's door of his Capri and sat in the seat.

'Why is he sitting there with the door open?'

They watched as he rooted around for a few minutes, then he emerged out of the car with a packet of cigarettes in his hand. He closed the car door and leaned against it as he lit one up and inhaled, the red tip glowing in the dark. Jacob lifted his hood away from his eyes a bit more. 'He's a smoker.'

'And he has access to a lot of cars and each witness has described seeing a different vehicle. Mrs Swadling thought she saw a brown or dark-blue car. Lowe is known to drive a white van and his friend, Tyler, had a silver car. The vet said she saw a black hatchback. Mavis the shopkeeper thought she saw the loitering man standing by a grey car or SUV and here Finn is with a marine-blue Capri. He has access to a lot of cars, we know that. Only he could have access to that many different vehicles.'

Finn pulled his phone from his pocket and held it to his ear.

'I need to find out what he's saying.'

'Guv, he might hear you getting out the car and if he does,

we'll blow it. Not only that, it could spell the end for Darcie and Shannon.'

'I can do this. He won't hear me.' She reached up and switched off the interior light, then she turned her phone onto silent. The door handle made the slightest click as she pulled. Gently, she pushed it open. Jacob scrunched his nose in dread at the door creaking. One centimetre at a time. Soon the gap widened enough to allow her to slip out onto the pavement, knees first. On impact, she held still for a few seconds before leaning back and pushing the door to an almost closed position. A lump of grit dug into her knee through her trousers. The hum of Finn's conversation carried in the air but she couldn't make out anything he was saying. She needed to get a lot closer. If she could reach the fence that divided his drive from the public path, she'd hear everything.

As she went to stand, her knee clicked. Heart in mouth, she remained behind the car trying to control her panicky breaths. He stopped talking. She hoped Jacob had slunk down in the car. She couldn't see Finn but in her mind's eye, she envisaged him staring across. Finn cleared his throat and began muttering again. Slowly, she raised her head above the boot and glanced through the windscreen of her car. She could see that Finn had his back to them and Jacob had indeed ducked. It was time to make her move towards the fence.

Creeping, she reached the fence and took a couple of silent deep breaths as she waited for her heart to calm down. The booming in her chest filled her ears as blood pumped around her body but she just about heard Finn's voice.

'You know what we did was wrong,' he yelled to the other person on the call. 'I can't leave my dad... no... he hasn't had a good night. He's not well.'

Gina tried to think who he might be talking to. One thing she knew for sure was that he wasn't talking to Corey Lowe right now. Corey was safely tucked away in a cell. Maybe he was involved and this was bigger than they were imagining.

'Look, it could be a few hours but I'll come over when he's settled. If he does go to sleep in the meantime, I'll sneak out. My sister is coming to take care of him at eight so she's able to let herself in.' He paused. 'With all that's happening, I don't think we should carry on.' He threw his part-smoked cigarette to the tarmac and it landed in Gina's eyeline at the end of his drive. 'Shut up. I wish I'd never met you. My life was easy before all this.'

A light cast across the drive. Gina looked up to see an older man at the window, his hands trembling as he almost tugged the curtains down. He placed a flat hand on the glass as he looked down at his son.

'I've got to go... no, I'm not lying... forget it if you're not going to listen. I'll call you again in a bit when you've calmed the hell down... this needs to end.'

Gina accidentally elbowed the fence. She heard each of Finn's footsteps as he reached the other side of the panel, then she almost jumped as he cleared his throat and spat before hurrying back into the house. With jellied legs, she hurried back into the car.

'Anything?' Jacob waited expectantly for her to reply.

'He said to the caller that what they did was wrong and he was angry at them. He thinks they shouldn't carry on with whatever it is they're doing and that they need to end it. Problem is, we don't know who he's talking to. I want to go in there and arrest him so we can dig deeper, but who knows if they have some sort of arrangement should the other not call back or check in. I don't know what to do right now, Jacob.'

'I know. The tightrope we're walking right now is a flimsy one. If we go in all guns blazing there will be repercussions for Darcie and Shannon, if we continue to hold back, we might leave it too late. I wish I had the answer.'

She leaned back and bit her lip as she toiled with her thoughts. She rubbed her knee, then noticed that her trousers were damp. She bit her bottom lip and grimaced. The stone she'd kneeled on had cut her.

Jacob's phone lit up. He snatched it and held it to his ear. 'Ooh, yep. That's great!' He ended the call and smiled.

'Don't keep me in suspense.'

'Jamie has come around and the officers taking over from us are just around the corner.'

FORTY-EIGHT

Gina had barely had any sleep but she'd arrived back at the station for seven in the morning. The press had thrust microphones in her face as she'd rushed in. Everyone's eyes were on them now.

She entered the incident room, trying not to spill anything as she gripped the plastic tray. The team were already getting on with the tasks they'd left open the night before to grab a bit of sleep. O'Connor continued to research the past with Kapoor and Wyre. Gina placed the tray of coffee and cans of energy drinks in the middle of the large table. 'Morning. Any updates?'

O'Connor turned away from his computer screen in the corner of the room. 'There are so many mentions of Cleevesford High during the years our victims would have attended. I've come across a few incidents. A gang wearing their uniform was discovered hanging out at lunchtimes in a derelict house when a girl got injured by a smashed window, putting her in hospital. A pupil got badly hurt in a hit-and-run. Bus crash on a class trip. Two pupils charged with assault on a teacher. One accusation of inappropriate behaviour, a teen boy accused a teacher of sexual assault. That teacher died five years ago.' He glanced back at his screen. 'Many instances of shoplifting, minor assaults and vandalism. One alcohol poisoning death after a party at a disused warehouse, an incident involving a horse that put a pupil in a coma, and a few other accidental injuries, including one death following drug or alcohol use. A drowning. The list goes on. In fact, the school had quite a bad reputation around then.'

Gina grabbed a coffee and hugged it between her cold hands. 'That's a lot to work through. Are any of our suspect or victim names matching up with any of the incidents?'

'Not so far but we've barely touched the surface of all the information we have. I've tried to call the school, but there is no one there yet.'

Gina glanced at her watch. It was barely half seven now. 'I'm not surprised.'

Jacob entered the room, his face covered in stubble and his eyes dark underneath. He hadn't had much time off to recover after the last incident but it was obvious that coming back to work was tiring him out faster than the others. He grabbed an energy drink and sat at the end of the table.

'We're just talking updates.'

He yawned. 'Sorry, guv. I'll come around in a minute.'

O'Connor piped up. 'How did the visit to the hospital go last night?'

'When we got there, Jamie was awake but it was as if she wasn't there. Doctor Alessi said it might be best if we come back later. As far as he was concerned, he thought she was still affected by the sedation or her silence might be trauma related. I think I'm going to call her sister, Layla, to see if she can visit again. A familiar voice might help bring her out of herself.' She tapped her fingers on the desk. 'Has anyone heard from the officers who were watching Finn's house last night?'

Wyre leaned back in her chair. 'I spoke to them about half an hour ago. He hasn't left his house all night.'

Gina's phone rang. 'Hello.' She nodded at the team. 'It's one of the officers.'

They all watched and listened.

'Has he left?' she asked. Everyone in the room sat in silence, waiting for news.

The officer on the other end of the call continued speaking in his deep voice. 'A woman with a baby has just turned up. They exchanged a few words at the doorstep. She went in and he left. He's just driven out of Brickford Close so we're following him now.' A police radio crackled in the background. 'We're now turning onto the Cleevesford Bypass.'

'Keep talking. I'm just going to place you on loudspeaker so the team can hear what you're saying.'

The officer continued. 'Heading down Grove Street now. Two other undercover cars have been despatched and are close by. If he spots us, we can turn off and one of the others can pick up on the tail. So far so good, he hasn't even checked his mirror.'

Gina held a thumb up to the team. Deathly silence filled the room as they all waited, hoping that Finn would lead them to Darcie and Shannon.

'He's just taken a left onto Sycamore Road and he's parking up outside a lock-up. We're staying back.'

'Can you describe the lock-up?'

'It just looks like a large garage. Wait, a man is coming out. He's about twenty-five, maybe thirty at a push. Red hair, approximately six feet tall. He's gone back inside, leaving our suspect outside, alone.'

'Is there any signage on the lock-up?'

'No, nothing that I can see from here. The red-headed man has come back out.'

'What is he doing?'

The officer on the call blew out a breath. 'He's passing our suspect what looks like a tyre. Suspect has just put it on the passenger seat of his car and now he's driving off. We're going to continue. Wait, my partner is just passing the other side and there is a sign. Bill's Tyres. It looks like he's just collected a tyre.'

Gina's shoulders slumped. 'Keep following and keep talking.'

'We're back on the bypass... he's indicating to come off onto Cobblers Road. Taking a left, then first right onto Woburn Drive. Left at the end.'

'He's heading towards Shoreford's.' She folded her arms and shook her head. Looks of deflation spread around the room.

'He's just got out at the back of Shoreford's. He's heading around the front on foot. I'm getting out of the car and I'm going to follow him.'

'Don't let him see you,' Gina said.

Everyone listened from the incident room as the officer left the car and walked. 'A man who looks to be in his early sixties, wearing a suit and tie is walking up to him in the showroom. He's quite broad and large.'

'That sounds like the owner, Mr Shoreford.'

'Wait, they're arguing. I have to run. He's coming back out.'

A few moments passed and Gina felt like she'd been holding her breath throughout.

'I'm back in the car. Finn has just thrown the tyre out of his car and kicked it against a unit at the back of the showroom before getting back into his Capri. He's leaving.'

Gina could tell that the team were also wondering if the argument had been about Shannon and Darcie. Had Finn been talking to Gordon Shoreford in the early hours? She tensed up in the hope that Finn was about to lead them to the victims and she dared to hope that they were still alive. 'Where's he going now?'

'We're still on his tail. Wait, he's turning... Oh.'

'What?'

'He's getting out of his car and going into McDonald's.'

'Maybe he's getting them some food.'

'He's taking a bag from the server. He's sitting by the window and he's pulled out a bun and now he's eating it. He's staring out of the window and leaning back.'

Fifteen minutes passed and the officer told Gina that Finn had bought another drink.

'I think we're going to hang up for a bit,' Gina said. 'Stay with him and keep us posted.'

'Got it. It's probably for the best. He doesn't look like he's leaving anytime soon.'

Gina placed her phone on the table. 'We know Finn and Gordon Shoreford were arguing. We don't know what about but it shows there's tension between them. Damn.' She stood straight and turned away from the team so they wouldn't see the disappointment written across her face. 'O'Connor, can we try the school again?'

He turned away to make the call and began to speak when someone answered.

'What did they say?' Gina asked as he placed his phone down.

'There is one teacher there today who happened to work at the school during those years. The acting head is happy for us to head over at lunchtime to speak to her.'

'Not until lunchtime? That's ages away.'

O'Connor leaned back in his creaky chair. 'She's having an emergency tooth extraction unfortunately.'

Gina walked over to the window and saw Briggs heading across the car park. Several reporters tried to call him over but he charged right through them. She glanced back at the board. 'Can I have a printout of all those school incidents that you collated?' she asked O'Connor. 'We need to share them out if we're to get through all that work.' She stared at the board again and tried to consider each suspect or interviewee and how they could be paired in the crime.

'What are you thinking, guv?' Jacob asked.

'O'Connor, it was you who interviewed Corey Lowe's friend, Tyler Job, wasn't it? Did he say which garage Lowe's van has been taken too?'

O'Connor flicked through his notes. 'Button Lane Garage.'

Gina did a quick Google search on her phone and found Button Lane Garage Limited registered with Companies House. 'It's registered to Finn Sampson. He and Lowe have a connection. Wyre, can you wake Lowe up and interview him again? Kapoor, you can assist. We need to put some pressure on him now and arrange for a plain-clothed officer to head over to Button Lane Garage to check it out.'

PC Ahmed entered.

'Anything from the search of Lowe's house last night?' Gina asked him.

He shook his head. 'Nothing that connects him to any of the kidnappings. Sorry, guv.'

'Great!' She glanced at Jacob. 'I was hoping that Finn Sampson would lead us straight to Darcie and Shannon, but it's not happening. I'm going to call Layla Purvis now. Jacob, we should meet her at the hospital. Like I said before, maybe seeing her sister will help Jamie and just maybe she'll tell us something that will help us save the others. There are two women out there and we have no idea what's happening to them right now.' She began to pace as Briggs entered. 'They took Jamie. They held her and then dumped her. She was found emaciated with a missing finger and water in her lungs. The women are stalked from their own attics before they are taken. Clocks are a clue. Eleven o'clock is a clue? We have the toy boat and a box with boats on them. What the hell have boats got to do with it all?'

She scrunched her brow. 'Joel, the trainee, said that Shannon hadn't seemed herself on the morning she was taken and it wasn't the first time. Do they gaslight them first, make them think they're losing their minds? With Darcie, it looked like whoever was watching her made Cleo think he was the bogeyman. Does he, or do they, drug them? I think Corey Lowe is definitely a waste of space and won't be winning any parent-of-the-year awards but I still don't know if he'd leave his young daughter at the roadside to fend for herself, which begs the question, did he take Darcie? If he didn't, was he partnered with someone who did?' She stared hard at the board. 'We're being gaslit. Someone, or an alliance on this board, is trying to lead us astray and I don't know who to trust here.'

She glanced at all the photos of the garage employees, then there was Anna, Finn and Jamie. They had a break-in where ketamine had been stolen.

'Who do you suspect?' Briggs waited for her to answer.

She bit her lip and scrunched her nose. He'd tried to call her in the early hours but she'd ignored his call, not wanting to discuss her cut knee or the bruise on her face. She was glad the room was busy and he'd only asked about the case.

'Dammit. I can't see the wood for the bloody trees. I need to go to the hospital and see if Jamie can be interviewed. Jacob and I will call Layla on the way. Just bear in mind, all is not what it seems whenever you consider anyone's statement. I think someone on this board is toying with us like they toyed with the victims. Not one of these people can be believed right now.'

FORTY-NINE

'Layla, thank you for coming.' Gina walked over to the woman and they headed up the corridor towards Jamie's private room.

'When I got the call, I couldn't wait to be here. My son is at his grandmother's house and I literally got on the next bus. When I was told she might not make it, I felt like my whole world was falling apart but she has a second chance and I'm going to be there for her.'

'I was hoping that you'd help us. We need to find out who took Jamie and where she was held. Two other women are in serious danger, they might already be dead. We hope that isn't the case and if they are still alive, they won't have much time and Jamie might be our only chance to save them.'

Gina needed Layla to know how important Jamie's account of what happened was to them; that it was a matter of life and death. Jacob followed them with three coffees all bunched up between his hands. She nodded to the officer sitting outside Jamie's room and he smiled and let them through.

'I'll do everything I can,' Layla said in a hushed tone. The young woman crept over to the other side of the bed and sat on the visitor chair. Jacob placed the drinks on the bedside unit and

Gina took one and began sipping it. For now, they would have to give Jamie a bit of space to open up.

'Hello, sis.' Layla placed her hand on Jamie's and lay her head on the pillow so their noses were almost touching. Jamie's brown hair splayed over the white pillow and a few clumps stuck to a tape patch on her shoulder.

Gina slowly moved to the end of the bed and watched the sisters. Tears filled Jamie's sunken eyes but she didn't blink. Her stare was looking right through Layla as if she wasn't there.

Layla glanced at Gina and frowned. She continued to speak gently. 'My little baby boy, Sonny, wants to meet his aunt. He's so cute with his little button nose. He has your eyes, you know. Beautiful big brown eyes that make me melt. Do you want to meet him when you're better?'

Looking at Jamie, Gina knew she would be in recovery for ages. She not only had her injuries to deal with, she had pancreatitis to manage and then there was the trauma on top of all that.

Layla stroked Jamie's hair. 'Remember when we use to lie like this at home when we were scared at night? You'd get into my bed and we'd talk about all the places we were going to visit one day.' She giggled. 'I wanted to go to Paris because I liked chocolate eclairs and you wanted to go to Australia so you could cuddle a koala. You wanted to live in Cornwall and paint seascapes for a living.' Layla scrunched her brows and tried to look into her sister's eyes but Jamie still stared right through her. 'We can still do those things, when you're better. We can take Sonny to Oz and Paris. He would love that.'

Gina swallowed the lump in her throat.

Layla sat back up in the chair, pulled her phone out of her pocket and scrolled. She placed the phone where her head had been, showing Jamie a photo. 'This is Sonny.' Tears rolled down her face as Jamie gave her no response. 'I had a baby. I bet you can't believe it. Me and his dad adore him...

Jamie, it's me Layla,' she cried. 'Please say something. Anything.'

A whisper came from Jamie's mouth and it got louder. 'Tick-tock. Tick-tock. Tick-tock.' She reached out for her sister's hand and gripped it hard.

Gina felt her heart rate picking up. Jamie was saying those words when she came into hospital.

'There are two police detectives here. They want to help you, Jamie. Can you tell them anything about your kidnapper or where they took you?'

Jamie withdrew her hand and placed her hands over her ears and bawled loudly. 'Don't make me go back.'

'You're safe, Jamie. You're safe. You're in hospital and there is a police officer outside your door. No one is going to hurt you.'

The machine began to beep faster as Jamie's heart rate picked up.

Gina stepped around and stood behind Layla. 'Jamie, do you know where you were being kept? Shannon Calder and Darcie Fletcher are missing and we are really worried for their safety,' she said as softly as she could.

Jamie let out a piercing scream and she pulled her blanket over her head. The monitor above her shrieked, setting an alarm off, and a nurse ran in.

'You're going to have to come back later,' the nurse said as she nudged them all out of the way.

Gina hoped what she said hadn't just made things worse for Jamie. A part of her wanted to demand that she stay until Jamie had calmed down, but she knew that Jamie couldn't take any more right now. The nurse held the needle up and Jamie screamed. 'I...' As the syringe emptied into her arm, Jamie's shrieks turned to a soft mumble. 'I escaped. She... chased... me...' Then Jamie sunk into the bed and stared at the bedside unit.

'Sorry,' the nurse said. 'You need to leave.'

Gina walked down the corridor with Jacob and a sobbing

Layla.

Layla pulled a tissue from her bag and blew her nose. 'I'm staying here. I am not leaving her.' She sat on a chair next to the vending machine. 'Not until I know what happened there.'

Gina's knees ached as she crouched down in front of Layla and she hoped Layla wasn't upset with her for speaking back there. 'I'm so sorry for what you're going through. If when you speak to her again, she says anything else about what happened, can you please call me? I think your sister wanted to talk then, but it was too much for her right now. The officer won't leave her so you can also speak to him if you'd rather.'

'I just want my sister to be okay and if talking makes her react like that, I'm not going to push her. I know two other women are depending on her right now but she's my sister, I have to put her first. I can't lose her.' Layla gripped the tissue.

'She's in the best hands. If you need anything, call me, okay.' Gina meant that. She was finding it hard to leave the distraught woman.

'Go, just find the evil person who did this to her.'

A short while later, Gina and Jacob exited the hospital. She took a couple of breaths and swallowed her emotions down.

'That was tense, guv.' He lightly kicked the wall, scuffing his shiny black shoe.

'It was. Did you hear what Jamie muttered in there?'

'No, I couldn't hear much above the beeping.'

Gina repeated what she was sure she'd heard. 'I'm ninety per cent sure that Jamie said, *I escaped, she chased me.* That means the perp didn't let her go. Firstly, she can't have got far looking at the state of her. She was kept close to Broadwas Mews. That covers Shoreford's, Finn's house and Corey's place. Secondly, I think we're looking for a woman too and there is one woman who I know lied to us. As we can't afford to screw this up, work on the assumption that one or both of our victims are still alive. Let's get a tail on her too.'

FIFTY

'Do we have eyes on Anna Heard?' Gina asked Jacob as they walked towards Cleevesford High School's reception.

'No, she's not at home.'

'And Finn Sampson?'

'He's left McDonald's and is sitting in his car.'

'It's like he wants to be seen in public. What else did O'Connor say? I saw your face light up.'

'An officer went to check out the Button Lane Garage and a man on a neighbouring unit said that Finn is winding it down as he has new premises, which he is currently preparing to move in to. O'Connor said he's liaising with the officer while trying to find out where the new premises are.'

'I think we have to consider that he may be keeping our victims there. We're so close, I know we are. Stay on it and let me know when you have a location. Jamie said something at the hospital. She mentioned a she. This had led us to think a woman is involved and Jamie also said that she escaped. If it's Finn Sampson, his new premises have to be close to Broadwas Mews, the location where Jamie was found. We're at the school now. Let me know immediately if there are any developments.'

Gina pushed open the main door and was blasted by a burst of heat as she and Jacob walked through the door. She hurried to reception and was greeted by a young man.

'Morning. Who are you here to see?'

'I know we are a little early but we were hoping that Mrs Chandler was in now.'

The man raised his brows. 'She came in a few minutes ago. Are you from the police station?'

Gina nodded before introducing herself and Jacob. They passed their identification to the man, who photocopied it and gave it back to them. He then handed each of them a visitor lanyard after they'd signed in.

'Come through.' He led them into the staffroom which was empty. The smell of coffee hung in the air and a box of opened cereals had been spilled onto a counter. 'It'll be too busy to talk in here come twelve so we're putting you somewhere more private.' He led them out of the other end and into a small room containing a round table and three chairs. 'Take a seat. I'll just go and find Mrs Chandler. I think she was just dropping some books off at her classroom.'

Gina and Jacob sat and then the lunch bell rang. He took out his notebook and she sat and looked out of the window as the courtyard began to fill up. Students jostled and pushed to get through the crowds.

A woman with long brown hair with two grey stripes framing her face stepped in. Her sleek black trouser suit and super thin physique made her look quite statuesque. She pushed her thick-rimmed red glasses up her nose. 'I'm May Chandler, how can I help you?' She made a slurping sound and Gina could see that her one cheek was slightly puffy. 'Sorry, I'm talking a little funny. I had a wisdom tooth removed this morning and it hurts like hell.'

'Thank you for speaking to us. We wanted to know if you remembered some students who were here twenty years ago.'

'Gosh, that's going back a bit. I see a lot of kids come and go, so I'm not sure how much help I'll be.'

'Have you seen the news over the past couple of days?'

'Only briefly.' She winced and held her mouth. 'It's horrid when the injection wears off.'

'We were trying to identify a woman who was found left for dead and who is now fighting for her life in hospital. We also have a kidnap case. A young woman taken after leaving her friend's house last Thursday night. Her name was Darcie Fletcher. We still haven't found her. We now also have another missing woman called Shannon Calder. The first woman who was taken is called Jamie Purvis.'

'Purvis, that is such a standout surname. I think I taught two Purvis's and they were sisters. Not at the same time, mind you. I think there were a few years between them.'

'Do you recognise the other names? None of them have changed their surnames since school.'

The teacher closed her eyes for a few seconds. 'You're really testing my memory now, but I vaguely remember Darcie. She had this on-off boyfriend and I think his name began with a C.'

Gina piped up. 'Could his name have been Corey?'

'Yes, that's it.' She closed her eyes for a second and clicked her fingers. 'Corey Lowe, that was his name. I didn't really like him. He was a bit of a bully from what I remember. I'm sure that group of girls were always arguing about boys and they probably argued over Corey, but I can't say for sure. I'm trying to picture Shannon but her face isn't coming to me. I remember her name though. But Jamie, I remember her as clear as a bell for some reason. She was adorable and would always help new students and I remember thinking that when she started to hang around with the rest of that group, she was starting to get into trouble.'

'In what way?'

'Drinking and smoking, not doing homework. I remember

that Jamie's mother didn't seem to want to get involved as she never turned up when I tried to call meetings to air my concerns. It was early in the new year. It had been such a cold Christmas and winter, then something changed. It was like the group had broken up and my concerns seemed like nothing after that.'

'Do you remember anyone else they used to hang around with?'

She let out a laugh. 'I'm sorry, it was so long ago. I'm still in touch with a couple of colleagues. I could ask them if they can recall anyone if that will help.'

'That would really help, thank you. I'll get an officer to come by later and take a bit more information from you if that's okay.'

'That's fine. I finish teaching at three fifteen.'

'Do you know why the friendship group might have become distanced from each other?'

'No, and teenagers don't really talk a lot to the teachers. Jamie was the one who got distanced from the pack. Corey became sidelined for whatever reason and the other two girls just hung around quietly.'

'Did anything memorable happen that year? Any major incidents?'

She shrugged. 'I don't know how relevant this is.'

'Please, go on.'

'There was another girl and I don't remember her name but she was friends with Darcie and then Darcie friend-dumped her for Shannon. There was so much upset between them and a lot of nastiness. I broke up a couple of scuffles between that other girl and Shannon. It's not often I break up a fight between the girls so I remember these ones.'

Gina needed to know who the other girl was. 'Did you have a student called Anna Heard?'

Mrs Chandler clicked her fingers. 'That was her name.

Anna. She was so emotional and I was sad for her loss when it came to the friendship group. Girls can be cruel to each other. Is she okay?'

Gina felt her stomach flutter in a nauseating way. Anna was not at home. Had she been taken like the others had, or was she their number one suspect?

FIFTY-ONE
UNKNOWN

I'm back. Last night went as planned but we need to move fast and fade back into our everyday. The police have nothing, which is a bonus, but it is our hard work that has kept them confused.

I think about all the things I asked him to do and now I regret it. This was my battle all along and I feel like shit for getting him involved but the reality is, I couldn't have done this on my own. I love him with all my heart but he's not cut out to do the things I'm used to doing. For some reason, I don't feel sad when they feel pain and I have a stomach of iron for the jobs that need doing. I bite my blood encrusted nails. Gross, I know, but right this second, I literally do not give a stuff. I took my time with Jamie but right now, time is a luxury I don't have. The police are everywhere.

As I walk the boards, a few drops of stagnant water leak on me. I inhale my jasmine perfume to try and conceal the stench of this place.

There's the shuffling sound again. She's awake and she's staring at that clock.

I snatch the syringe full of liquid and the kindest thing

would be to take away her anxiety for a few hours. But I'm not feeling very kind. No one can hear her. She's gagged and tied up and we are underground.

'Tick-tock. Tick-tock,' I whisper. 'Eleven o'clock is coming.' I adjust my night-vision goggles, hold my phone in one hand with the torch activated and the cheese wire in the other. 'Look after that finger for me.'

FIFTY-TWO

LAYLA

Layla popped her bag of crisps on the hospital chair next to her and grabbed her ringing phone. 'Hello.' She wiped her greasy fingers on her jeans and waited for the caller to speak.

'Layla, sorry to call you again.'

'Elle.' She recognised the voice. It was the woman who called the evening before, asking how Jamie was.

'Yes, it's me again.' The woman paused. 'I can't stop thinking about her.' Elle's voice cracked and she sniffed.

'How do you know my sister?' She knew nothing at all about Elle and she had hung up on her abruptly last night.

'We, err...' She blew her nose and coughed. 'We live together on the streets. You are her emergency contact and she said I had to call you if anything ever happened to her. We share a tent, or we did until just under a couple of weeks ago.'

Layla swallowed the lump in her throat. Her sister had been with that monster for nearly two weeks.

'I love her. We love each other and we were getting sorted.'

Eyes welling up, Layla held her hand over the mouthpiece while she let out a sob. 'I didn't know.'

'She was about to contact you, to tell you that she was on a methadone programme. We've been each other's strength through the worst of it. We wanted to get better, get jobs and then get a flat together. Jamie loves cats. She wanted a cat and I wanted one too. We want a life together. So, you see, when you told me that she's in a coma and she might not pull through, my life was ripped apart. All those dreams are now in the air and I keep thinking about how I'll cope if I lose her. After I called you, I stormed out of my tent and straight up to my dealer and I bought the first wrap in months. Since then, I've held it in my hand and...' Elle burst into tears.

Layla felt the woman's pain, the same pain she was also suffering. If her sister loved Elle then the best thing that Layla could do for Jamie was to make sure Elle didn't inject herself with that poison; the same poison that had ruined Layla's relationship with her sister. 'Please don't take it. Jamie wouldn't want that. I know my sister and I know she loves deeply. She's sensitive, she's kind and she'd want you to get better.'

'But she's not coming back,' the woman spat as she choked out another sob. 'I can't live without her. I keep thinking if I just inject a large dose in my veins, I can be with her. There is no reason to live without her.'

The pained scream coming through the earpiece reached straight into Layla's heart.

'Have you ever loved someone so much it hurts when you're not with them?'

She wiped her damp cheeks and thought of Sonny's dad and she wasn't sure he was the one. It appeared that her addict sister had reached a much higher level than her when it came to loving intensely. Layla could honestly say that she'd never had a love as intense as Elle and Layla have, although she loved Sonny more than anything. He definitely counted as the love of her life. If she lost him, she'd be beyond devastated. She loved her sister, that hurt like hell too, but the years had separated them.

'Jamie knows you have a baby. She loves him, you know.

You haven't seen her but she has seen you and she wanted nothing more than to be the best aunt one day. That's why she was trying so hard to recover. She loves the nephew she's never met and she loves you. That's why I love her. She has a huge heart. I can't believe I've lost such a beautiful human being.' The words through her tears were barely coherent but Layla knew exactly what Elle was saying.

Anger mixed with Layla's sadness. Why had Jamie not come up to her to say hello? She imagined her sister, scared while she hid and watching in the hope that being a part of Layla's and Sonny's life was her future. 'I lied to you earlier.' She choked on a tear. 'She woke up briefly. She's sedated at the moment but I think she'll be okay.'

'Why would you lie to me? That's horrible.'

'I had to, I'm sorry. I didn't know who you were when you called.'

'You made me think she was dead. Is she at Cleevesford General?'

'I'm not allowed to say.'

'Says who?'

'A police officer is guarding her room. No one can hurt her. The police want us to keep that information quiet.'

Elle went silent.

'Elle.'

After a while of tussling with her inner thoughts, Layla knew she had to call DI Harte. 'Hello, I think I've just made a huge mistake.'

FIFTY-THREE

UNKNOWN

'No, no, no, no, no!' I tap my head over and over again as I pace above them, my low heels clacking on the stone floor. This isn't how I planned it. Everything is out of hand and I don't know what to do. Think, think.

Hurrying downstairs, I pull the goggles back on so I can see. I almost slide down the stone steps on a pile of slimy moss where the water has constantly leaked on it. This building needs so much work but really, that isn't my problem. My main problem is not breaking an ankle and getting stuck down here. After regaining my balance, I take the steps slower and I turn into the first room. I've been so used to the mouldy smell, it barely affected me before but now, it's making me want to heave. I flick the apple-scented car air freshener in the hope of getting something from it but the scent is overpowered.

I stare at the lump under the old grey blanket, the type my grandmother would use to make a bed with, the type that would have a person scratching all night. To me, they're nothing more than dog blankets, destined to end up at animal shelters but Shannon and Darcie are animals. Darcie hasn't moved all morning and that's probably for the best. I noticed that her finger was raging and infected so given that deep down I'm a compassionate person, I gave her a shot of ketamine. That's when her shallow breathing became even shallower. Nature is nicely taking its course; besides, no one will find us here. No one knows about this place. I press my lips together as I contemplate my failures. Jamie escaped. I was too trusting with her. She looked so weak, I had no idea she even had it in her to get so far but I should know, life finds a way. As for Darcie, I should really just finish her off.

Taking a few steps closer, I feel the rough blanket for that rise and fall. Why am I so reluctant to pull the blanket back? It's not like I haven't seen death before. Maybe I'm going soft or maybe this is too personal.

The past brings a tear to my eye but now is not the time to get all emotional.

My chest starts to tighten so I hurry out of the first room, avoiding the dripping water as I unlock the second door and scoot in.

'Shannon, it's time.' Mask on, goggles on and gloves on, I pick up the cheese wire from the stainless-steel table on wheels. Now this is more like it. 'I know I said to look out for eleven o'clock but things are moving faster than I hoped.'

A part of me wants to know if she remembers but another part doesn't want to hear her speak. If I hear her, I might crumble and that can't happen. If that happens, the person I love the most will be at risk. No one has seen his face but they will make the connection if I'm caught. Or will they? These two aren't going to live to tell the tale and Jamie might not have seen me properly.

Shannon lets out muffled cries so I pull the gag from her. Maybe I do want to hear her scream when I slice her finger off. She needs to know how it felt for the one I loved so much. She came into my life last year, I didn't infiltrate myself into hers. This is all her doing. Jamie and Darcie's suffering are on her. I was happy until then, well, as happy as can be. I guess I'd buried the past. I definitely hadn't accepted it; it was more like I lived with it. Yes, Darcie, Shannon and Jamie just continued without a care in the world. Jamie had her problems but that was because of her alcoholic mum. If anyone wanted to know who the psychopaths in this scenario were, it's them, not me. A tear drizzles down my face.

'Let me go, you psychotic bitch,' she yells as she coughs and spits water from her lungs. Okay, not quite what I expected. Darcie was gentler. She begged and pleaded.

'You still don't know or get it, do you?'

'I know enough. You're deranged.'

No, that's not true. She's the deranged one. They all are. They're the psychos.

'You know something?' she splutters. 'I'd planned to beg you to let me go and I thought, well Darcie probably already did that and I can no longer hear her so I guessed you killed her anyway. Pleading won't work with you. You might kill me but I'm not giving you the smug satisfaction of seeing me beg.' She jerked on the table, making everything rattle.

She is everything I remembered, the 'it' girl, the bully, the one who took him from me so I let rip. I tell her everything like I'm spelling it out to a five-year-old and then I see the shock on her face. She wasn't expecting any of that. Her screams bounce off the walls, sending me hurtling to the back wall. I can't stand it. It's time to show the bitch that I mean business and that means getting a move on. Jamie is awake and my time is limited.

With a snot-filled nose and teary eyes, I grab the cheese wire, wrap it around her finger and pull hard on the sticks it's tied around until I slice through her finger, finishing it off with a bone saw. 'I don't care if you beg or not. I don't care if you hurl abuse at me. This is for him,' I yell as I finish cutting her finger off and place it in a bag. I have an urgent delivery to make and it can't wait.

Now is the time to implement plan B. I leave Shannon screaming and swearing and shut all the doors, containing most of the noise.

Grabbing a pen and a sheet of paper from my bag, I start writing. I will go down for this to protect *him* and I'll do it in style. I hear a cracking sound from above so I hide the paper underneath my metal tray. Someone is coming. I'm guessing it could be over.

FIFTY-FOUR

Gina drew the call from Layla to an end and threw the rest of the sandwich that she'd bought from the garage onto the back seat of the car in its packaging. She had a feeling she wouldn't be eating again until much later that night. 'You have to take that phone straight to the station, see if we can get the caller's location.' She doubted that the caller would have the phone any more but it was worth a try.

Jacob finished eating his wrap.

Layla replied, 'I'm so sorry. Please make sure Jamie's okay and that no one will hurt her.'

'There is an officer outside her room and no one can enter intensive care without being buzzed in.'

'I'm going to the station now.'

'Thank you, Layla.'

'Are the other women going to get killed now, because of me?'

Gina felt her throat swelling slightly so she cleared her throat. Layla had told the kidnapper everything, now they had nothing to lose. There was every chance that if Shannon and

Darcie had been alive, they were in huge trouble right now. That thought was making her nauseous.

As Gina put her seat belt back on, she filled Jacob in on the other side of her phone conversation. 'Can you message O'Connor, please? Update him and let him know that Layla is on her way. Also tell him that we think the kidnapper knows that Jamie is alive which puts the others at even greater risk.'

'I'm so worried for them, guv.'

'I am too.'

He began tapping away as Gina started the car and pulled away. Her phone rang. She accepted it on loudspeaker while she continued to drive. 'Hello.'

'Guv,' O'Connor said. 'I'm just including you in on the call from the officers tailing Finn Sampson.'

Her phone signal wavered, making what she and Jacob were listening to a bit choppy. '... heading along Birch Road... straight on at the island. He's speeding up. I'm not sure if he's in a hurry or he's spotted us... sharp left.' Gina pulled over to continue listening. 'Straight on over the island. Straight on again. Right at View Place.'

'He's heading home,' Gina said as she pictured View Place in her head. That road led to another that joined Brickford Close.

'You're right,' O'Connor said.

The officer tailing him continued. 'Yes, we're just entering Brickford Close. Another car has pulled up behind us. We're on standby.'

'What's he doing now?' Gina asked, hoping the officer would hear her. She also wondered if the person claiming to be Elle had already called him with the news about Jamie.

'He's just parked on his drive. A woman has opened the door. She looks angry and she's holding a baby. He's barging in and now he's closed the door.'

Gina hit the steering wheel not knowing how to play the

next move. Do they go in and arrest him under suspicion at the risk Darcie and Shannon might be hidden somewhere else, a place they might never find, or do they continue to watch? Was he arguing with the woman about Jamie being a threat to them, or is it something else?

'Guv?' O'Connor said. 'One of Finn Sampson's neighbouring businesses said that he's been asked not to tell anyone where the new premises will be. It's not registered under Finn's name with HMRC or Companies House because it's a new onsite service that Shoreford's will be offering. Gordon Shoreford owns this unit and has applied for permission to turn it into a garage. It's the closest one to the showroom, directly behind Shoreford's.'

Gina's heart began to race. All that time, a possible scene was under their noses. 'Send a team over now and keep eyes on Finn. He cannot get to Darcie and Shannon. We have reason to believe that they are being held there.' She swallowed. 'If we're wrong, we could put them in more danger. Be ready to arrest Finn and the woman on my say.' Gina wondered if she was Elle.

The officer watching Finn murmured an acknowledgement.

'We're heading to Shoreford's now.' Gina ended the call and put the car into gear, ready to hopefully release Darcie and Shannon from the hell they'd been living in before it was too late.

FIFTY-FIVE

Gina waited until three other police cars turned up, each containing two officers. There was no way Briggs would be happy if she barged in with just Jacob, putting them in potential danger. PC Smith got out of one car and PC Ahmed hurried out of another. Gina cleared her throat and gestured to Jacob to follow her.

Gordon Shoreford was sitting at the main desk in the empty showroom. He dropped his fork into a Pot Noodle cup and leaned back in his chair. 'What's happening? Why are there so many police officers here?' He grabbed a tissue and wiped his mouth.

Gina stepped to the front. 'Mr Shoreford, we need access to your unit at the back of the building.' The way he stared back at her was like he wasn't expecting her to ask for that at all.

'Really? It's not even fully operational yet.'

'Who has a key to it?'

'Er, just me and Finn. We'd been toying with the idea of bringing his mechanical and valeting services on site here and then we decided it would be the best idea.' He looked down. 'We're not fully or officially set up yet, but I know Finn brought a van there to work on. He dropped a tyre off earlier and he may have left it in the unit. I can't be in trouble for that, so has something happened? Have you found Darcie and Shannon?'

Gina glanced back and saw PC Ahmed holding the battering ram.

'Why is he holding that thing?' Gordon asked.

'We have reason to believe that Shannon Calder and Darcie Fletcher are being held in that building and I need immediate access. If you can't give us access, then you leave us no option but to gain entry by force. Two lives are at risk. I'd really appreciate it if you gave me the key.'

He stood and nodded. 'Of course, you should have just said that in the first place. I'll get you the key.' He began to back away towards his office. Gina knew the building would be surrounded should he try to run. 'It's ridiculous that you think they're in there. Don't you think I would have noticed someone shifty coming and going?'

Gina knew he wouldn't even blink an eyelid at seeing Finn around. She followed him into his office and watched as he slid his top drawer open. He rummaged and scrunched his brow before opening the second and third drawer. Only then did he pull out the key. 'There they are. I must have accidentally put them back in that drawer.' He passed the key to Gina. 'There are two keys. The main key and the padlock key.'

Hurrying out, leaving Gordon sitting in his office with a PC, she left the main door of Shoreford's with several PCs following and ran around the back with Jacob to where the unit was situated. She unlocked the padlock. As it clicked open, the thin chain that had been threaded through the handles fell to the pavement. She inserted the main key into the keyhole, unlocking the huge car-sized doors. The two-storey industrial building stood oppressively above her, almost blocking all the light from the little that was cast from the dull sky.

As she pushed the door open, she could see that the unit

was almost bare except for a large workbench alongside one wall. She led the way into the large, vacuous building, each footstep echoing. Corey Lowe's van was parked up in the middle of the huge room. Gina noticed that the tyre the officer saw Finn deliver had gone from outside and there was now a tyre on the workbench. Someone had been in the unit since and it wasn't Finn. The woman, someone else helping Finn, or Gordon Shoreford had to have left it there. She snapped a pair of latex gloves on and headed to the back of the room where she opened another door. It led to some stone stairs leading up and another set leading down. Jacob flicked the light switch and led the way down.

Gina called out. 'Darcie, Shannon. It's the police.' She was well aware that the unknown perpetrator could also be down there and with nothing to lose, they might be entering a hostage situation. She questioned how sure she was that Finn was the perpetrator.

As they reached the bottom, there were two doors. She nudged the first one and there was a filing cabinet in it. A smell of rot hit her nostrils as Jacob went to open the second door. That's when she spotted the dead rat in the middle of the room, underneath a desk. She recoiled and stepped back, relieved that the smell of rot wasn't coming from Darcie or Shannon.

An officer called down. 'Upstairs is clear. It's just a mezzanine full of tools and equipment.'

Jacob led the way back up the stairs. Gina's shoulders slumped. As they reached the main room again, she glanced around for anything that might help. There were no clocks and no boats. Those were clues left by the kidnapper or kidnappers, and they weren't leading them here.

She walked over to the tyre on the bench and gasped at what she saw positioned in the middle of it. A little plastic bag and a bloody finger. Gina felt her sandwich rising at the back of her throat and she swallowed. How the hell had they missed that? She grabbed her phone and called O'Connor. 'Go ahead and arrest Finn and the woman.'

'The plot thickens,' he replied. 'Anna Heard has just turned up at Finn's, her eyes streaked with tears.'

'Bring them in, all three of them. We'll bring Gordon Shoreford in, too. He has a lot of explaining to do, too. And call Bernard. We have another scene.'

FIFTY-SIX

SHANNON

The pain in Shannon's hand began to throb. It was all making sense now. How could she not have known?

The baby kept crying. Was it real? No one would bring a baby to such a horrid place. It was her imagination. The drugs she'd been given were playing with her mind again. The cries turned into Barney's whines. She prised an eye open and watched the clock above.

Tick-tock. Tick-tock. That sound was like torture. So loud and intrusive. It was as if each tick and tock had wormed their way into her ears. That's when she felt the worms and the itching. Then a slimy wriggler dropped from the ceiling onto her neck. She closed her eyes. There is no worm. It's the leftover drug in her system. It was just a leak.

The more she tried to ignore the crying the louder she imagined Barney's cries. Tears slipped from her eyes and she let out a sob. There was no point screaming.

The whining and the ticking boomed through her mind. She sobbed until she was breathless. Her breathlessness turned to choking and gasping. She couldn't breathe.

FIFTY-SEVEN

'What do we have?' Gina asked O'Connor as she burst into the room. Jacob closed the door behind them. Wyre rolled on her chair from a desk to the central table and Kapoor remained in front of a screen. Gina could see that she appeared to be reading newspaper articles.

O'Connor walked over from the window and closed the blinds to the reporters who were hungry for more of the story. It had swept the nation almost immediately and now all eyes were on how Cleevesford handled the investigation. 'We have Finn, Gordon and Anna in custody. The other woman was Finn's sister, Joy, and she had her baby with her. She couldn't leave the baby with their father as he is too ill to look after the little one and she was just there to care for him.'

'They were arguing.'

'Yes, because Finn's father has a hospital appointment later and Finn failed to tell her and she was meant to be home by then. She showed the officer the appointment card.'

'What happened when Anna turned up?'

'From what the officer who arrested her said, she started shouting when Finn answered the door but the PC couldn't hear what she was saying. They were both bundled into separate police cars and booked in. Their solicitors have turned up and are speaking to them now. We have everything from Shannon's phone through now. It makes interesting reading, especially if you read some of the messages that Finn sent to her.'

She glanced at the printouts that O'Connor passed her. 'He was terrorising her.'

'There was a tracking app on her phone too so he would have known where she was at all times.'

'Damn.'

O'Connor thrust more pages at her. 'We also have everything from Anna's phone and Finn's phone here.'

She quickly scanned over the pages. Finn's were the same as the ones she'd read on Shannon's phone and there were a few more of him flirting with women he'd appeared to have met on a dating app. Anna's contained messages to Darcie arranging their night at hers. Nothing sinister came before or after the night Darcie was taken, Anna had tried to call Finn over and over again. 'How about Gordon's phone?'

'Gordon Shoreford called Finn around the time that Shannon was taken.' O'Connor passed her the last printout.

A PC pushed the door open. 'Anna Heard is ready for interview. I've taken her to interview room three.'

Gina thanked the PC and looked back across at O'Connor. 'Good work. Keep digging. The answers are in the past. Also, Wyre can you head over to the school to speak to May Chandler. She was going to call a couple of colleagues who worked at the school at the same time our victims attended?'

Wyre nodded.

'O'Connor, could you and Kapoor take a bit of time out of reading old articles to interview Gordon Shoreford?' There may not be anything on his phone but the search of Shoreford's that was taking place could reveal a hidden phone. With all of them in custody on suspicion of kidnap, she was feeling the pressure to get results. Her mind bounced back to Corey Lowe who was still also in custody and then his friend, Tyler Job. They were juggling too many balls right now.

Gina left the room with Jacob. As they entered the interview room, Anna sat hunched forward over the desk, streaks of make-up down her face. She was alone. 'Where is your solicitor?'

Anna shrugged. 'Probably gone out for a late lunch. I sent him away. I don't need a solicitor because I haven't done anything, let alone kidnap anyone.'

Jacob introduced them for the tape, ready for the interview to begin.

Time was running out. The words that Jamie had spoken filled Gina's thoughts. Tick-tock. Tick-tock. 'It's your right to not use a solicitor so we'll begin. Anna, where are Shannon and Darcie?'

'I don't know.' Her blonde hair had clumped and one of her nails had chipped.

'Why were you at Finn Sampson's today?'

'I wanted to talk to him so I went to his house. Is that a crime?'

'Elle?' Gina had to try and see if Anna responded.

Anna scrunched her nose and furrowed her brows. 'Sorry?'

'Elle, that's a name you use, isn't it?'

'Are you crazy? First you accuse me of kidnapping my friends, then you think I'm pretending to be someone else.'

Gina shook her head. 'Friends. It's funny how the past never leaves a person. It's hard being rejected. They rejected you, didn't they? Darcie got that job with Shannon and they left you out. I can understand why you'd want to take it out on them, but how did you get Finn Sampson involved?'

'I didn't. This is mad. I haven't taken anyone and you think I'd go as far as kidnap because Darcie and Shannon were leaving me out of things. I'm not a child.'

'Finn was in the area on the night that Darcie was taken. You told us yourself. I've also seen the messages he sent to Shannon. He was begging her to give him another chance only this week.'

Anna leaned back and folded her arms. 'I guessed as much. That's why I went over today. I wanted to have it all out with him but I am not involved in any kidnapping and you don't have any proof. Why? Because I didn't do it. You've taken my house keys off me. Go there, search everything. Take my car, check my phone, do what the hell you like.'

Gina knew that a team of officers would already be there given that she'd been arrested. 'Where were you this morning?'

'With my sister. I stayed there last night. Call her and check. Her number is in the phone that you have under Little Sis. I spent half of yesterday evening crying in my wine over Finn. I called him and spoke to him in the early hours but he was being horrible, so I went over to his earlier, fuming and wanting answers about our relationship. It's that simple.'

Gina now knew who was on the other end of the phone conversation that Finn was having on his drive. 'Has Finn told you where Darcie and Shannon are?'

'No.'

'Have you been to Shoreford's this morning?' She wondered if Finn gave her his key so she could plant the finger in the new unit.

'No, ask my sister. Or better still, check my maps records on my phone. They'll show you everywhere I've been. I never travel without satnav even when I know where I'm going, just in case there's traffic. I haven't been anywhere near Shoreford's.' She paused and unfolded her arms. 'I don't trust Finn. He hasn't said anything to me but he's cold and he's a great liar. It's a shame it took all this to make me see. His intensity scares me a little. At first, I thought it was attractive but right now, I'd say he's behind all this.'

'Has Finn ever mentioned Jamie Purvis to you?'

Anna shook her head. 'No, but if Jamie is a woman, he knows a lot of women.'

A few minutes later, Gina wrapped up the interview and Anna was taken back to her cell. Once a search of Anna's house and car had been completed, along with a check of her whereabouts, they'd have to let her go if nothing was found.

Jacob stood and gathered up his interview pad. 'I think she's telling the truth.'

'I do too which pins everything on Finn and Gordon. We still have an unknown woman potentially called Elle. I still can't link Finn to Jamie. What the hell am I missing? Shoreford's is central to this. We're looking for someone who drives and smokes cigarettes. Again, Jamie is the confusing piece of the puzzle. There is no link to her and Shoreford's, but we found what probably is Shannon's finger there earlier. The kidnapper is either toying with us or maybe they're trying to frame Finn. We have to consider that. We need to keep Corey Lowe for longer. It's still on my mind that he went to school with all three women and his connection to Shoreford's is Darcie and Shannon. I know he's here but if he's working with someone, they might be continuing with the plan. Who is Elle? She is the key to all this. I have a feeling Elle is right under our nose.'

Just as they were about to leave the interview room, O'Connor walked in. 'Lowe's solicitor has stepped in and we've had to bail him until he appears at the Magistrates Court, which will be in three to four weeks. The CPS have agreed the charges of common assault of Monica Bell and assault of an emergency worker for yourself, guv.' O'Connor glanced up the corridor and left them to take in the news.

'Damn.' Gina slammed her fist on the table. The last thing she needed was Lowe back out there while they were still trying to work out who had kidnapped Darcie and Shannon.

FIFTY-EIGHT

O'Connor came back five minutes later, his face a bit red and puffy from all the darting back and forth. Jacob had kept refreshing emails to see if anything had come back from the searches at Shoreford's. 'Finn Sampson is with his solicitor in interview room one and Kapoor and I are about to interview Mr Shoreford.'

'Thank you. Question Mr Shoreford about his call to Finn near the time Shannon was taken. We'll do the same with Finn.' They left one interview room and stepped straight into another.

Finn's dark hair shone under the light. He hunched over the table with his head in his hands, avoiding anyone's gaze. Jacob and Gina sat, then Jacob did all the introductions for the recording again. Finn's solicitor sat in the corner, steely eyed and still.

Gina couldn't believe how time was escaping them. It was almost five. Darcie and Shannon were depending on her getting what they needed from Finn Sampson but experience told her that he'd answer mostly with 'no comment'.

'This afternoon we found a severed finger at your new workshop, the unit behind Shoreford's. How did it get there?'

She knew that Finn hadn't actually placed it there as their officers had been tailing him all day. Her mind bounced back to Gordon Shoreford but, then again, Jamie Purvis had mentioned a woman and their mystery caller, Elle, was also a woman. Racing thoughts took over her mind. Maybe Gordon Shoreford had used some sort of software to disguise his voice. He had a key to the unit. Jamie – had she really been held by a woman? Maybe the ketamine and other drugs used to treat her at the hospital did nothing more than confuse her. Panic struck. If a look into Anna's whereabouts came back clean and she had an alibi, then she'd be ruled out as a suspect. Gina was fast running out of suspects, especially female ones.

Finn hadn't said a word in response to her question.

'Mr Sampson, two women are missing and one nearly died in hospital. This is serious. Who did you get to place the severed finger in your new workshop?'

He huffed and smirked. 'You lot followed me all day. You tell me. Oh wait, you can't because you can't prove I did anything.'

'I saw the messages on your phone to Shannon. It sounded very much like you were stalking her. You stalked her, you scared her, then you kidnapped her, didn't you? You knew that her security light was broken because you broke it. She is your ex. You had a key to her house and you let yourself in, where you watched her from her own loft. Where is she?'

'You really are a shit detective. For the record, I'm admitting that I sent her a few messages and that I had a key, but I gave the key back to her. I have never been in her house without her being present. I know Shannon's routine and I went to her house to try to talk to her just before she got home from work and I noticed that her security light was broken so I sent a few pranky messages. Stupid – yes, especially as I knew she'd be out walking alone in the dark, but at the end of the day, I wanted her to meet up with me so we could talk and she wouldn't.'

'So, you thought scaring her was the answer?'

He shrugged. His solicitor whispered a few words in his ear but he continued. 'It was a joke. Besides, as I was leaving, another man turned up and went straight into her garden.'

Gina knew that Finn was referring to Kyle Fletcher. He'd already told her that he visited Shannon that night but it got her mind whirring. Kyle had an alibi for the night Darcie was taken and why would he conspire with someone else to take his own sister? And if he did, why also Jamie and Shannon? She swallowed. Maybe she hadn't investigated Kyle hard enough. Had Kyle's husband been telling the truth about Kyle's whereabouts? She quickly flicked a few pages and saw a note stating that the family liaison officer, Ellyn, had been with him during the time Shannon had been taken and she'd reported nothing suspicious.

'Where did you go after that?'

'Home, to look after Dad.'

'Anna Heard claims that at seven thirty on the evening of the twenty-ninth of February, you were heading to hers. She contacted you to tell you not to come but you stayed there watching them, didn't you? A witness describes seeing a man loitering at the back of Anna's garden gate around eight on Thursday and on that same evening, another couple claim to have seen a man sitting in a dark-coloured car by the Welcome to Hutton sign around ten thirty.' Gina know the Swadlings' didn't mention a midnight-blue Capri but Mrs Swadling did claim to see a dark-coloured car and Finn had one of those. 'One of the witnesses saw the man smoking. You're a smoker, aren't you, Mr Sampson?'

'Yes, but so are lots of other people.'

'We have cigarette butts taken from the scenes. When the forensics report comes back, if they are yours, we will know.'

'They're not mine. I wasn't there. Anna told me not to come over and I was pissed with her because I don't get much time with Dad needing me. He was fairly settled that evening which is why I was heading to hers, but after she contacted me I went home. In fact, I think the neighbour was just going out as I pulled up. He's always admiring my car and talking about it. I had new wheels and he said they were cool. He'll remember.'

'What's the neighbour's name?'

'Fabio. Don't know his surname.'

Gina waited for Jacob to list that as something to check.

'Where were you on Saturday the second of March at eight that evening?'

'I stayed in with Dad that night.'

'Was anyone else with you?'

'No, but I called my sister to tell her that Dad hadn't had the best evening. His emotions are all over the place but then they would be, wouldn't they? He's got Parkinson's. He gets scared and angry at times, not to mention frustrated when he can't do some things. Check my call log on my phone.'

'We have. Why did Gordon Shoreford call you on the evening Shannon was taken?'

'He just wanted to talk about a car I needed to fix.' He glanced to the side and then his gaze met hers again.

'Who are you working with?'

'I'm not.'

'How do you know Jamie Purvis?'

He raised his dark brows and tugged at a loose thread that dangled from his sweatshirt. 'I don't think I know a Jamie.' He looked aside. 'Do I?'

'Do you?'

'Name rings a bell but I can't think why.'

'Who's Elle?'

'Seriously.' He shrugged.

'Answer the questions, please.' Gina gripped the side of the plastic seat in her hands, frustrated at the lack of useful information coming from Anna and Finn.

'I don't know anyone by that name.'

'Back to the finger. How could it have appeared in your lock-up.'

He grabbed his hair and roared. 'It's not my bloody lock-up.' He took a couple of deep breaths and paused. 'It's Gordon's. I can't afford the rent on mine any more. He threw me a lifeline. I don't even own or rent it. I'll be working for Gordon. I have started planning the refit but that's it. I don't go there.'

'But you had Corey Lowe's VW Caddy van in there. You collected a tyre earlier and left it outside.'

'Yes, I was meant to fix the van. It needs a few minor repairs, including a tyre change, and I was going to do them at the new unit, to give it a whirl. A lot of my tools are on the mezzanine. Mr Lowe said it wasn't urgent as he had another vehicle to use. I'd been busy with all my other jobs and dealing with my dad. Before you get any ideas, Gordon wouldn't have gone in there either. He has zero interest in that building and the man is scared to death of blood. I cut myself once and the bloke almost puked. There's no way he could cut someone's finger off and then pick it up and move it.' He stopped speaking and combed his fingers through his hair. 'I know there was a prick harassing Darcie, trying it on with her when she went out with him for test drives. Maybe it was him. I know Darcie had fallen out with her brother. Maybe it was him. Both of these people will have met Darcie and Shannon. Who knows about the other person you mentioned, Jamie. I sent some stupid messages to Shannon—'

'Harassing messages.'

'Whatever. I sent those messages, I admit that. You've seen what's in my phone and you've probably come up with the word, player. I am that. I am not a nice person, but I'm not a bloody kidnapper and I wouldn't cut anyone's fingers off.'

'What were you and Anna arguing about earlier when she came to your house?'

'Her, she's clingy and a pain in the arse. I can't believe she came. I didn't even know she had my address.' He scrunched his brows. 'In fact, how did she get it? That sounds stalkerish to me.'

Gina raised her brows and sighed. Anna had already told them; she'd seen a letter with Finn's address on it. She glanced at the wall clock and the tick-tock sounded through her mind, reminding her that the kidnapper knew about Jamie and they were running out of time.

'Wait, I knew I recognised the name, Jamie.' He held a finger up and closed his eyes in concentration for a few seconds before continuing.

'Go on.'

'Shannon was quite an emotional person and really clingy. I admit, we used to drink a lot together. I just thought it was a bit of fun but she read more into what we had. I never lied to her. I told her I didn't want a relationship.'

'Tell me about Jamie.' Gina needed him to hurry. She was glad Finn hadn't gone no comment all the way through but the man could talk and she needed him to get to the point. Right now, she really didn't like Finn, but her instinct screamed that he was speaking the truth.

'Anyway, she thought she saw someone from her past on one of the occasions when she took her riffy dog to the vets last year. She said that she and this woman had gone to school together. Shannon seemed quite upset after. Next to the vets was a takeaway and this woman was going through the bins and eating whatever food she could find. She said she felt like the most horrible person in the world for not going up to her and helping her. In fact, I sat with her while she berated herself for not buying the woman some food. Anyway, we both got quite drunk and she started crying, saying that she'd done something terrible when they were at school. I told her not to worry about it, that I'd done lots of things I wasn't proud of. She said this was different and seeing that woman at the bins had brought it all back. I'm sure that she said the woman's name was Jamie.'

FIFTY-NINE

LAYLA

The kind nurse at the hospital had told her to go and rest for a while. Jamie was still sleeping and they didn't want her to get upset, like she had been earlier. Layla had taken her phone to the station earlier but it looked like Elle, or whoever the messenger was, had used a burner phone. As she approached the bus stop, she shivered as she waited. All she wanted was to go home and cuddle Sonny until she could speak to Jamie again. She tried to call *him* but as usual, he didn't answer.

She gazed up and down the road, watching the tail end of the work traffic pass by. Her phone rang. She answered immediately. 'Where have you been?'

'Just busy, sorry. I have Sonny so I can pick you up and take you home now. Where are you?'

She hadn't asked him to pick Sonny up but he'd done her a favour. She had no energy for small talk of any kind today. 'I'm at the bus stop on Lamburn Road.' She was angry that he hadn't been there for her when she needed him but she understood he had a job to do too. It's a good job Sonny's nan had stepped in to help. There was no way she'd have left him with her mother.

'On my way. Love you.' Just as he hung up, she heard her baby crying and her arms longed to soothe him. She was so lucky in every way and it had taken such tragedy to appreciate that. Jamie had nothing and no one. Layla had her baby, she had a good job and her own home, and she had a man who she thought she loved. Who was she kidding, she did love him, despite him going a bit AWOL recently. People would look at them when they saw them as a couple, but she was no longer going to let that hold her back. He was Sonny's father and they were going to be a family. She had to give him a chance to prove himself, despite her mind telling her to run away and bring Sonny up alone.

He pulled up in the brown Volvo and smiled. She glanced through the window at the back seats and saw that Sonny was fast asleep in his baby seat, his dummy dangling from his bottom lip. She got in and kissed her man but then recoiled. He stank and it wasn't pleasant. The apple-scented air freshener dangling from the rear-view mirror could not disguise the scent of decay emanating from his pores, or was it urine? He was wearing overalls and work boots.

'What is it?' he asked, his genuine-looking smile reaching his eyes. Normally, she'd love nothing more than to grab his smooth face and kiss him again but not now.

'It smells bad in here.'

'Does it?' He grimaced. 'I can't smell anything. Are you sure you're alright?'

She leaned in to smell the air freshener and she could smell apple. Did that mean there was nothing wrong with her nose? She knew when she was being gaslit. 'Why are you wearing those clothes?'

'I had to, err, unblock a drain.'

He never mentioned any blocked drain to her. She went to open the door but it was locked. 'What's going on?'

'Oh, just child locks. I want Sonny to be safe in the car.'

'He's only a few weeks old and you've locked the passenger door.'

'Have I?'

She felt a chill running through her as he pulled away. 'Stop the car, now.' She glanced back at Sonny. 'Stop!' She went to grab the steering wheel to force him to pull over.

He went hurtling towards a lamppost and slammed the brakes on so hard the airbags filled their faces just as he clipped it. 'Do that again and I won't brake next time. Do you hear me?' His clenched teeth and white knuckles told her not to mess with him. He reached under his seat and pulled out a knife. She screamed as he sliced through the airbags and popped the knife back under his seat. Turning her head, she could see Sonny stirring but he was secured safely.

Tears ran down her cheeks. She had heard him loud and clear. He wasn't the man she knew and, in that moment, she knew it was him who'd hurt Jamie. Why, why, why is all she kept repeating in her head as she stifled her sobs. One wrong move and she knew he'd hurt her and their baby. He pulled over a little way down from the lamppost. After snatching the knife again, he pressed it against her neck, his arms shaking and rage in his stark eyes. 'I can't believe I bloody well got you pregnant. It was never meant to happen like this. It's just me and him from now on. He doesn't need murderers in his life.'

Murderers, where did that come from? He poked the tip of the knife into her skin and she screamed and banged on the window, but it was too late. No one was coming to help her and her precious baby boy.

SIXTY

Gina rushed back into the incident room with Jacob. Kapoor settled back into her chair and began reading old newspaper articles again and O'Connor joined them at the main table. Briggs appeared from the other end of the room and stared out of the window, pacing as he quietly rehearsed what he'd written for the next press release. 'O'Connor, how did the interview with Gordon go?'

'He prepared a statement that his solicitor read out which claims that he never went into the unit today and that he knows nothing about Darcie and Shannon's kidnappings. It also stated that he called Finn on the night Shannon was taken and they spoke about a car. Apart from that he went no comment all the way. It was over in no time. We've kept him in for now as Shoreford's is still being searched. I called PC Smith to ask how things were going but they haven't found anything incriminating. All the computers are being brought back to the station and handed to tech, but going through those will take a while. Garth in tech is happy for it to be a long night and he's making a start now. How about you? Did interviewing Anna and Finn yield anything?'

Gina relayed what had been said in the interviews.

Wyre hurried through the door, throwing her bag on the table.

'Did the teacher manage to contact her colleagues?' Gina's heart raced. They needed a break and she hoped the look on Wyre's face meant they had one.

Wyre smiled and brushed a stray hair away that had got caught in her lips. 'Yes. There was an incident about twenty years ago just before that group of friends went quiet and started falling out. The whole school had been quite subdued so this group of friends hadn't really stood out from the rest, but the one teacher knew that the boy involved had hung around with the girls a lot.'

'What incident?' Gina had just realised she was clenching her hands.

'A boy drowned that year. He'd apparently been out on a boat in a disused fishing lake. Do you remember Arundal's Fishing Lake and Lodge?'

Gina furrowed her brows. 'That hasn't been open since the mid-eighties.'

Wyre nodded in agreement. 'Well, a sixteen-year-old boy drowned there. There were drugs and alcohol found in his system and get this, it looked like his finger had got caught on some twine in the lake and it was severed. This information wasn't released to the public but it was released to his family at the time. I think they spoke to other people as the teacher said it had become common knowledge around the school. There was no suspicion surrounding the boy's death. As far as the coroner was concerned, it was an accident.'

'Do any of the teachers remember anything else?'

Wyre nodded. 'One seemed to think that the boy had a girl-friend but she only lasted one term before her dad removed her from the school and moved. There were rumours she was preg-nant but there wasn't any proof.'

'Do we know her name?'

'The teachers couldn't remember. As I said, she was only there one term.'

'What was the boy's name?'

'Oh, my goodness. Guv, you have to see this.' Kapoor moved away from her computer screen so that Gina could see the article she'd found.

Gina quickly scanned the article. 'The boy's name was Oliver Summers. Kapoor, get a team over to Joel Summers's address and bring him in now. He's been right under our noses all this time. I'm guessing that the others were involved in his father's death but they were never reported. We need his mother too. She's called Tina and she drops him off and picks him up from work all the time. He must have used her car. He doesn't drive or has he been driving her car?'

In her mind, she pictured Joel sneaking the keys from Gordon's drawer, maybe making a copy. He would have had access to Darcie and Shannon's personal things, which meant he could have easily got their keys and had them cut too. As for Jamie, she would have been a much easier target. 'Is Tina's surname Summers? Who checked Joel's alibi?'

Wyre spoke. 'I did and no.' As soon as Wyre reeled off Tina's surname, Gina knew exactly who she was.

'O'Connor, Wyre, Jacob – we need backup to assist us at Arundal's. If that place is still standing, Darcie and Shannon are likely to be there. Joel has gone back to where it all started on the year he was born. Let's go!'

As she went to follow the others out the door, Briggs pulled her back. 'Remember what I said about sticking to the rules. Don't just rush in there. Wait until all the backup officers have arrived and are in place. I don't want a repeat of the last case where you go it alone and put your life at risk.' His gaze lingered on hers for a few seconds. The last case was different and he knew it.

SIXTY-ONE

SHANNON

Barney is licking her face. 'Stop it, boy. Okay, okay. I'm getting up,' she mutters.

She opened her eyes and all she could see was the same blackness that she'd woken up to several times. There was no Barney. She was still trapped in the hellhole of a pit she knew she would die in, and she was still lying under the leak.

Was she dead? Shivering, she knew she needed the scratchy blanket that had been placed over her to be pulled up over her torso, not that it was doing much to keep the damp from seeping through to her core. 'Help,' she called. She tried to wriggle her legs a little to warm her up, but she was numb.

The woman ran in, a piece of paper in her hands and tears running down her unmasked face. A shaft of light reaching across the room made Shannon wince.

'It's you,' Shannon said, barely able to force her words out through her chattering teeth.

'You three took him from me that night and I have never been able to forgive you. When I saw you early last year, it hit me, like it was yesterday. It didn't take me long to work out where you lived and worked. I told *him* what you did and I've never seen him like that...'

Him, Shannon had no idea who she was on about.

'The way you ignored Jamie was ugly. You must be ashamed now. All year I boiled with rage from what you did, the fact that you were still walking around free after what you did. We watched you all the time and then you gave us Darcie on a plate. It was so handy, you and her working together. Still, all we did was watch and fantasise but you still kept coming back to me again and again.'

Going back where? Shannon wracked her brains, trying to think of where that could be.

'I knew that was a sign, it was like fate was saying, what the hell are you waiting for? I'm giving her to you on a plate. Then, just before Christmas, I finally listened to that persistent voice in my head. Of course, there was poor Jamie, always lurking around the streets trying to sell herself or score, she was by far the easiest. I knew she would be the first.' The kidnapper sighed.

'You didn't take me. It was someone else.' Shannon knew that a man had bundled her into the car. The woman in front of her was shorter.

'No, it was me. He knows about you but he has nothing to do with any of this. This was all down to me.'

'I know it wasn't.' The woman was lying. Shannon knew she was trying hard to protect the man. 'Where's Darcie?' Shannon coughed, her dry throat making her voice croaky. She tried to shift on the table, then a sharp pain went through her foot, making her wish she'd remained still.

'He lost a finger too, on the night you all left him.'

'He?' Shannon whimpered as the burning pain radiated out.

'Oliver. You three killed Oliver.'

Shannon swallowed down her tears. No way. That night

had finally come back to haunt her. 'He fell into the water. We all did. It was an accident.'

Her kidnapper slammed her hand down on the slab, rage in her eyes. 'You all ran away. I saw you. Not one of you stayed and called an ambulance or tried to save him from the lake. I was on the other side. I tried to call for you to help him as I ran around closer to where he'd fallen but none of you saw me. None of you had any idea he'd arranged to meet me there later that night, had you?'

'It was freezing...' Shannon cried through chattering teeth. The cold room was taking her right back to that night.

'And you couldn't handle being cold for a bit longer to save him?'

'We couldn't even see where he was in the lake.'

'So, you just ran away...' She paused. 'You felt what it was like to drown, didn't you?'

Shannon turned her head so she didn't have to look at the woman. After she waterboarded her, Shannon knew exactly what Oliver must have gone through. The fear, the panic, the powerlessness and finally death as his lungs filled with the filthy lake water. If she could go back now, she'd have insisted that they all stay there and try to get him out. Jamie had been anxious to leave with her little sister, Layla, who she always called Shrimp. The little girl had been vomiting after swallowing a lot of water. Their mother was pretty evil and would probably have beat them up if they weren't there when she got home from working at the petrol station. Darcie had simply given up and broken down and was talking no sense. It had been Shannon who had insisted they couldn't do anything else. It had been Shannon who told them all that there was no point calling an ambulance as they'd get done for murdering Oliver. That sounded pathetic in her head now. It was an accident... but then again, people put two and two together and get five. Would there be a question mark over all of their heads forever more? They were taking drugs and drinking. Murderers or victims of an accident?

'The fact that you encouraged them all to leave him and did nothing hurts, doesn't it? As soon as you all got out of that lake and ran away, I trudged in and swam over to that boat. It was eleven o'clock. I'll never forget. However hard I searched; I couldn't find him. I dove into that murky water over and over again.'

'I'm sorry.'

'Don't say that.'

'Why didn't you call the police?'

The kidnapper let out a laugh. 'It's ironic, isn't it? I shouldn't have been there either. I wasn't allowed to see Oliver any more. My father totally disapproved. He took me out of school once I told him I was pregnant and he said we were moving. He said if I saw Oliver again, he'd kill me and him. My own dad said that and I actually believed he would. I feared for my baby's life. I did what you lot did. I sneaked back in through my bedroom window, changed and went to bed with a broken heart, but at least I went to bed with a clear conscience. I did everything in my power, under the threat of death, to save Ollie. You lot left him to die.'

Shannon had been scared, they all had. They were just stupid kids not knowing how to handle a crisis that big and they had all grown up regretting every minute of that night. 'It was my fault. Please let Darcie go, if she's still alive. I told them all we had to go as soon as we'd dragged Layla out. Please, Darcie has a little girl. Cleo needs her. Do it for little Cleo.'

Her kidnapper sobbed as she untied Shannon's binds.

Weak from the drugs and the torture her body had survived, Shannon fell to the stone floor as the kidnapper dragged her off the cold slab of metal.

'Get up.'

'I can't.' Shannon lay like a jellyfish on the stone, unable to get her arms and legs to function properly. Her kidnapper started to drag her towards the door and into a small square space that led to the stone steps and another door. As she was dragged into the other room, a drop of rusty water from the leak above landed on her tongue. She needed a drink so badly. The kidnapper hurled her into a corner against a mossy old beer keg.

'Darcie.' Shannon spotted a lump under a blanket. 'Darcie,' Shannon croaked out again, but there was no movement. Shannon tried to hold her breath but all she heard was her own blood pumping through her body. She cried out as a more intense pain radiated from her hand to her elbow. There was no rise and fall of the blanket. Darcie had to be dead.

'It's time to end this.' Her kidnapper pulled a scalpel from her pocket and raised it above her head, not an inch of regret in her face.

'Please, it was an accident. My dog, Barney, needs me. You know he does.' Shannon furrowed her brows, wondering if she could remember the woman's name. She recognised her, but it was vague.

She shrugs. 'My son needs me more and as a mother, I will do everything in my power to protect him and his family. You know too much. It's over, Shannon.'

Shannon gasped as everything fell into place. She knew exactly who this woman was and she knew who had taken her. It was game over.

SIXTY-TWO

Gina drove up the bumpy mud road that led to the old fishing lodge and Jacob stared out the window at the trees towering over them. Surrounded by pitch-black dense woodland, Arundal's fishing lodge and lake had once been a popular estate until the owner folded the business, but did nothing more with the property. For years it had sat there, getting mouldy and crumbling. Gina felt her stomach fluttering with nerves as they got closer. She turned her car lights off as they neared the back of the lodge. The mud track was the only way in. If anyone tried to leave by car, they'd have to go through hers. The bare bones of the Swiss chalet-style roof stuck out above the trees partly open, allowing the elements to invade it.

'There's a light coming from inside.' Jacob paused. 'We should wait here for backup to arrive.'

She pulled up on the single-track road and killed the engine. Jacob's phone rang. He listened to the speaker then ended the call. 'A team of officers are on their way. Two cars are at the end of the mud path waiting for the others to arrive, and another two have pulled up on the main road. Several PCs are now making their way through the woodland on foot so we can surround the lodge from the back end. If anyone runs through the woodland, we'll have them. A police helicopter has been despatched should the suspects try to hide.'

She heard the whooshing of blades above. 'Can you grab the bolt cutters, just in case?'

He nodded and grabbed the tool off the back seat of her car.

'Let's go.'

They stepped out of the car all togged up with tasers, stab vests and truncheons at the ready. She was prepared to do whatever it would take to save their victims. She thought of Briggs. He'd be reeling if he knew she hadn't waited for the team to join them on the front line but Shannon and Darcie didn't have any more time. Gina tried to swallow but struggled as her heart palpitated in her throat. There was a chance she'd find them dead.

Her feet sunk in the mud and squelched with each step. Creatures rustled in the bushes and the helicopter circled, awaiting further instruction from the team below, the very team that were still at the entrance to the long path. She grabbed her phone and called Briggs.

He answered instantly. 'Gina.'

She spoke in a hushed tone as Jacob followed her. 'Backup will be with us soon. They're just waiting for the others to arrive. The chopper is in place. There are some PCs coming on foot through the woodland. In fact, I can see a torch wavering in the distance. Jacob and I are approaching.'

'Gina, I urge you to wait.'

She stopped. 'If I do, Shannon and Darcie might be killed. Every second matters right now. I have to do this. I would have done this before the last case.'

He paused for a few seconds and she knew he'd be pacing and running one of his meaty hands through his hair as he weighed up the dilemma they faced. Every second counted now the kidnapper felt threatened. 'Do you even have a plan?'

'Yes, the plan is to save Darcie and Shannon from Joel Summers and Christina Everly or Christy or Tina or Elle or whatever name she's going by today. I know I'm dealing with a twenty-year-old man and a thirty-five-year-old woman. Jacob and I are armed with tasers and we will use them if we need to, so there is no need to worry. The officers with torches are getting closer.'

He tutted. 'Put this conversation on loudspeaker so I can listen in. Are your body cams on?'

'Yep.' Gina shook her head and quickly turned hers on, glad that Briggs had mentioned them.

'Approach slowly and keep this call open. I won't speak again.'

She placed the phone sticking out of her pocket and beckoned Jacob to follow her alongside the trees. The closer she got the sicker she felt. The PCs in the woods were even closer now, she could hear their steps nudging through the brambles and twigs.

'Here,' Gina whispered to Jacob as she dragged him out of view from anyone that might be standing outside the lodge. As they got closer, she could see the back of what was left of the building. Scrawny trees had grown through the roof and the fence had fallen down. They wouldn't be needing the bolt cutters. Most of the walls still remained upright but all the windows had long gone. The half-moon shone above and reflected in the lake next to the lodge. Wind whistled through the trees sending a shiver through her. The weight of all the gear was making her sweat like mad underneath. Or was it nerves?

Two male PCs came around the building and she saw another approaching from the other side.

'Backup has arrived,' she whispered, hoping that Briggs could hear.

After checking each direction for movement, she beckoned

them all to close in on the entrance. That's when she spotted the body lying face down amongst the reeds. She did a quick check of the entrance to the lodge and the PCs had it covered.

'Body in the lake,' she called out as she darted towards it. She unclipped her stab vest and dropped that, along with all her gear and her phone, onto the slimy bank before stepping into the water fully booted. Trudging in, taking one laboured step after another, she pushed past the reeds until she reached the body. Facing down, hair splayed across the top of the lake, Gina grabbed the woman and gasped as she turned Christy over, before dragging her back to shore. She lay her flat and began administering CPR immediately. Breathing for the woman, followed by chest compressions.

'We need an ambulance,' she yelled as she continued. A PC ran to Gina and took over the chest pumps but it was too late. Christy Everly, the vet, was dead. Gina knew right then that she'd lied to them about being broken into. There was no intruder or black SUV parked outside the practice watching her. She'd sent them off on a fool's errand looking for intruders that didn't exist so she could take the ketamine from the practice she lied about owning. They'd also discovered that she only worked there.

'Joel, he could be in there.' Gina glanced back. There had been no sign of a car anywhere near the lodge.

Jacob called back. 'We're going in, guv.'

She stood and began putting her gear back on. While panting to get her breath back, she grabbed her phone with her dripping wet hands. 'Christy Everly is dead. We tried to revive her but she's gone. I'm going to hang up now. We're going in.'

Sopping wet and shivering, Gina tailed behind Jacob and four PCs. Several others joined them in surrounding the building and the helicopter remained above. She stepped through the doorless gap in the brickwork onto several collapsed beams. Old sofas with lichen and moss growing out of them had been tipped up and torn apart. The old bar remained in place but years of neglect and vandalism had taken its toll. A beam above creaked.

'Step with care,' she called out. A torch had been left on the ground. That's where the light had been coming from.

'I've found stairs to a basement,' one of the PCs called out.

Gina hurried to where his voice had come from, stepping over the debris consisting of old bottles, broken glass, damp wood and litter. 'This must have been the beer cellar back in the day.'

Drip sounds came from below, leading the way. She shuffled towards the doorframe and followed the PC and Jacob down the slimy stone stairs. Their breath echoed in the tiny space. 'Darcie, Shannon. It's the police. Shout if you can hear me,' Gina called through chattering teeth. Her limbs were stiffening in the cold.

A murmur came from below.

'There's someone down there.' She stopped. What if they continued on and Joel was waiting to ambush them? 'Take it slowly. We are one perp down but we believe there is another perp.'

The PC nodded and continued slowly while gripping his truncheon.

'Help,' said a woman in a croaky voice.

'Go.' Gina followed them to the small square bit of flooring that led to two closed doors. Torch light filled the tiny space. She pressed the door handle to the left down and recoiled as the smell hit her. In the middle of the room was a metal tilting table on wheels with a stainless-steel table next to it. A bin containing empty syringes sat next to the door, but there was no one in the room, and a pair of night-vision goggles lay on the floor, tangled in wire.

Jacob opened the other door and Gina nudged through. The woman on the other metal slab pulled the coarse blanket over her head and whimpered underneath it. 'Guv,' Jacob said as he pointed to the corner of the room. Gina stared at the grey blanket covering a mound. Only a foot poked out.

'Can you back off a moment and give me a minute please?' She needed the PCs to wait outside so as not to scare the terrified victims. 'Darcie, Shannon, I'm DI Harte. You can call me Gina.' She went over to the mound in the corner of the room and pulled the blanket away. She almost stumbled back in shock when she saw that Shannon had been stabbed in the heart and her finger had been cut off. Reaching in, she checked for a pulse but there wasn't one. Jacob stared at her in anticipation. She shook her head. They all now knew that Shannon was dead.

Slowly, Gina approached the woman on the stainless-steel table. 'I'm just going to pull the blanket back, okay?' As Gina reached down and began to tug at the coarse grey blanket, Darcie tugged it back and screamed. 'Darcie, it's okay, you're safe now. We need to get you out of here and home.'

After a few seconds, Darcie stopped fighting Gina for the blanket and allowed it to drop. Gina could see that Darcie's hands were bound together and the rest of the rope had been looped around the table, giving her just enough slack to pull at the blanket. Jacob hurried over and began to untie it.

'What did they do with my daughter? Where's Cleo?'

Gina kneeled and kept Darcie's focus on her as Jacob struggled with the binds. 'Cleo did as you told her. She ran away to safety and a lovely lady who owns a B&B called Beryl helped her. Cleo is safe with your brother, Kyle.'

Big sobs escaped Darcie's mouth. 'I thought he'd go back for her and hurt her. She said that Cleo was dead and that I'd never see her again. I thought they'd killed her.'

The binds dropped to the floor. Gina helped Darcie up and was happy to hear the sirens of an approaching ambulance. 'She's safe and she can't wait to see you.'

'Thank you,' Darcie cried. 'What about Shannon?'

Gina looked down. 'I'm sorry.'

Darcie glanced to the side and stared at Shannon. A cry escaped her lips. 'He has her?'

'Who has who?' Gina waited for Darcie to answer. Her furrowed brows told her that the woman was struggling to think. 'I heard them. He took the baby and was going after Shrimp.'

'Who's Shrimp?'

'It's Jamie's little sister. Layla. We called her Shrimp.'

As soon as they reached the main doorway, the paramedics took Darcie from her. The woman's eyes rolled back and she collapsed.

Gina turned to Jacob. 'Find out what Christy Everly drives. We need all units on the lookout for her vehicle. Joel has Layla and we suspect he's illegally driving Christy's car. Can you call in to see if there are any updates?'

He nodded and made the call. Gina watched as Darcie came around slightly and was loaded onto the ambulance. Jacob hurried back over. 'It's a brown Volvo estate. It's just flagged up on an ANPR camera off the Cleevesford Highway. The chopper is heading there now.'

Mrs Swadling had been right about seeing a brown car on the night of Darcie's kidnapping. Joel had taken Darcie using his mother's car. She thought of all the other cars described. She could only surmise that some were used by Finn and that Joel possibly sneaked some of the car keys from the showroom, ensuring he always drove a different car. Why did Joel have Layla?

'Guv,' one of the PCs yelled.

'What?'

'There is a note on the bar.'

SIXTY-THREE

Gina ran back into the building and flashed her torch at the bar. The note had been left on the end. She pointed the light at the scrap of paper and read.

My name is Christy Everly and this is my confession. I kidnapped Jamie, Darcie and Shannon and I did it alone. Everything that was done to them was down to me. I also stabbed Shannon and I removed one finger from each of them.

The writing got worse. Gina could tell that Christy had written it in a hurry as it was sparse.

Fifteen years ago, they left Oliver, the boy I loved, to drown. They could have saved him, but they didn't. Shannon started using the practice that I work at to treat her dog and it angered me that she didn't recognise me and was happily walking around and getting on with her life. That anger just got worse and worse until it ravaged me inside. I killed Shannon because she told them all to leave Oliver when he fell in the lake to his death. They could have saved him but they let him die. They are murderers.

I'm sorry. I hated Shannon that much, which is why I had to kill her. When I knew Jamie had survived, I intended to kill them both and run, but when it came to Darcie, I kept thinking about her little girl and what it would be like for her growing up without a mother, just like my son had grown up without his father. I couldn't do it to her.

Something else happened and it changed my life. My boy had a baby and I felt I needed to protect him from the evil in this world. There's something about new life that almost makes a person primal in the lengths they'll go through to protect their own. Now he will grow up in a better place because of what I've done.

There is only one way out for me because I know you won't understand and really, I know I can't run. You will find me. I have no other option and I prepared for this. I saved one last syringe for myself. I'm now going to walk into that lake to join Oliver forever.

My son is a good lad. This was all my doing. He doesn't know what I've done so please tell him how sorry I am. Tell Sonny I love him too and that I did this for him and Oliver.

Christy

A wooden strut fell from above, sending Gina's heart pounding as it landed next to her. She took a quick snapshot of the letter and ran out of the building, knowing it would now need to be made safe before anyone else entered.

'That was close, are you okay?' Jacob ran over to her.

She bent over, hands on her knees as she got her panic under control. If she'd have been a little to the left, she was sure she'd have died. 'Yes.' She stood and took another deep breath. 'We need to get to Joel. The letter is a confession. Christy said it was all her and that Joel didn't know, but we know that's not true and now he has Layla. Let's go.'

She began to jog across past the PC who was cordoning the building off until she reached her car. She and Jacob got in and before he could even clip his seat belt on, they were already halfway up the dirt track. 'Call O'Connor, we need to know where that Volvo is now.'

Jacob called and quickly updated O'Connor as Gina followed the rural road towards the highway. 'Guv, take the next left, then a right. Traffic police are trying to carefully pull him over on Hartlebury Road. He's heading that way. They're saying that there's only one person in the car and he fits Joel's description. Should they deploy a stinger ahead?' Jacob went back to his call and grimaced.

'No,' Gina yelled as she drove. 'There's a baby in the back.'

Jacob continued. 'Damn. He's just veered off and crashed into a fence.'

The lump in Gina's throat threatened to choke her as she continued to drive onto Hartlebury Road. She pulled up on a verge as a queue of traffic began to form. Several police cars pulled up and officers blocked the road. She ran as fast as she could towards the brown Volvo. An ambulance dodged through the traffic, parking next to the car. Gina reached the officer and held her identification up. 'I'm DI Harte, SIO of this case. Is there a baby in the back?'

The PC nodded and pointed to another PC who was standing right back from all the commotion. He held a baby carrier in his arms. A paramedic ran over, taking the baby seat from the PC before returning to the ambulance. Gina joined them. 'Is the baby, okay?' She glanced at the tiny baby who was sucking on a dummy and she knew that the baby was going to be fine. His huge eyes met hers and he began to cry.

She hurried back to the car. 'What's happening with the driver?' She glanced through the window and could see that the airbag had been slashed, and that Joel's head was bleeding and slumped against the steering wheel. His open eyes were expressionless.

The PC moved back. 'We have to leave him to the paramedic. He has a pulse but hasn't communicated with us at all.' Another ambulance pulled up and another paramedic hurried through.

Gina furrowed her brows. Darcie had told them that he had Layla but where was she? 'We need to open the boot. We have a missing victim.'

Jacob snapped on a pair of latex gloves and reached for the keys in the ignition just before a paramedic came with a neck brace for Joel. His overalls matched the description that Cleo had given.

Gina stood by as Jacob opened the boot. She held her hand to her mouth as she saw Layla crunched up in the foetal position with a bloodied arm lying on top of a scrunched up white mask. Reaching in, she placed her fingers on Layla's scratched neck to check her pulse, then Layla opened her eyes and grabbed Gina's wrist as she yelled. 'Sonny, Sonny.' She flinched as she thrust a leg out of the car and followed that with the rest of her body. Rubbing her head, she aimlessly walked around calling out her son's name.

Gina followed her. 'He's in the ambulance. Let me take you to him.'

They both ran together. Layla jumped into the ambulance and cried as they handed Sonny to her. He had come out of it all unscathed and Gina felt herself welling up. Jacob turned away and she knew the scene had touched him too. They had a lot to unpack.

SIXTY-FOUR

Wednesday, 6 March

After taking what felt like hours of statements followed by a couple of good night's sleep, Gina stepped into the ward where Jamie had been moved to. Staying back, she watched as Jamie held Sonny and smiled at Layla. The patient in the next bed had gone walkabouts, which was perfect for Gina. She hated having to talk to witnesses and victims on wards but she guessed the private intensive care room was needed for someone else.

It warmed her heart that the two sisters had each other and she could see a better future on the cards for Jamie. Gina slowly walked over to them and smiled. 'It's lovely to see you awake and talking, Jamie.'

Jamie flinched in pain as she handed Sonny back to Layla who snuggled him against her chest.

'And how are you, Layla?' Gina asked.

'Thank you, just thank you. I thought he was going to kill me and take Sonny. I trusted Joel but he turned out to be a monster.' She looked away. 'I trusted him and all this time he'd only got with me to try and find out more about the others and Jamie. Not once did his mother, Christy, mention that she'd seen my sister by the practice looking through bins. I'd have hurried right over to take her home.'

Jamie placed a hand over Layla's as Layla continued to speak. 'You know I met him while going on a coffee run at work. He followed me into the café and now I know him bumping into me and being kind and nice was all an act. He was manipulating me.' She paused. 'I keep thinking that me getting pregnant was the only thing that saved me up to that point. Even his mum was kind to me. I thought it was lovely how she'd been so nice when we told her I was pregnant, despite Joel only being twenty and me being thirty. I thought she'd be angry, especially as she had him at such a young age, but she was lovely and...' She wiped a tear away. 'Now I know what she did, I can't reconcile the two sides of her. The Christy I knew was kind and loved looking after Sonny and the Christy who tortured my sister in a dungeon, I don't know her.' A sob escaped her mouth. 'I feel like I should have seen that something wasn't right and maybe I could've prevented all this and Shannon would still be alive.'

Jamie placed a hand on her sister's arm. 'Sis, he'd have found a way. Or they'd have taken Shannon or Darcie first. It's no one's fault.'

Layla wiped her eyes and rocked Sonny as he nodded off in her arms. 'But it was. We left Oliver all those years ago.'

Jamie shook her head. 'It wasn't like that and you know it. We were all shivering cold and half delirious. I'd dived in several times to pull you out, while all the time I had no idea you were crying on the bank. I was spent at that point. We'd lost Ollie. It had been too long. We couldn't have saved him. What we did wrong was not call the police and you know what Mum was like, she'd have beat the hell out of us for not being home when she got back. We were terrified.'

Layla glanced at Gina. 'That night, when we were soaked through and late, we were terrified... we were just terrified kids, and we did wrong by not calling the police to save ourselves from being hurt. We can never change that. We didn't know that Christy had been calling us to help him and we didn't know then that she tried to pull him out after we ran away.'

Jamie piped up. 'I heard she and her father moved away after that. I never saw her again, until Joel took me.'

Layla spoke. 'I didn't really know Christy back then as I was only ten and the others at the lake were my sister's friends, but she must have known who I was all along.'

Gina would never know if Oliver would have lived had they stayed but she knew that the girls hadn't set out to hurt him. She glanced at Jamie's cheeks that were now slightly pink, the paleness subsiding. 'How are you feeling now, Jamie?'

'Like I've been hit by a truck. My hand still kills and my pancreas is in a state but I'm determined to battle on for this little one. I want to sort my life out, get completely clean and I want to be there for my sister and Sonny now, if they'll have me.'

Layla leaned over and half hugged Jamie with Sonny in the middle. 'I'm sorry I left you with Mum all those years ago. I'm sorry about a lot of things.'

'Me too,' Jamie replied. She turned to Gina. 'What happens now?'

'In relation to Oliver?'

'Yes.'

'At most, you will be interviewed about the events of that day and a report will be prepared for the coroner. It's nothing to worry about.' Gina knew that an inquest wouldn't be likely. It would fail the evidential threshold test due to lack of evidence and it wasn't in the public interest. She hoped she'd put Jamie and Layla's minds at rest. They deserved some peace now.

After saying goodbye, Gina left the two women. She knew that Joel Summers had been taken to another hospital and that the swelling in his brain wasn't looking good. Hooked up to a ventilator was where he'd be for a long time and she had a feeling he wouldn't make it.

She headed to the other ward, the one where Darcie was recovering in a side room. She could see that Darcie also had visitors. Cleo sat on Kyle's lap, eating a little jelly that must have been served with Darcie's lunch. Kyle waved at her. Gina stepped into the room. 'I just thought I'd come and visit.'

Darcie looked down. 'Could you take Cleo to the café to grab some cake?' she asked Kyle.

'Of course. Let's go get cake.' Cleo giggled and skipped as she followed him out.

'How are you doing?' Gina sat on the chair, taking in the warmth that Kyle had left behind.

'I can't believe Shannon is dead. I told Kyle that we owe her. I overheard her telling Christy to let me go because I had a little girl. I think she died for me, if I'm honest, and I'll always be grateful to her.' She paused and scrunched her brows. 'I'm going to adopt Barney. Shannon loved him. He was her baby.' Darcie hiccupped a slight sob and took a deep breath. 'Joel was the one watching me from my loft, wasn't he?'

'It's looking likely that it was him who had been watching you and Shannon.' Gina knew they were still waiting for DNA matches on the drink cans and the cigarette stubs.

'I think I'm going to put my house on the market as soon as I'm out of here. I'm going to stay with Kyle as I can't go back there. Cleo saw him and I dismissed her as having a nightmare. He was in my house, watching me in bed, messing with my clock and scaring my daughter and I couldn't see it.' She shook her head. 'I didn't see him at the fishing lodge. Once he'd taken me there, he left me with Christy. That was his job done.' Tears ran down her cheeks. 'When she cut off my finger, she said she wanted the world to know there was more to it than some loony, as she put it, taking women for nothing. I think a part of her wanted to get caught so that the world would know that we left Ollie in the lake that night. None of us cut his finger off. It was an accident.' She flinched and Gina could see Darcie cradling her dressed hand. 'I guess I have a permanent physical reminder.' Her face flushed and she turned away.

'You've been through a lot.' Darcie was going over the same things she'd spoken about in her statement but Gina knew she'd need to talk a lot to process what she'd been through.

Her bottom lip trembled. 'When I see Cleo, I tell her I'm okay but I can't keep it together. As soon as she goes, I'm a mess. I thought Christy was going to kill me and all I kept thinking was, I'll never cuddle my little girl again. We didn't kill Ollie, he drowned.' She paused. 'When I left my friend Anna on the night I was kidnapped, I was so upset with her for seeing Finn and upsetting Shannon. We both said some horrible things.' She hesitated. 'While lying on that metal table, all I could think of was how petty it all was. After storming out and saying goodbye, I kept thinking it was the last goodbye I'd ever say and all I wanted was to see Anna again and say I was sorry for flying off the handle like that. I kept thinking how horrible she'd feel and that's all she'd remember of me when I was gone. I treated Anna badly as a friend sometimes but right now, I miss her so much.'

Gina turned as someone tapped at the door. Anna peered around holding a box of chocolates. 'I miss you too.'

Gina smiled and left the two women to spend some time talking.

SIXTY-FIVE

LAYLA

'I promised I wouldn't tell and I didn't,' Layla said. Once again Sonny was sleeping in Jamie's arms.

'It's a hard secret to keep and the weight of it crushes me some days but we can never tell. You, me, Darcie and Shannon, we promised to never tell and we won't. Pinky promise to the end.'

Thinking back to that night, Layla shivered as she recalled bits of what the others were saying behind Ollie's back. Jamie had fancied Ollie but his girlfriend, who Layla now knew had been Christy, had pushed her away from him and called her a slag. That had riled Jamie. Shannon then thought they should all try to make him pay in the name of the sisterhood for leading Jamie on. They'd intended to get him drunk and throw him into the lake as a prank.

Layla hated that they had to keep such a horrible secret but the only outsider who really knew the truth was dead and that secret was now buried with her. She thought back to that night as Jamie dragged her away shivering from the lake. Darcie was screaming because the rest of them weren't meant to fall in. Jamie's teeth were chattering and they'd been genuinely scared of their mum. Shannon had been the one to make the decision that they leave Ollie. Jamie had kicked him as he tried to grab her in the lake but he had surfaced again. He thrashed in the middle of the lake as they ran away, too scared to go back into the freezing cold water and too scared to call the police and get into trouble with their parents. She decided that an ambulance wouldn't make it in time to save him as if that could absolve them from their decision to leave him to drown. None of them knew that he couldn't swim.

Their legs had stiffened and all their clothes were frostily clinging to their bodies, sending them ever closer to hypothermia. They knew they'd left him to die. What they never knew then was that Christy saw everything but she was too far away to get to him on time.

Had they tried to help him, he would have lived. Christy tried to do what they should have done and she was right to blame them. She, Jamie, Shannon and Darcie had killed Ollie and left Joel without a father.

EPILOGUE

A Week Later

Gina stood in the kitchen, waiting for her meeting with Briggs. She nervously exhaled and took a sip of the coffee she'd just made. He'd tried to call her at home but she told him she needed time to think and she had done a lot of thinking and she was now ready to talk to him.

He walked past the door. 'I'm free now if you want to come to my office.' He smiled warmly at her which just made things worse. Her stomach was churning away. She followed him through and sat opposite him around his desk.

Briggs started. 'The DNA results have come back and the saliva on the cigarette butts that were found at the scenes match Joel's, as does the DNA found in Darcie's and Shannon's loft.'

It still sent a cold shiver through Gina as she imagined Joel peering through his little peepholes as the women thought they were alone.

Briggs continued. 'A trace of a commonly prescribed

sleeping drug was found in an open bottle of wine in Shannon's house, suggesting that he'd drugged her. There were also traces of the same drug in her orange juice and cheese spread. He'd been determined to drug her one way or another. You spoke to Joel Summers's doctor. What did he have to say?'

'The swelling isn't getting any better, which isn't good.'

'So, he might have escaped justice?'

'It's looking that way,' Gina continued. 'His grandfather came all the way from Cornwall to be with him. That must have been where Christy's father had taken her to have the baby. From what he'd said, he was strict with Christy. He brought up Joel during his early years and had insisted that Christy study hard to provide for Joel and she had, qualifying as a vet. He'd been upset when Joel was seven and she moved back to Cleevesford, knowing that being there would dredge up memories of her loss. He told me that Christy had never stopped grieving for Oliver and that she'd even insisted that Joel take Oliver's surname when he was born. They decided not to tell Oliver's parents of his birth, not wishing to complicate things.'

'That all sounds complicated.'

'It is.' Briggs cleared his throat and went to speak.

Gina cut him up. 'I need to say this so can I go first?'

'Okay.' He picked up a pen and nervously twisted it between two fingers.

'I know you mean well, but I feel stifled by your protectiveness and it's too much. The last case was unique and I hope we never have a repeat of anything like it. Yes, I did go it alone but we both know I had no choice.' She swallowed the lump in her throat. 'I need the space to do my job. It's dangerous, what we do is dangerous and I know I could sit behind a desk and send Wyre, O'Connor and Jacob off to do the groundwork but that is never going to happen. The truth is, I love being there. I love the chase and the dangers it comes with.' She stroked the bruise on her cheek.

'When I see you get hurt like that, it makes me think of what Terry did to you. All I want is to protect you.' He dropped the pen and clenched a fist. 'If I could go back to when he was alive, I'd like to grab him by the neck and punch the hell out of him. It goes through my mind sometimes, the things he did to you. That makes me want to make sure no one hurts you again.'

She stood and leaned over his desk. 'I've been hurt in the past; I've been hurt recently and I will get hurt again in the future. We all get hurt as a life in a bubble is no life. I need you to ease off a little. I love that you're concerned but you know me, my role here has always been my life and it always will be until I'm forced out of the building.'

He exhaled and leaned back. 'I'm sorry, okay. Maybe I need to work on myself a bit. Can we do something later?'

She knew it would be easy to say yes but what she really needed right now was a bit of alone time to digest the case and clear her head. 'I'll call you, okay.'

He smiled. 'Okay.'

A LETTER FROM CARLA

Dear Reader,

I'm so grateful that you chose to read *Her Last Goodbye*. If you enjoyed it and would like to keep up to date with all my latest releases, just sign up at the following link. Your email address will never be shared and you can unsubscribe at any time.

www.bookouture.com/carla-kovach

The idea for the book began with the tiniest of sparks. I pictured a little girl hiding out scared in a barn. In my mind, she'd run away after seeing a scary person take her mother from the roadside. From that spark the story developed into a full-blown plot. I love exploring an idea and developing it into a full novel. In this case, I really enjoyed writing the Layla and Shannon chapters and delving into how their pasts had come back to haunt them.

Whether you are a reader, tweeter, blogger, Facebooker, TikTok user or reviewer, I really am grateful of all that you do and as a writer, this is where I hope you'll leave me a review or say a few words about my book.

Thank you,

Carla Kovach

KEEP IN TOUCH WITH CARLA

 facebook.com/CarlaKovachAuthor

x.com/CKovachAuthor

instagram.com/carla_kovach

ACKNOWLEDGEMENTS

I'd like to say the biggest thank you to everyone who has helped to create *Her Last Goodbye*. Editors, cover designers, people working in every aspect of publishing from admin to management are all a part of this big team and I'm so grateful and proud to be a part of team Bookouture.

My editor, Helen Jenner, is brilliant and I couldn't have written this book and all the others without her editing, her encouragement, and her support. I don't know how she does what she does. Thank you.

The first thing readers see is the cover. I'm grateful to Lisa Brewster for the cover design. It's another belter!

The Bookouture publicity team are fab. As always, they ensure that publication day is made special. Super huge thank yous.

Thank you to the blogger and reviewer community. I'm always grateful to the bloggers who choose my book. I know there are stacks of books out there so it means a lot that they chose mine.

Much gratitude to the Fiction Café Book Club. I love what they do for authors. This group is awesome.

I also love being a member of the Bookouture author family. Thank you to each of the authors who show the most amazing levels of support to me and each other. My other author friends are lovely too. Authors are just fabulous people.

My beta readers, Derek Coleman, Su Biela, Abigail Osborne, Jamie-Lee Brooke, Anna Wallace and Vanessa

Morgan, are all brilliant and I'm thankful that they read my work at different stages before publication.

Special thanks also to Jamie-Lee Brooke, Julia Sutton and Abigail Osborne – again. I love our, 'Hot Dog Cringey Crew' support group. Big apologies but this is an in-joke.

I'd like to give special thanks to expert, Stuart Gibbon, of Gib Consultancy. He answers my policing questions and without his knowledge, I'd definitely be making a mess of the police procedures and charges. Any inaccuracies are definitely my own.

Lastly, super big thanks to my husband, Nigel Buckley, for the coffee, the admin, dealing with my website and a whole host of other jobs I'm useless at, and mostly for being there for me throughout the whole process.

PUBLISHING TEAM

Turning a manuscript into a book requires the efforts of many people. The publishing team at Bookouture would like to acknowledge everyone who contributed to this publication.

Audio
Alba Proko
Melissa Tran
Sinead O'Connor

Commercial
Lauren Morrissette
Hannah Richmond
Imogen Allport

Cover design
The Brewster Project

Data and analysis
Mark Alder
Mohamed Bussuri

Editorial
Helen Jenner
Ria Clare

Copyeditor
Jane Eastgate

Proofreader
Shirley Khan

Marketing
Alex Crow
Melanie Price
Occy Carr
Cíara Rosney
Martyna Młynarska

Operations and distribution
Marina Valles
Stephanie Straub

Production
Hannah Snetsinger
Mandy Kullar
Jen Shannon

Publicity
Kim Nash
Noelle Holten
Jess Readett
Sarah Hardy

Rights and contracts
Peta Nightingale
Richard King
Saidah Graham

Milton Keynes UK
Ingram Content Group UK Ltd.
UKHW010900080524
442402UK00004B/103

9 781835 251898